The Asking Price of Stars

John F. Baeyertz

ISBN-13:978-0692074916 (Victory)
ISBN-10:0692074910

Cover Design by John Baeyertz

Foreword

Welcome to The Asking Price of Stars. One night five years ago I started writing Stars. I had lost Ruth my beloved wife of many years. I was at a point in my life where I needed to focus on a project beyond my grief. After finishing a science fiction novel, I thought I could have written a better book. The result is this book. I leave it to the reader to judge its merits. I claim no literary skill; it is unpretentiously a story of an adventure in the far distant future.

This book would not be possible without the help of many people. Katherine and Gene Henson who read many versions and offered numerous suggestions and added a character to the mix. My thanks to Brian Shirk who reviewed all the versions and offered worthwhile ideas.

Next, my special thanks to Janice Lehman who I met a year after starting the book. She was the first to proofread Stars, she told me when a chapter was poorly constructed, and creatively named a character. Jan also made coffee and put up with my obsession to complete the book. We recently married and live a full life traveling, reading, and enjoying life.

I'd like to thank the members of the Writers Club at Four Seasons Beaumont. Thanks to the past president Joseph Laurin who welcomed me into the club as a novice author. Roland Harrah, Ed Paules, and the late Phil Bond all read sections and offered suggestions.

Next, my deepest appreciation for Jean Laurin Lawrence of the writer's club who volunteered to be my editor in the first draft of the book. Her fine talents, as an editor, made Stars a readable book. Finally, I thank all the staff at Victory Publishing, Jenae Noonan, and their highly skilled editors for bringing a final polish to the book.

A few quick notes: The book uses the metric system, who knows what system will be used in the distant future, but metric is at least logical. Also, much of the science in this book is fiction. No claim is made for scientific accuracy. Next, the command structure of the Free Space Force based loosely on the United States Air Force, not the Navy as in many science fiction books. Whoever commands a ship or base is a Commander and Captain is a rank just above lieutenant. Finally, for those of you who are very sensitive, a warning, this book contains violence, adult language, and adult situations. I not do believe it contains anything you would not see on television today.

All names used in this book are used fictionally and bear no resemblance to anyone living or dead.

Major Characters

1. Tracey Mills-Watkins - Lieutenant 3rd Class PO (Parliamentary Officer) in the FSF (Free Space Force). Just graduating from OTS (Officer Training School).

2. Shane (Kat) Jang - Ex Lieutenant 1st Class PO (Parliamentary Officer) Now broken to the rank of 2nd Class FO (Fleet Officer). - Looking for any ship in The Free Space Force that will take him.

3. Nirabella Freestar - Fleet Physician Assistant 1st Class FO. (Fleet Officer). Recently dumped by her doctor lover and looking for a new ship.

4. Shadow - The son of a prostitute. Shadow lives in New Haven the main space port of the planet Freehome. He is eighteen, bright and quick but totally uneducated. Killed two men so far.

5. Light - Twin of Shadow. A bar girl in New Haven. Killed her first person at ten. Uneducated but has impressive survival skills.

6. Cici De Santis - Chief Sergeant a Warrior and also a ship's Supply Chief. Close friend of Nirabella.

7. Peter Guderian - A half Trocnavar cadet. Lieutenant 3rd Class PO (Parliamentary Officer). Just graduating from OTS (Officer Training School). His existence is the result of extensive Trocnavar genetic manipulation.

8. Tara Vasta Freeborn - Owner of Freeborn Farms. Lady with a mysterious history.

9. Artystaar Tiigano - Trocnavar pirate gang leader. -- Ex Imperial Blue Fleet cadet. Kills for excitement.

10. Fidelity Stone know as Fi - Free Space Force crew member, a cute young redhead. Just a year of FSF service.

11. Demitrianna Constantine - (Spider) A very young Captain and the Chief Time Wave Navigator of Green Fleet.

Other Characters

1. Capitan Gunson Montgomery - Weapons Officer in the FSF
2. Colonel Harrison Chung - Executive Officer of Green Fleet
3. Baryic Chahill - Chief Sergeant – Older Engineer popular with the ladies.
4. Centari Shamir - Lady of seventeen years' leader of the Lost.

5. Rhonda Santacruz- Seventeen-year-old member of the Lost

6. Mark Bittman - Crewman - one of the Lost

7. Neil Marsborn - Van driver.

8. Erica Nguyen – FSF Crew Member.

9. Czajka - Female Weapons Officer on the Ms. Weldon II

10. General Alexander Bridgeford – (The Ax) - Fleet General, Commander of Green Fleet

11. Anna Morgan - Daughter of an innkeeper on the Pangerbar Space Station

12. Niikia Kaiii-var - Tough young female Trocnavar pirate commander

13. Count-Viceroy Markiii - commander of Troc forces."

14. Lord Markiii - his son

15. Lord Erasmus Sunstar - Prime Minister of Horizon

16. Lord Clovis - of Rarkiikar Clovis

17. Xiggott - A pirate

Chapter One –
The Planet Freehome – 06-15-517 - The Year Five Hundred and Seventeen, After Freedom, Month Six, Day Fifteen of Thirty

Tracey turned the glider trying to sense the column of rising air. She had disabled all the safety devices, locked out the lift engine, and turned off all the instruments except the air speed indicator, the altimeter, and the artificial horizon. She wanted to feel the air; to be part of the glider herself. Great clouds boiled up into the sky from green fields below. Suddenly she felt the glider shudder and it began to rise as she caught the lift. Tracey tightened the turn further to keep in the column of rising air. *Damn, I love this,* she thought. She turned her head to see how much the left wing was flexing. It flexed upward almost two meters, well beyond where the safety devices would have allowed.

If any of the instructors or officers at the school knew she was flying with the safeties disabled, lift engine locked out, and limited instruments they would surely set her back a half year. The risk made the flight even more exciting.

Tracey's ear plug buzzed as Pat Richman, the student air controller said, "Tracey you better head back they are posting."

Tracey responded, "It is two weeks early. They have only had our final test results for a few days."

Pat explained, "I'm telling you the Great White Sheets are going up as we speak."

"By all the gods this may be the last time I fly a glider for years. I am going take her up to the limit!" Tracey exclaimed cutting Pat off.

But, Tracey knew this was the most important day for the graduates. No data packs, no electronic transmission and no computer. By tradition, lists of each student's ranking and their first assignment in the Free Space Force were hand written on large sheets of white paper. These were nailed to the wooden wall at the end of the old meeting hall just as it had been done for the last 356 years.

She kept the glider in rising air for another 15 minutes until she reached 4,600 meters which was the limit on Freehome without oxygen masks. She then turned and set a course for the school's landing field. She prided herself on reaching the field by her skills as a pilot and the glider's 45 to 1 glide ratio. Tracey began resetting the safety devices and instruments for normal operation. However, to test her skills as a pilot, she did not restore lift engine power until she landed on the school's vast grass field.

The Officer Training School of the Free Space Force was located in a wide green valley covered with forests and farms. Great mountains rose to the east and low hills bound the west side. Numerous streams fed The Guderian River as it flowed slowly down the center of the valley.

Tracey popped the canopy as the first-year students reached her and began rolling the ship to the glider hangar. "Ma'm you're the last graduate down. They are all over at the old meeting hall," one of the freshman students told her.   Tracey noted all the lifters parked along the field edge. The school's old 20-person Space Lifters had been moved down the field and the big 40 and 60 person Space Lifters were now parked close to the flight center building. Some were marked as the personal lifters of generals and some were marked with the names of battleships, battle cruiser, and other major ships of the Free Space Force. One was marked with a bright green band. The freshman pointed to it and said, "You know what that means?" Tracey nodded yes, she knew.

An hour later Tracey, freshly showered and in clean utilities, walked across the quad toward a large high stone and timber building. The Old Meeting Hall had been here almost from the start. She passed a group of second year cadets. One called out, "Hello, beautiful! Come see me if you want to spend your last week here with a real man."

Tracey yelled, "I didn't know you had an older brother! I sure as hell hope he is better looking than you!"

Tracey did not consider herself a beauty. She was tall, just over 170 centimeters, and well-muscled thanks to years of playing Field Ball as a Soft Bat Forward. Her hips were wide with muscles and her breasts small. She did not match the voluptuous soft curves currently popular in Vid Stars. On a smaller woman, her face would be called cute with a small up turned nose, large blue eyes, and just a dusting of freckles across the bridge of her nose, but on Tracey, handsome would be a better description. Tracey kept her blonde hair cut exceedingly short. In early days of the Free Space Force too many women and men died when their long hair caused a leak in their space suit helmet seals. Tracey continued on to the hall. As she entered she looked right and left and saw the names of every Space Force Officer who died while on fleet service carved into the high stone walls. There were many names and room for many, many more. She passed two sobbing cadets *Looks like those two lovers won't be serving close to each other.* Tracey found there was still a large group of third year cadets gathered at the white sheets.

The Officer Training School had five levels of rating; Above Standard, High Standard, Standard, Low Standard, and Below Standard. At the end of the third year by graduation few if any of the last two low ratings were left. Everyone with a Standard or higher rating would receive a Parliamentary Commission as a Space Force Officer, a Lieutenant 3rd Class Parliamentary Officers (P.O.) and would become the leaders and masters of the Free Space Force.

However, class rankings were also critical; the higher the ranking the better the first assignment. The two highest ranking levels were assigned directly to the fleets. Cadets ranking Standard were assigned to fleet support. If a cadet performed well on the ground or on an orbiting station he or she could be sent to the fleets in a few standard years. Of course, a rating could be overlooked if the cadet's father, mother, aunt, or uncle was a General, a Member of Parliament, or extraordinarily wealthy.

Tracey was concerned because her grades and athletic evaluations ranked her in the gray area between High Standard, and Standard. Her athletic scores were high and her scores were solid in Weapons Systems, History, Languages, Ship Systems, and Ship Administration, but she just passed the classes in Advanced Mathematics, Time Wave Drives, and Time Wave Navigation.

Two hundred and three Cadets were on the list. Tracey traced down lines with her finger looking for her name. The first nine names were *Above Standard.* She kept moving down numbers 20, 35, and 40 and there was still no Tracey Mills-Watkins. Below 60 were the Cadets who were rated Standard. At last she found her name at number 56. Tracey shouted, "By all the gods and hells I am going to a fleet!"Her finger traced over to see which fleet and ship she would serve on.

"Damn, Damn, Damn!" she exhaled.

Chapter Two
– New Haven City on Freehome, the Capital of the League of Free Stars, 06-15-517.

Shane Kat Jang (Kat) slowly awoke with his head feeling like it was being crushed in a vise. He managed to get his left hand up to his head and found there was no vise. Still, a large number of things were awfully wrong. His head hurt beyond pain. The "bed" in which he lay was hard as stone, wet, cold, and smelled like a sewer. Kat's mind raced, *"My gods I smell a sewer full of vomit. If I can open my eyes: O my gods, it is so bright. How could I, Shane Kat Jang PO Lieutenant 1st. Class, be in this mess? I will raise my head just a bit. My gods I am beaten black and blue and laying in a sewage gutter! My data pack is gone along with all my money in it! The pack contained all my identification. My shoes are gone!"*

Kat was even dressed in the wrong uniform. He was wearing what was left of a 2nd Class Fleet Officer's uniform. *"Why by all the hells do I have this uniform on? Fleet Officers were levels below any officer who held a Parliamentary Commission."* Slowly Kat's memory returned. He began to recall the Board of Inquirer months ago and, in particular the ruling affecting him.

At the end of that inquirer, Colonel Brashear looked down on Kat and had said "This board finds you, Shane Kat Jang, to have been drunk on duty. You are reduced to the rank of Lieutenant 2nd Class." *Not too bad,* thought Kat. The Colonel's next words were, "We also find you guilty of being drunk in uniform at a formal public event, The Annual Parliament and Military Officers Ball. You are reduced to the rank of Lieutenant 3rd Class" *Not good,* said Kat to himself.

Brashear continued "Next, the Board finds you guilty of hitting Lieutenant Cynthia Chin after she slapped you twice for what you said to her. For decencies sake, I will not repeat your words, but Chin should have slapped you twenty times. You should have taken the slaps like an officer and a gentleman. Your Parliamentary Commission is withdrawn and you are further reduced to the rank of Fleet Officer 1st Class" *Very bad, exceedingly bad,* was Kat's only thought. Next the Colonel said, "Shane Kat Jang you are found guilty of breaking the nose and wrist of Captain Gunson Montgomery when he tried to stop you from hitting Lieutenant Chin." *My gods Gunson was my friend,* sped through Kat's mind.

Colonel Brashear concluded, "You are further reduced to the rank of Fleet Officer 2nd Class. Shane Kat Jang, you are a disgrace to the Free Space Force and the League of Free Stars. Were it not for your outstanding record in combat, you would be dismissed from the Free Space Force!"

Kat's friends told him he was lucky to be kept in the Space Force and that he better stay dry. But that admonition had not stopped him from drinking last night. Kat remembered: *I was in a tavern called The Last Wave, near the space port just outside New Haven. The Last Wave is not a place you often find officers even Fleet Officers, but bar girls are very friendly and the yellow spiced liquor cheap. What the hell happened to me? I remember walking out of one of the back rooms after some fun with a bar girl. I paid her what she asked. Did she set me up? Next I seem to remember ordering more yellow liquor and dancing with the bar girls. Then I found myself on the floor. After that it's a blank.*

Kat's mind returned to his present problems. He managed to drag himself up to sit on the curb. Two enlisted crew, in sharp clean utilities, walked past him. One said, "It's a joke to see an officer like that. What a drunken scum." Kat tried to respond, but it came out as "fucee goo." The two crew members laughed and walked on.

Half an hour later a voice asked, "You need help space man?" Kat turned and saw a bar girl but not the one he had been with last night. Her small body was thin and strong, her muscles like steel cables. Light brown hair capped her fine cut face. She moved with quick smooth motions to help him to his feet. "You need to wash, and get some clean clothing. We shall trade."

Trade what? Kat thought.

Chapter Three
– The Planet Green Four, Orbiting Green's Star – 6-16-517

It was early morning at the Space Force ground base on the planet Green Four. Many of the crews were out on the balconies of the enlisted barracks getting ready for a day's work or packing gear for a lifter ride up to their ships or to the space station. Nirabella heard a crewman on the nearest balcony yell down at her, "You sure are good looking for a fatty!" The Chief Sergeant driving the power cart asked, "Shall I go up and kill him for you?" Nirabella knew the Chief Sergeant would do it if she asked, but she wouldn't ask. Nirabella recalled meeting the sergeant a standard year ago. She had reattached the sergeant's leg that was cut off during a nasty battle between the Free Space Force *Republican Lady* and a pirate light cruiser. The sergeant, Cici De Santis lost 50% of her blood and was clinically dead. The Doctor was occupied with four higher ranking officers who were also seriously wounded. So, Nirabella as a physician's assistant along two nurses pumped the sergeant full of blood, drugs and then restarted her heart and breathing. Two hours later when Cici was stable Nirabella's team began reattaching Cici's leg blood system, bones, muscles, and ligaments. Six hours later Nirabella undertook the delicate process to start re-growing the nerves. If she had waited for the doctor it would have been impossible to restart Cici's heart. Doctor Tommy told Nirabella, "Few physicians could do the surgery as well."

If she was so damn good, then why was she out of job? Nira took stock of herself. She was the best PA in the fleet. It was said if you came in dead Nirabella could walk you out. She was thirty years old, short, fewer than 125 cm tall. However, she had a beautiful face with green eyes framed by light brown hair. Nirabella had the soft curves seen on vid actresses. She just had too many curves; about 20 kilos too many.

It was on the Last 3rd watch on board the heavy cruiser *Republican Lady*, when Doctor Tommy revealed what a scum bag son of a bitch he is. Tom and Nirabella had been lovers for the last year. She worshipped him and did everything in bed and out for his love. During the 3rd watch the sex was wild and uninhibited. Just as they awoke for the first watch, Tom told her he was transferring her off the *Republican Lady*.

While I spent nights in his bed, the pig bastard worked out my transfer! Nirabella thought.

Tommy unceremoniously told her, "I am deeply in love with my third wife and she will be the new PA on board. It would be best if you left quickly."

During last 3rd watch Doctor Tommy even had the crew pack her gear while he and Nirabella had uninhibited sex in his bed. She was sick to her stomach. Next, he told her, "You have to find a new ship on your own." He had not even bothered to arrange even that much for her. She hit the 'pig' and kept hitting him until some of the crew came in and pulled her off.

Chief Sergeant Cici De Santis told the ship Commander, "I am going with Nirabella, shoot me if you don't like it." The Colonel avowed she was not about to shoot the best supply sergeant in the fleet. An hour later Nira and Cici were onboard a lifter on their way down from orbit to the ground base.

Nirabella looked at her friend. Cici was tall with black hair forming a close cap to her head. Somehow, she was both very muscular and feminine at the same time. Her eyes were black and sexy. Cici's nose was straight and her face was eye-catching. She possessed a white skin tone that Nirabella rarely saw.

Chapter Four

'Light' watched the space man pull himself out of the cot. He walked into what passed for a bathroom and pissed. He then took a long drink from the only water faucet in the ramshackle apartment. At least he was clean. Yesterday she washed him in the makeshift shower. 'Light' and her twin brother Shadow built it out of scrap metal and plastic sheets. A sun tank on the roof provided warm water via a hose. After the shower the space man slept twenty hours except for getting up to piss blood.

The space man was a fine-looking man, young, handsome, muscular, with black hair and eyes like black diamonds. Light guessed he was 180 cm tall. Great purple and blue marks covered him, he was badly bruised. His un-bruised skin was a light tan except the white scars of four holes which laced his chest and back. Light thought these appeared as possible rocket pistol hits from years ago.

She asked, "What is your name space boy?"

He responded, "It's Shane, but those close to me use my middle name, Kat. What's your name and where in all the hells am I?"

"My name is Light. You are in my brother's and my apartment in the Space Port District. As you know, it's the poorest damn area of the city. We live above the Summerfield's. They run a clean building and keep the rats and motans down. We have power and water most days."

Kat nodded. Light instructed, "Kat please look at the two sets of clean clothing on the table by the wall."

Kat looked blankly at the clothing. One was a set of civilian work clothes and the other was a near new full set of Space Force utilities with cap, socks, and under garments. The boots were old but clean and polished. To top it off, all the insignia taken from his destroyed dress uniform were correctly placed on the utilities.

"Try to focus!" Light instructed. "Ms. Summerfield and I worked very hard to tailor that uniform. You will need it to get back on to the Space Force base tomorrow."

Kat muttered, "Without my data pack I can't get past the guards. They will want the details of how and where I lost it. Colonel Brashear's staff will check every aspect of my story. The Colonel will find out I was out drinking again and that will be the end my career."

Light tossed him a data pack. He turned it on and found it was his pack. "It's mine," he answered.

Light responded, "That's right, it's your pack. To get it back cost Shadow two first-rate rocket pistols and 100 rounds of rockets. You will find all your money is gone. What little the thieves didn't get, we spent on your uniform."

Kat asked, "Who in the hells is Shadow and why are you doing all this?"

Light replied, "We shall trade!"

******

It had been ten days, one week, since the man his twin sister called 'Kat' had left. Kat said he would meet them within a standard ten-day week. Shadow sat at the only table in their apartment recalling that Kat said he would return within a standard ten-day week. Across the table were two empty chairs that Shadow had bought at a used yard instead of stealing them. Kat instructed them not to steal and to quit working as a bar girl. Shadow and Light did as Kat asked. Light even had saved funds for the trade 'plan' so they could live for months. Shadow was not sure if this trade plan would work. *Maybe he and Light were riding a hopeless dream.* He mused.

The door buzzer announced someone downstairs. A minute later Kat, clean, neat, and sober, walked through the door with a lady on his arm. Shadow thought, *not another person in on the trade.* The lady on his arm was old, close to 45 standard years. She had space cut short white hair. She was trim and in good shape for a woman that old. She must have been a beauty in her youth. Kat introduced her, "I would like you to meet your aunt, Ms. Tara Vesta Freeborn. Auntie Tara will be helping us with your project."

Auntie Tara said, "My dearest niece and nephew, it's been years since we were together! In fact, I can't remember the last time I saw you two."

A few minutes later they all sat drinking tea while seated at the table. Auntie Tara continued, "In the

16

notebooks before you, there are three documents; two are tests which you will take today and one is a history you will read tonight."

Shadow spoke up, "I'm not much on tests or history. Furthermore, our mother never had a sister as elegant as you or as well spoken. Our mother was a space port whore who was knifed by a customer when we were ten. Light and I have been on our own for the last six years."

"Dear Shadow, I am terribly disappointed that the only memory of your history is the story you just related. My memory is far different," Auntie Tara said. "Let's move ahead. We only have seven weeks for this phase of the plan and Kat and I feel it is important that we set a baseline of where we start. The tests will help set that baseline. I am also most disappointed dear nephew that you don't want to read the history of your Freeborn Family. The history contains information any member of the family would know. It has maps and descriptions of The Planet Vista and of Freeborn Farm, which I am sure you "know" is located on Vista. If you remember, you were both born at the farm. You really should know the family history and the layout of the farm before a visit. Shadow, my dearest you need to clearly remember your mother died at the farm giving birth to you two dear children. Now shall we begin the tests?" Auntie Tara concluded as she handed them test tablets.

Four hours later Shadow and Light finished the tests and a half hour later Auntie and Kat finished scoring them. Auntie Tara spoke first, "The negative news is that you each lack almost any of the required formal education. On the positive side, you both have exceptional scores in raw intelligence. I now believe phase one may just be possible."

Kat continued, "You leave here early tomorrow. Please bring only clothing for a week, the history note book, and a few personal items. Box up all the guns, drugs, and anything that was stolen and bring the box. It should look like you are travelling for a week or so. We have paid your landlords a year's rent in advance. However, I don't believe you will ever come back here. Finally, say no goodbyes to friends. Also, you must burn all the tests and scoring sheets tonight."

Light was quick to ask, "Auntie Tara why are you doing this? It will cost much more than the money we saved. We sincerely thank you both, but how can we pay for it?"

Auntie Tara responded, "The Space Force Commanding General and I have a tad of history together. It is going to be fun to put one over on my old friend and help two young people who deserve a better life. Be ready for the hardest seven weeks of your lives!"

Kat only said, "A trade is a trade."

Chapter Five
- Officer Training School on Freehome, 06-26-517

The clerk announced, "Lieutenant Tracey Mills-Watkins, General Bridgeford will see you now."

Tracey rose and walked into the inner office. She hoped that wearing her new dress uniform she at least looked the part of an officer and a lady. The light gray blouse, with her six-pointed lieutenant's star pinned to it, trim cut dark black pants and fitted short black jacket, cost all four of her parents a month of savings. Her two dress uniforms were the minimum an officer needed.

Graduation was completed and the colonels and generals were using borrowed offices all over the school to interview the new Lieutenants assigned to them. The man behind the desk rose and motioned her to one of two chairs in front of the desk. They had talked briefly at the celebration after graduation, but this was their first formal meeting. He was a striking man, tall, thin, with short cut gray hair. His handsome face was narrow with cold blue eyes. On his right chest, a fleet general's red round "saw blade" marked his rank. The red twelve pointed star was pinned through a green ribbon.

"Welcome to Green Fleet Ms. Mills-Watkins. I hope you were not too disappointed in this assignment. I asked for you specifically. I believe your talents will fit Green Fleet's unique roll," the General said.

Tracey thought, *It sure in all the hells is not my first choice, it's really only half a fleet. But the gods know I'm glad to be going to any fleet even the Green Fleet.*

The clerk entered with ice tea and served them each a cold glass. General Bridgeford sipped his tea and asked, "Do you know why the school encourages the flying of gliders, light aircraft, and mini-lifters?"

"Sir, I believe it's to improve our coordination and give us a feel for working in three dimensions," she responded.

The General asked another question, "Why do you think the school also encourages competition in Field Ball?"

"Sir, I believe the game is played to develop strong bodies, quick reactions, and teach working together in an ever-changing environment," Tracey responded.

"One final question, Lieutenant," he said. "How many cadets were killed during your three years at OTS?"

It was a strange question, she thought.

Tracey answered, "Four died and a half dozen were so badly crippled they could not continue at OTS."

Trace thought, *all died flying or playing Field Ball except Raj who died climbing in the high mountains east of the school.*

The General called the clerk, "Please send in the other new Lieutenant, perhaps he knows why the school allows Cadets to dance on the edge of death."

Tracey was totally shocked as she turned to see the new Lieutenant.

The General said, "Lieutenant Mills-Watkins I believe you know Lieutenant Peter Guderian."

Tracey's mind raced erratically, *what in the hells was Peter doing here? He is a hopeless disaster! Peter is not in the top 60 graduates. Short and ugly, he somehow makes his new uniform look disheveled. I know it was hand tailored by the finest military tailors on Freehome. Why is he getting a fleet posting? Did his Stepfather buy him the posting? The Guderian family is powerful and rich. They own more than 100,000 hectares of land on Freehome alone. Also, they own trading companies throughout The League of Free Stars and even within the Empire. Why did Bridgeford select this half Troc?*

The General interrupted her thoughts, "No, I did not accept a bribe to post Peter to Green Fleet. In fact, his Mother and Stepfather don't know yet about his appointment. I chose Peter because, like you, his talents fit Green Fleet's unique role."

The General spent an hour explaining Green Fleet's operation and what was expected of them. He then ended the meeting and asked Tracey to stay for a moment. Peter excused himself.

After Peter left, the general continued, "I selected Peter because he never, never ever gives up. He may have wrecked two gliders, a light aircraft, and a mini lifter, but he learned to fly. Peter spent hours each week until he mastered flight. He will never be a great pilot, but he is a fair pilot." Bridgeford continued, "He also never gave up on sports. Each year he tried out for every sport offered at Officer Training School. He finally made the field ball D team in his third year."

"When Raj fell up on the mountain and all you heroes were up on top trying to find him and the lifters could not fly in the blinding snow storms, who made trip after trip up the mountain carrying supplies to high camp? Your search efforts would have come to a quick stop without the food, fuel, and equipment Peter packed up to your rescue team. Ms. Watkins, did he even get a thank you?"

Tracey stared mutely at her hands folded in her lap.

Chapter Six
– Freehome and onboard the ship *Blue Lightning*. 06-27-517

The trip from Freehome to Vista was both intimidating and spectacular. Auntie Tara picked up Light and Shadow in an unmarked electro van. She told the driver to destroy everything they left in the van including the box with the guns and drugs. Light and Shadow kept only their few personal items. Auntie then provided both of them with new clothing and a completely loaded travel kit. Next, she gave them each a new data pack. For the first time in their lives they had last names; they were now known as Light and Shadow Freeborn.

The space lifter ride to the station was amazing. The surface of Freehome spread out below, white clouds, blue seas and green and brown land masses. The orbiting station was even more amazing. At 20% of standard gravity they walked and skipped through vast spaces with Auntie. The other travelers never gave them a second glance. In their new clothing, the Freeborn twins now looked the part of the high-middle class. Time wave travel was extremely expensive and only the wealthy and well-to-do could afford commercial travel.

They arrived at docking port 27. Light and Shadow looked outward at the space liner which would take them to Vista. The spherical ball of the

Blue Lightning floated outside the grand observation window. Shadow exclaimed, "It must be over 100 meters in diameter."

The ship was a silver ball with many hatches and small projections for antennas, sensors, and control jets. The aft was covered 25% by the smooth black surface of the Time Wave Drive (TWD). The TWD surface was only pierced by a circular hole at the exact center of the back of the sphere. Two long tubes projected through the hole, each covered by a myriad of piping and armored control wiring. These were the nozzles for the main plasma and dark matter engines. At the center of the front of the ship was a clear bubble some twenty meters in diameter. This was the Navigation and Control Center and an observation area for the passengers.

Many power cables and lines attached the *Blue Lightning to* the dock. Two large transparent tubes also ran from the station to the ship. Shadow could see the lower tube was being used to load cargo containers. The crews on the dock guided passengers into the smaller tube to board the ship. Each person became weightless as soon as they left the station's gravity field until they reached the ship and its gravity field. Crew members stationed along the tube helped anyone who was not accustomed to weightlessness.

Light noted, *Auntie Tara appears to have spent considerable time weightless.*

Once aboard a steward welcomed them, checked them in and said, "I see all three of you are returning home to Vista." Next, she updated their data packs with a full set of ship information.

Light wondered, *by all the gods, how did Auntie get the records changed so Shadow and me are now citizens of Vista? She must have major pull with someone in the government.*

Auntie Tara led Light and Shadow to their undersized suite. The suite contained a small bedroom, a living room with a foldout bunk and a tiny bathroom. Auntie Tara and Light were assigned the two bunks in the bedroom. Shadow got the foldout. Their baggage was already in place in the suite. Light declared, "This is the nicest place I have ever lived in, it's beautiful!"

Auntie Tara thought *you should see a Premier Class suite*!

Three hours later Auntie Tara, Light and, Shadow were all reclining in seats in the observation dome. The room was filled with rings of reclining seats.

Auntie Tara told the twins, "If you recline back and look straight up you will be looking out the nose of the ship. Passengers can reserve seats in the outer two rings. The control area in the center is blocked off from the passengers by the low ring wall."

Light thought, *within the wall there appears to be 20 crewmembers most likely officers.*

Her years of experience as a bar girl had taught Light how to identify an officer. Each of the inner rows of reclining seats inside the wall had numerous controls, displays, and instruments in a swinging module. Once seated, the module would be swung in front of the person. In the very center of the circles were just five seats.

Light asked, "Who are all those people in the control area? Is the woman with the gold cap The Commander? Or is the man with the dark blue cap The Commander?"

A steward serving drinks to the passengers replied, "The lady in the gold cap is the Chief Time Wave Navigator and the Commander is the gentleman in the blue cap. Two other Time Wave Navigators and the Chief Engineer will fill the other three inner seats. The others are power engineers, sensor engineers, communication specialist, life support engineers, and subsidiary technicians."

Half an hour later the *Blue Lightning* using control jets, pushed off from the dock and turned outward. As soon as she was 100 km out the Commander fired the main plasma engine. The ship soon reached one standard gravity of acceleration. The Chief Engineer turned off the gravity field and they felt the pull of one standard gravity. At 100,000 km. out the Commander fired the dark matter engine and cut the plasma engine. They accelerated to ten Gs'. The Chief Engineer reversed the ships gravity field and brought it up to negative nine Gs' keeping the perceived acceleration within the ship to one standard G.

Twenty-six hours, an excellent dinner and breakfast later, Auntie Tara, Shadow, and Light returned to their seats in the observation dome. Aunt Tara pointed out the three filled navigator positions.

As the ship approached critical speed the Commander said, "You have control CTWN. Start the Time Wave Drive whenever you wish."

"Thank you, Commander. I have full control and I am initiating TWD on my mark - Now!" She ordered.

Light only felt mild disorientation as the ship rode a wave of compressed time and space. Auntie Tara told them, "The ship is now well above light speed. We will cover the two and a half light years to Vista in about a week."

From watching Vid shows and hearing talk in the bars, Light knew with the slightest navigation error the ship could disappear and never be seen again.

Chapter Seven

Nirabella and Cici sat on the patio of the Noncommissioned Officers Club; it was warm and humid on the big island near the equator of Green Four and the ice-cold beers were a welcome relief at the day's end. So far, they were scoring zero in finding new ship board assignments. Nirabella and Cici spent days at the base headquarters talking to various officers and then finally to Major Samuelson the Chief of Personnel.

The next day Samuelson sent them to the Green Fleet's Executive Officer Colonel Harrison Chung, who in turn told them to wait. Nirabella yelled, "With all due respect sir, wait for what? That big black and red c-cat of yours is more active than Green Fleet." The c-cat was sleeping on a table in the corner with his paw on a half-eaten motan.

Colonel Chung replied sharply, "Ladies you will maintain Space Force discipline! Until General Bridgeford returns I am just as much stuck here on Green Four as you are. The *Republican Lady* returned to their home base. Green Fleet is now without a battleship or battle cruiser. I am here at the Space Force ground base arranging supplies and repair parts for the ships that remain in orbit. Within the next eight standard weeks, I expect the General to

29

return from Freehome with two rebuilt long range battle cruisers. If you two would like to volunteer to assist in arranging supplies and parts, it would certainly help me. I cannot promise you assignments to Green Fleet. However, it would demonstrate your sincere interest in the fleet."

Nirabella asked, "When can we start sir?"

Chung replied, "Now would be an exceedingly good time!"

By the end of the day, Nirabella discovered that the process of ordering medical supplies was a disaster. The doctor in charge was a brilliant surgeon who could replace a heart blindfolded. However, as an administrator, he was a total disaster. He had let everyone run wild. What was on the order lists did not match the ship's doctor's requirements and even those few orders which were the correct items were the wrong quantities. She thought *no wonder Colonel Chung needs help.* She began putting together a plan to fix the major problems. It would require twelve hour days and on Green Four the days were only twenty hours long.

At the same time, Cici found the ordering of food supplies was also plagued with problems. The local suppliers on Green Four wanted to supply food to Green Fleet. The supplies met or exceeded Space Force standards but for some unknown reason many of the food supplies were ordered from off planet, at great expense. The civilian buyer running the effort was more concerned about going home rich than the needs of the fleet. "Someone is getting dreadfully rich on this and I know who it is," Cici told Nirabella. Tomorrow she would inform the Colonel and recommend they shoot the civilian parasite.

Nirabella and Cici knew they would have plenty of work for the next eight weeks.

Chapter Eight
- Freeborn Farms on the Planet Vista 08-14-517

It had been five weeks since Light and Shadow arrived at Freeborn Farms and they were mentally and physically exhausted. Auntie Tara had driven them through five weeks of intensive training. Now, Light and Shadow rested on the edge of the pool enjoying a beautiful spot. The large round pool was built into the deck in front of the rambling farmhouse. Sweeping views opened to the entire valley below. It was midsummer in the South of Vista, fields of Aki-Aki, wheat, corn, and imperial beans filled the bottom lands. The hills which rolled up to the house were covered with a dozen types of fruit trees. As the twins relaxed for the first time in five weeks, they watched two brightly colored c-cats hunting rats or motans in a rock pile near the deck.

Auntie Tara appeared with Ms. Jamison the housekeeper. Aunt Tara announced, "I have a tray of Rackiy Nuts and Ms. Jamison has ice tea."

Light was amazed because she had heard of Rackiy Nuts. On Freehome they were imported and dreadfully expensive. She had only seen them on the Vid. Light took one, bit into it and as the outer shell cracked, she bit into the white worm inside. The white worm squealed as it died. The rich, wonderful and unique flavor filled her mouth. She took another nut.

Auntie Tara told them, "We grow them here at Freeborn Farms and export them all over the League of Free Stars. The trees and worms only grow here in the Southern Mountains of Vista. They are one of the few crops expensive enough to warrant the cost of shipping off planet."

When the last worm had squealed Auntie, Tara asked, "Are you two ready for the tests and evaluations in four days?"

Light spoke, "I believe we are ready for athletic evaluations and most classes but we are still weak in history."

Auntie Tara asked, "Who will give me a quick overview of human history?"

Shadow answered her, "I will give it a try."

Shadow continued, "Home Planet was a blue green ball. We humans lived there in farming societies. Only the simplest manufacturing existed. Over 1,000 years ago a Trocnavar trader in a long range armed merchant ship discovered Home Planet. When he sent down lifters, the Trocs found us humans who looked to a great extent like Trocs. However, we are totally unrelated to Trocs. Humans are taller, thinner, with eyes that are just a little closer set. Of course, the humans had dull black, brown, and blonde hair with only a few red heads. The Trocs loved the red heads.

The Troc trader jammed as many humans as possible into his ship. As soon as he was back in the Trocnavar Empire he sold the humans for bound laborers and went back for more. The trader then built a much larger ship. Over the next 90 years, tens of thousands of humans, their farm animals and wild animals were taken and sold. Many plants and seeds were also brought back. Finally, the trader's granddaughter and her ship disappeared and the location of Home Planet was lost forever with her.

The Trocs found humans worked exceptionally hard and could live on any planet that the Trocs could live on. Slowly over the next two hundred years the Trocs came to use humans in their military as servants and in low clerk positions. Many of these humans were unbound and freed. A small population of free humans developed within the Empire.

From the Trocs point of view, human's major fault was that they were prone to revolt. Each revolt was brutally suppressed. Many humans were killed; the Trocs would wipe a planet clean of humans to stop a revolt. Any human who revolted were captured and faced a slow and painful death. Still, the humans continued to dream of freedom and home on the blue green planet with its ring and four moons."

Auntie Tara stopped Shadow by saying, "Very nice job nephew." Turning toward Light she said,

"You may continue the history later. But now it's time for Field Ball. Ms. Jamison, please have my mini lifter brought around."

"Dear ones what is the two most important things to remember in Field Ball?" Auntie Tara asked.

Light and Shadow answered in unison, "The goals move at random speeds and in random directions and the goal's aperture changes size at random times."

******

Dinner was semiformal that night as it was most nights. Auntie Tara planned to hammer upper middle class manners into the twins. After dinner that night Auntie Tara, Shadow and Light gathered on the deck near the fire pit. The night was cool and the fire's warmth pleasant. Auntie Tara said, "At the game today you both played well. You two are naturals at the Runner position. But, allow me to change the subject. Earlier today I asked Shadow to outline our early history, Light would you continue?"

Light continued the narrative, "As Shadow said we humans were prone to revolt. 520 years ago, a mutiny broke out on a transport. It was an old ship and except for the Troc officers the crew was human. Six Troc officers and a free human crew of forty manned the ship. The ship carried 210 bound humans and supplies that were being shipped to a mine on a planet at the edge of the Empire. Robert Smithson, a free human, led the mutiny. He and others of the crew had been planning mutiny for months. The mutineers took control and pushed the officers out an airlock. Janet Guderian, a mutineer trained in Time Wave Drive, set a course far out of the Empire.

Three years and a 1,000 light years later they found the planet we now call Freehome. The star was in the center of a cluster of stars and hidden away. The new planet was lush and green with seas covering more than half of it. The gravity was 95% of imperial standard. They set down the first settlement at the mouth of a great river flowing through a fertile valley. Robert named the settlement New Haven. The date was set at year one day one of freedom. We are now, of course, in year 517.

Four years later Robert, Janet and a crew of volunteers took the ship back to Empire and captured two more ships. Next, they raided farms and towns on outlying imperial planets. Within another four years 5,000 freed humans were settled on Freehome. The Next year Janet and Robert married. However, Janet kept the Guderian name and her independence. She began raising the first of their five children. Ten years later Robert and his crew disappeared on a raid, Janet was home with family. She and their five children lived on to establish the Guderian dynasty.

The Free Star Group continued to raid the Empire and bring back people, ships, farm animals, plants and supplies. Much of Freehome was settled. Mining and industry developed and cities were built. Ships were built and more planets settled. A group moved to a planet orbiting a nearby star. They called it Vista.

The League of Free Stars grew over the years without the Empire being aware it existed. The League of Free Stars developed into a group of planets loosely governed by a Parliament and the Prime Minister in the Capital of New Haven. The League was populated by humans and by a miniscule number of Trocnavar, taken of their technical knowledge.

The Free Space Force was formed in the year 162. It was an amalgamation of pirates, private warships, and merchant warships. Wars were fought with two invading alien fleets. Each time the Free Space Force gained victory. They were exceedingly costly victories.

Two hundred years ago the major event in our history occurred. Ships from Free Space Force met a group of long range ships from the Imperial Fleet off the planet Morgan's Abode. The contact quickly developed into the 1st Battle of Morgan's Abode. The Free Space Force was barely victorious. A truce was signed and League remained free. Long periods of both peace and war followed.

In the next years, the League grew to fifty-four planets and while the Empire expanded to over one hundred and fifty. Three times the Empire and

League combined to drive off invading aliens. Twice they fought deadly wars against each other. The Free Space Force grew. Both of the Imperial and League built ships comprised our fleets. Some Imperial ships were given to the League when we fought a common enemy and some were captured when fought each other and some were bought in times of peace.

An uneasy peace was broken thirty years ago with the 2nd Battle of Morgan's Abode. The fleets of the Space Force destroyed the Empires' fleets. Again, it was a costly victory. Once more an armed truce restored the uneasy peace. Today we live in a period of peace as fragile as a striker fish's egg.

"Thanks Light, it is a good summary of our Human history. I believe you two are ready for the next step of the plan," Auntie Tara affirmed.

Chapter Nine
– The Battle cruiser Lady Delapasse at the FSF Space Doc Above Freehome 08-07-517

Six weeks after General Bridgeford had selected them, Tracey and Peter crawled through the main wiring tube on the rebuilt battle cruiser *Lady Delapasse* checking the new wire harnesses installed during the rebuild. The battle cruiser had just undergone a complete rebuild from hull up. The ship's hull was old, built over 140 years ago and this was her third rebuild.

Tracey reflected, *new electronics, new rail guns, new missile racks, new life support systems, new plasma engines and new dark matter engines, both of the old imperial Time Wave Drives were overhauled. The Lady's' old TW drives were superior to any drives currently manufactured by suppliers in the League of Free Stars. The Lady was originally the imperial battle cruiser Vermillion Empress who at some point was captured by, sold to, or given to the Free Space Force. Exactly how the transfer happened depended on the state of relationships between the League and the Empire at the time.*

Tracey focused on the task at hand. She thought *Peter, the team and I have kilometers of wiring to check.* Tracey, Peter, and six crew members and two sergeants were visually checking thousands of connections in the wiring. The computer tests had

39

already confirmed the wire cables were OK, but the Chief Engineer Major Sasha Kedrova wanted visual confirmation. The team had already found several connections that were good electrically but were poor mechanical connections that could break under high G forces or vibrations.

Tracey looked at Peter as he worked and observed that he was short, stocky, clumsy, bungling, ugly and unkempt. But she also thought that the words "strong" and "smart" described him to a tee. He was grown not born, the product of Trocnavar genetic manipulation. Peter was far from their best effort. He had the body of a Troc and his head was a mix of Troc and human except for the turquoise and lime green spotted hair. He kept his hair so short that it was hard to determine the colors. His right eye was surrounded by fine scars. It was said his stepfather and mother paid for three replacement eyes. Finally, the third one functioned correctly.

Peter did possess two valuable qualities. Number one, he aced advanced math, wave navigation, and drive classes with the best scores in the last five years. General Bridgeford pointed out the second quality when he told Tracey that he selected Peter because he never, never ever gave up. All Bridgeford told her was true; however, now Peter was going to be trained as a TWD Navigator.

All the gods together could not save us if he ever guides us in a Time Wave was Trace's estimation.

Chapter Ten
–The Battlecruiser *Lady Delapasse* in orbit
above Freehome 08-10-517

Kat, riding in the gunner's seat on the lifter was awe stuck by the sight of the great battle cruiser *Lady Delapasse*. She was very different from the spherical ships the League constructed. The Empire built their ships long and lean. *The Lady* was 280 meters long and shaped like a striker fish with a pointed nose. The control center was the "upper" side. The two launch tubes for medium missiles could be seen below the nose and aft twenty-five meters. The control center was shaped like a half tear drop and set into "top" of the hull fifty meters from the nose. It was covered with view ports, antenna and sensors that could be withdrawn into the hull during combat.

Aft of the control center was a hull section seventy plus meters in diameter with four turrets in a ring around the hull. Each turret was equipped with two heavy rail guns. The guns could fire in all directions except directly aft. The section also had two drop bays for the large missiles. Next was the added extended section which made the *Lady* a long-range ship. Extra fuel, water, supplies, rail projectiles, and missiles were stored within. This section also held the lifter bay.

The final quarter of the hull held engineering. Arranged around the hull in a three-pointed star configuration were three great structures. On "top" was the communications tower. Shaped somewhat

41

like a fish fin, it bristled with sensors and antenna most of which could be withdrawn during combat. It was also painted with a wide bright green strip which ran diagonally across the tower. To protect from attacks astern was another turret with heavy rail guns set into the rear edge of the com-tower. The other two structures were giant pods built on massive fins. The rear surfaces of the pods were domes with a smooth black surface. These were the dual Time Wave Drives. Finally, from the center of the fish tail protruded the tubes of the plasma drive and the dark matter drive.

With Kat onboard, the box shaped lifter docked inside the bay in the lower part of the extended section. There was space for four lifters, two 20 person models and two 40 person models.

The officer of the deck greeted Kat, "Welcome to your new home, Fleet Officer Jang. Captain Gunson Montgomery, our Chief Weapons Officer would like to see in his office as soon as possible. The crew will see your gear to your cabin. The Captain said he hoped you were not violent today. Is that some kind of a joke, sir?"

Kat thought, *Gunson helped me get this appointment. After what I did to Gunson at the ball, it was a generous act. It's going to be a tough job; the missile drops are automatic and controlled from the control center. During combat, the bays are open to the vacuum of space and the crew and I will work in space suits. Our function is to clear jams, fix problems, and defuse dangerous missiles. The greatest danger is that a missiles engine will fire inside the bay. By the gods, my hope is the team will not burn to death or tear our suits!*

At the time of the appointment Gunson's only comment was "The *Lady Delapasse* needs an effective leader in Missile Drop Bay One."

Kat followed a crew member to Gunson's office. He stepped through the hatchway and said, "Fleet Officer 2nd Class Jang reporting as requested."

Gunson greeted him and motioned Kat into a chair. "Good to have you aboard. As I told you planet side that I need an effective leader in Missile Bay One. You have a brilliant combat record, Kat. You know the dangers. Do you accept the risk?"

"I expected to be sent to a sentinel station on some cold airless rock," Kat said. "I thank you for helping me get this assignment. Yes, I accept the risk! I'll do my best to fulfill the post."

Gunson responded, "Just stay sober. Planet side your record is not so brilliant." Gunson then added a final comment, "The crew says, 'Only a few people can be a drop bay crew leader!' You must be smart enough to do the job and dumb enough to take the job!"

Chapter Eleven
– Farmington Capital of Vista, Mid-Winter in the North 08-13-517

It had been summer in the South. In the North, winter held the Capital of Vista in its grip. On a cold blustery day two hundred young people were gathered in an auditorium of government headquarters in Farmington the Capital of Vista. Along with the young people were parents, brothers, sisters, and other family members. There also was a scattering of teachers and family friends. The total audience was just over two thousand. On stage were the six members of the evaluation team.

A thousand students completing upper school applied for the training. After days of tests and evaluations, the two hundred in this room were the ones who passed the first screening. Today, the evaluation team would announce the twenty to thirty who had been selected for duty. Their names would be called in random order drawn from a dark blue glass bowl. No one could see how many would be selected. Today, the same process was going on at many planets in the League.

Light and Shadow sat between Auntie Tara and Ms. Jamison, the housekeeper at the farm.

Light whispered to Auntie Tara, "I think we did well in the evaluations but there are a lot of people here who also did well."

Auntie Tara whispered back, "They all spend three years getting ready and you two had just seven weeks and you both are in the final two hundred."

The evaluation team leader asked each member of the evaluation team to step up in turn and pull a single name from the bowl and read to the gathering. They would repeat the process until all the names were read.

Munif pulled the first name, "Jillian Smith."

The next name was read "José Sandston."

And so, it went. The first twenty names were read and neither Light nor Shadow's name was called. After twenty names, no one knew how many more names were in the bowl.

They reached name number twenty-two; it was read out "Shadow Freeborn."

The next name called was "Michael Starborn" with another very common last name.

Finally, name twenty-five was read out, "Light Freeborn."

One more name was read out making twenty-six young people from Vista. At first cheering and yells were heard. Then sadness swept over the crowd as they realized that one hundred and seventy-four fine young people would have to cope with the disappointment of not being selected.

That evening Auntie Tara took Light, Shadow, and Ms. Jamison out to an excellent tavern named The Roast Vraciek. The tavern was not the most expensive in Farmington but just the best. Light offered the first toast while they sat by the fireplace looking out over the wide river which wound through Farmington.

"Our deepest thanks to Auntie Tara, Kat, Ms. Jamison and all the people at Freeborn Farms, because of your efforts, both of us are going to crew training on Lancaster," Light said.

Auntie Tara offered a second toast, "To my true niece and nephew, you are the ones who achieved this. We only provided some help along the way."

Shadow's toast was shorter, "To one magnificent trade!"

Chapter Twelve
- Space Force Crew Training Base on the Planet Lancaster
9-23-517

The Space Force Crew Training Base was located on a wide plain which opened to a beautiful bay. The base was in the southern temperate zone of Lancaster. It was a late summer day, the third day of enlisted crew training. Light, Shadow and forty other recruits sat in a Spartan room attending a class on the Free Space Force organization.

"Victory, Honor, Ship!" The gray and scarred fleet officer said as he stood before the class of new recruits talking about the traditions of the Free Space Force. "As many of you already know, the battle cry of the FSF is Victory, Honor, and Ship. Remember the words. I know the cynical will say it means the ship's hull integrity. No! - It's the integrity of the ship and crew as a whole. After Victory and Honor each of you carries the responsibility for your ship and your fellow crew members. We do not abandon a ship if it can be saved. The Free Space Force has two hundred ships give or take a few. Big battleships and battle cruisers have crews of four hundred, cruisers three hundred, but most ship's crews are smaller. The average crew size is about a hundred eighty. Just 36,000 women and men crew our ships. Another 190,000 FSF personnel support those ships from ground bases and facilities in orbit. There are just 226,000 of us to defend the fifty-seven inhabited planets of League of Free Stars and the hundreds of millions who live on them. You hold each and every one of those millions in your hands"

****

Eight weeks later fall had come to the South of Lancaster. A brisk wind blew off the bay as fall leaves of red, blue, and pink tumbled in the wind to the ground.

Auntie Tara walked toward the reviewing stand and said to herself, *"By the gods I trounced you Robert Singh Khan, so much for you, General Asshole, you were a handsome devil. Once long ago when we lived together you told me, slum kids, even kids of the working poor, would never be able to meet Space Force Crew requirements. Only one in fifty applicants is accepted for crew training and the requirement that all applicants must complete upper school blocked almost all of the poor kids.*

Later when you became Commanding General of the Space Force, you made sure the screening process prevented the few who did graduate from meeting Space Force crew requirements. You believed that the parents were poor because they were stupid and their children would also be unintelligent. My dear Robert, today the twins will prove you wildly wrong. Of course, I won't be able to tell you about all this for a few years."

An hour later the graduation of new space crews began. The new crew members had just completed eight weeks of recruits' training. They were from twelve of the planets in the League. The next group would have recruits from twelve different planets.

The two hundred and fifty-four new Crew 2nd Class marched on parade in their sharp new uniforms. In the lead was the flag of the League of Free Stars. Next came the flags of each group's home planet waving in the cool wind. The group of fourteen from Vista was led by a small young woman dressed with light brown space cut hair and deep brown eyes with the look of cold steel. Of the twenty-six who started, only fourteen recruits remained to march.

Light posted the flag in its holder and returned to her place with the Vista group. After the speeches, it was time for each one to receive their three pointed red stars. Light had hope that Auntie Tara could be with them but she saw no sign of her in the audience. It was a long way from Vista to Lancaster; perhaps she could not make the trip.

On the reviewing stand was a group of sixteen officers, four of which were from the school's staff. The other twelve were officers from each of the planets the crew recruits called "home". As Light walked across the reviewing stand to receive her three-pointed red star she almost fell to the deck. Waiting at the podium was Auntie Tara in the full-dress uniform of a Space Force Officer with the eight-pointed star of a Major on her chest. The red star was pinned through a black and a white ribbon. Light had learned during training that the white ribbon marked Auntie Tara as a reserve officer and that the black ribbon was immeasurably more special. It marked her as a member of Free Space Force Intelligence.

Light heard Shadow whisper, "Damn! I knew she wouldn't miss our graduation."

As Light stood before Auntie Tara to receive her star Tara said, "This is a proud moment; you two have achieved so much in the last few months. It is my honor to pin these stars on each of you."

Light replied, "Ma'am, I could have no greater honor than to receive my star from you, Major Freeborn."

Shadow simply said, "Ma'am, I thank you more than I can ever say. I am proud to be a Freeborn!"

Auntie Tara smiled and continued pinning stars on the new crew members from Vista.

Chapter Thirteen
–The Battlecruiser Lady Delapasse in orbit and on Green Four 12-24-517

17,500 kilograms of provisions and 34,000 liters of water had been sent up to *the Lady* from Green Four. This would top off supplies for the upcoming fleet patrol. It was a task well done. As the officer in charge, Tracey was proud of her team. Chief Sergeant Cici De Santis was a wonder as a Supply Chief. The crew had broken their backs to ensure the schedule was met and nothing was damaged. The twins as the two new members proved excellent workers and much stronger than she would have believed given their small size.

De Santis told Tracey, "Ma'am, you can't arrive back on the *Lady* covered in mud, dirt and sweat. Officers are not supposed to join in and help the crew. I'll hold the last lifter till you clean up."

"Thanks, I'll grab a shower and clean utilities at the base shed," Tracey said.

They were loading the supplies from a small Space Force base in the heart of the northern farming zone on Green Four. A warehouse and the office shed were the only buildings.

Tracey walked into the shed. At the desk was a ground staff fleet officer who appeared overworked and disorganized. The two clerks were sitting at terminals with paper everywhere. The office needed a good cleaning. There were boxes sitting on any open space. One box in a corner held a pink and orange c-cat and one scruffy half grown kitten.

Tracey asked, "Can I use the shower?"

The fleet officer replied, "Sure it's in the back hall."

Fifteen minutes later Tracey stuffed her dirty uniform in her pack and headed for the lifter.

An hour later the lifter docked in the lifter bay of *Lady Delapasse.* The Officer of the Deck greeted Cici and Tracey, "Welcome back! Colonel Chung sends his compliments; your team is half a day ahead of schedule. However, you can't bring that aboard."

Tracey asked, "What in all the hells are you talking about?"

The officer pointed to her pack. The scruffy half grown kitten peeked out of the top of Tracey's pack.

"The Executive Officer must approve any animals -- **Before** -- they are brought aboard. I can space it if you want. It will die quickly."

Tracey was about to say "space it" but instead she said, "Let me talk to the colonel before we space it."

Cici's commented, "Good luck Ma'am."

Tracey picked up her pack with the little c-cat and headed for the colonel's office. Five minutes later she stepped up to the open door and knocked.

Colonel Chung said, "Enter" without looking up from his desk. He said, "Good job on the uploading of supplies. What do you need now lieutenant?"

Tracey said, "Sir, by accident I brought aboard a c-cat. I request that you authorize me to keep it."

"Ms. Watkins, are you aware that the regulations say an animal must have pre-approval before being brought aboard?"

"Sir, it was an accident. The c-cat crawled into my pack while I was in the shower at the ground base," Tracey explained.

"You pitched in again to help the crew load the lifters and needed to clean up? Watkins when will you learn that are an office and a lady, Colonel Chung admonished. "Well, let's look at the c-cat."

Tracey lifted the c-cat from her pack and sat it on the desk.

Chung looked over the little c-cat and said, "She's a female, small for her age. I don't think she will be over nine kilos when grown. Her purple color is considered unlucky by some. I would space her."

Just then a loud thud forced them to turn as a big red and black c-cat strutted across the desk and snuggled up to the purple c-cat. He had been on a shelf above the desk and Tracey had not seen him until he jumped down. The big male c-cat smelled the small female. She stood her ground but let him smell her.

Chung then said, "Well, Big Red appears to think she is acceptable. Perhaps you can keep her. Fill out form Pet88765G-27 and download it from your data pack. I'll make an exception this once and approve it. She better kill a lot of motans and rats!"

Tracey gratefully said, "Thank you sir."

The colonel then told her, "Lieutenant before you go, open the cabinet on your right. Inside you will find a safety carrier. It's too small for Big Red and he has a new larger model. Take it for Purple Cat. You will need to train her to use it."

Tracey thanked Chung once more and took the carrier. *What is a safety carrier? I have no idea. Better get out of the colonel's office before he changes his mind. Is her name now Purple Cat? I guess so.*

******

Tracey and the new Physician's Assistant, Nirabella sat in Tracey's cabin talking. Nirabella had finished telling the story of her doctor lover. She asked, "Tracey how did you come to join the Space Force?"

"It's a complex tale," Tracey began. "I was born into a quad marriage. They are very special families. Only five percent of quad marriages are stable. I was the youngest of three children. My two sisters were ten and eleven years older. My alpha mother, Kathy took care of the home and my alpha father, Richard made the money as a broker and trader in future commodities. My beta mother Kim-me was a professor of history at the Public University. In her view, even the upper middle class should have some chance of an education. My beta father, Brook took care of the estate and raised near-horses. We were rich and owned an estate of 10,000 hectors. The family lived in a great house with servants and large staff. My parents were part of the elite of the League. The Prime Minister and his mistress often came to my parent's parties.

My two older sisters both went to West Star University; the best and also the most expensive in the League. They both married and settled into great jobs when the bomb hit. My alpha father made a disastrous mistake. He invested everything in futures of imported frozen Cariiacan lizard. Cariiacan meat was costly; it has a special flavor and a euphoric effect. Cariiacan could not be raised on Freehome due to a virus. My father Richard gained control on all imports for the next ten years. However, a year later the government announced the development of a virus resistant breed. The family was ruined. I was twelve and in mid school.

My parents managed to retain the horse farm with 500 hectors. We moved into the farm manager's house. He had quit as soon as he heard we were broke. Only the cook and the lead stable man stayed. We lived on Kim-me's salary and what Brook could make selling near-horses. We were not poor, but a long way from rich. I learned to do laundry and muck horse stalls. I transferred out of Loyal Sons the best private upper school in the League, to Garrison's a good second rank school and ten times less costly. A year later my Alpha father found a position at a small local bank adding a bit more income.

At the end of my second year in upper school my parents sat me down for a talk. Kim-me said, 'You have only one more year of upper school before you must select a university. There is no way we can afford West Star. Your grades are not strong enough for a scholarship. An athletic scholarship won't help either; they don't care if you are the best field ball player at Garrison. Sports don't count for much at West Star unless you played for Loyal Sons or one of the other aristocratic schools.'

Richard continued, 'I am so damn sorry but the Public University is the best we can do. I advise you to study accounting or teaching for a secure future.'"

Tracey continued her story after taking a deep breath, "My heart stopped, accounting or teaching -

NO WAY! I had spent a lot of time in the stable and talking to Bob Redding our stable man. He had been an enlisted crewman in the Space Force. He spun out tales of the Free Space Force. I told my parents I wanted a life of adventure and planned to apply for Space Force Officer Training School!"

Brook said, 'You could have told us you wanted to be a tavern girl and shocked the family less.'

"Our family, going back generations, had no history of military service. They were bankers, traders, teachers, and horse people. No Mills or Watkins served any branch of military in living memory. They thought it was senseless to serve when you could live well here on Freehome. Alpha father Richard asked, 'Did you know what kind of salary an officer makes?' Kim-me said that the family would not pay for my education to be an officer. I told them Parliament pays the cost. After three hours of screaming, which got me and them nowhere; I went to my room and wrote out my plans. The next day Brook fired Redding. I told my parents to rehire him or I would be on my back in a spacer tavern before the week ended. Redding was rehired.

After a year of fighting with my family I went to Officer Training School," Tracey finished with a sly smile.

Chapter Fourteen
– The Battlecruiser Lady Delapasse orbit above Green Four 12-25-517

Nirabella was glad to be on board *the Lady* after spending weeks fixing medical supply problems on the Space Force Base of Green Four. Chief Sergeant Cici De Santis was standing next to her. Colonel Chung had been true to his word and recommended both of them for positions on the *Lady Delapasse*. General Bridgeford quickly approved their positions as soon as he arrived with the battle cruiser.

The general and the four senior officers were standing on the overhead walkway in the closed lifter bay. Almost all three hundred and sixty-five officers and crew were gathered in the bay.

General Alexander Bridgeford began, "I am going to keep this short. First, welcome aboard to the new members of the crew. I understand some very experienced crew members have joined us and some new crew members arrived from OTS and Crew Training."

"This ship will leave orbit in four hours and begin a long and dangerous mission," the general continued. "We will be accompanied by three other ships of Green Fleet; the destroyer *Fire Dancer*, a League built sphere ship, the fast escort *Summer Storm* an Imperial built ship and the sphere ship fast escort *Racing Lady*. The remainder of the fleet will provide protection for Green Four and convoys trading along the Green Line. As many of you know the Green Line is a line of stars reaching out from Green's Star on the outer edge of the Free Stars Cluster. The line reaches out into uncharted and unknown space. The inhabited planets that orbit these stars are independent and not part of the League of Free Stars. However, critical trade routes have developed along these planets. Many essential materials, metals, chemicals, bio-chemicals, drugs, and even luxury items are traded via the line. Just one example, the material used in your space suits comes from this trade. It's twice as strong and is more flexible than any material we can currently manufacture."

"Pirates are now threatening that trade with much larger and better armed ships than ever before," he warned. "For reasons, we don't as yet understand, the Troc Empire may be supplying the pirates with these ships. Together I believe we can destroy the pirates and protect the Green Line! May the gods protect us and give us victory!" the general said loudly and enthusiastically. The crew exploded into clapping, shouting ascent and joyful banter.

After the cheering stopped, Cici said to Nirabella, "Nice speech from Ax, short and to the point."

Nirabella replied, "You and I have been out along the Green Line; do you think the new crew members are ready?"

Cici said, "I am not sure about some of them but the new blond lieutenant and the twins sure as all the hells are." Cici quickly changed the subject. "Do you know how our General Alexander (the Ax) Bridgeford got his nickname? It's a story worth knowing." Nirabella shook her head. Cici leaned into her conspiratorially and spoke quietly. "Thirty years ago, at the space battle off Morgan's Abode," she said, "he was commanding a light cruiser which somehow took out an imperial battleship. His cruiser was badly damaged in the battle." Cici looked around to see if anyone was observing her and Nirabella. Everyone else was busy. Cici continued the narrative, "He landed at the main hospital on Morgan's Abode with three lifters full of critically wounded. A staff colonel told Bridgeford he didn't have the correct documentation to land and unload and new documentation would take several hours to prepare. Bridgeford was only a major at the time, the colonel out ranked him and was in charge. The staff colonel told Bridgeford that the wounded would just have to wait in the lifters. Bridgeford walked out of the colonel's office took a fire ax off the wall, went back into the office and with a single ax blow to the head killed the colonel. He then ordered the ground staff, "Move the wounded into the hospital NOW!" Next, he calmly asked to talk to the colonel's replacement. A Board of Inquirer was never held. The Colonel's family was told he died in an accident on base." Cici sighed as Nirabella raised an eyebrow.

Chapter Fifteen
– The Battlecruiser Lady Delapasse 02-01-518

The great battle cruiser had dropped out of the time wave two days earlier. The ship and her escorts were now three star systems out along the Green Line. The ships were turned so that the main engines faced toward their direction of travel. they were decelerating to approach the planet Pangerbar a major trading center.

Tracey heard the declaration, "Battle Alert, pull suit packs, and all crew to combat assignments!"

Tracey was lying in her bunk when the Battle Alert was sounded. Quickly she pulled her space suit and helmet pack from the locker in her small cabin. She heard Fleet Officer Nirabella next door getting her suit pack out. They shared a common bathroom and the doors were open. Tracey looked for Purple Cat to hastily push her into the safety carrier. But, the little cat was already in the carrier and ready to trip the sealed door closed. Purple Cat's training worked perfectly. After the door was sealed she would have two days' air and water if the ship's atmosphere was lost to the vacuum of space.

In the passageway outside their cabins, Tracey and Nirabella crossed paths, carrying their space suit packs. Tracey was heading aft to the backup control station for the rear turret. Nira was heading forward to the medical area.

They said the traditional words to each other. "Victory, Honor, Ship!"

In the main Control Center, Peter Guderian sat with his spacesuit pack hung on the side of his chair and a fire control panel in front of him. A Battle Alert had been called and he had absolutely nothing to do. The control panel in front of Peter had every function locked out. He could only watch, observe, and learn. Captain Montgomery did not trust him to operate the control panel. It was not because he was half Troc. It was because he wasn't very good at fire control. In fact, during a recent combat simulation he blasted one of the Space Forces' own ships. It was a clean rail gun hit mid ships.

The Captain's only comment was, "Which side are you fighting for Guderian?"

Battles could not be fought when the Time Wave Drive was engaged. All members of the Time Wave Navigation Team therefore had combat assignments in the control room. Demitrianna Constantine, the young Captain and the Chief Time Wave Navigator (CTWN) did not have much use for anyone who could not help in an alert. In fact, Demitrianna had little use for anyone who ranked below her. She was mid height, with a solid body. Her face was gorgeous with deep black eyes and meticulously styled coal black hair. However, there was nothing gorgeous about her personality. Her nick name was the Black Widow after the notorious spider the humans had brought into the Empire and later to the

League. She was only five years out of Officer Training School and already a Captain. Demitrianna was a superb CTWN and the most ambitious person Peter had ever encountered. She glanced over at him with a gaze that said, "I see a blank space when I look at you Guderian."

Peter's attention reverted back to General Bridgeford. The general ordered, "To all ships of the fleet, cut the dark matter engines on my mark. Turn all ships 180 degrees to face the nose in the direction of travel." Sixty Seconds later the General said, "Mark now!"

Bridgeford outlined the situation and his battle plan to the crew and the other ships of the fleet. "Our sensors show five pirate ships closing on the orbiting station of Pangerbar. There are eight merchant trader ships docked at the station and two more in orbit around the planet. If we continue to decelerate we will be too late to stop the pirate attack. If the fleet continues on at our current speed we will reach the pirates before they can attack the station or the merchant ships. But, we will get just a single pass at them as our velocity is five times the pirates'. To get a second pass we need to slow further and then go around the sun.

The *Fire Dancer, Summer Storm,* and *Racing Lady* will each attack one of the three small pirate ships. The *Lady Delapasse* will attack the two large pirate ships. All rail guns will fire on auto control by

Captain Constantine. All missiles will launch on auto control by Captain Montgomery."

Executive Officer Colonel Harrison Chung announced, "We will be in missile range in three hours, twenty-four minutes and 18 seconds and within rail gun range in three hours twenty-four minutes and 59 seconds."

Bridgeford issued a Standby-Alert for the next three hours. The crew could wait three hours to suit up. The cooks would distribute hot and cold drinks and sandwiches to all the combat stations. The crews could go take a piss.

Bridgeford closed with, "Victory, Honor, Ship!"

Three hours later Kat, Chief Sergeant De Santis and a dozen crew members were suiting up in the airlock above Missile Drop Bay One. Light and Shadow were two of the dozen members. On the other side of the airlock the drop bay doors were already starting to open to space.

Kat asked via his helmet mike, "Everyone sealed up? Is your air flow correct? All suit systems working?"

He counted thirteen "yes" responses, tapped his com and confirmed, "Bay one crew stand by for our dance with death!"

Tracey suited up in the backup control station of the rear turret. The backup control station was an armored chamber just below the rear rail-gun turret. With her were Chief Sergeant Baryic Chahill, who she did not know well and four crew members. The team had two functions. First, was to climb up to the turret if the auto loaders jammed and clear them. The second was to take control of the turret and aim and fire the guns if communications were lost with the main Control Center.

The four crew members were strapped into seats along the wall. Tracey and Baryic were seated in the center of the chamber with fire control panels in front of them. They were seated facing each other. Tracey could monitor all fire control actions but would only have control if the blue light flashed at the top of her screen.

The massive power cables around the chamber hummed as both large rail-guns above were charged. The twenty kilo projectiles were already loaded into the breach area of the guns. The projectiles would be launched at five thousand plus meters per second. But first the missiles would be launched.

Incoming missile tracks suddenly flashed onto Tracey's screen. The missiles appeared in space with no ship nearby. Tracey thought, *Drift missiles; they must have been planted by the pirates. These missiles drifted in space totally powered down until a tight beam signal turned them on and set a target. It was an extremely wasteful use of missiles. You have to place many of them to ensure one or two were close to your target. Where, by all the gods, did a bunch of dog licking pirates get that many missiles? There was only one answer!*

Tracey watched as seconds later Montgomery's team launched two mid-sized missiles from the two forward tubes in the nose section. Next came two more missiles. She watched as these four missiles destroyed the two incoming drift missiles

Inside Missile Bay One, Kat and Cici had arranged the crew along cat walks between each of the drop racks. These big missiles were over twenty meters long and a meter in diameter. They were pushed free by a blast of steam and their plasma engines only fired when well clear of the great battle cruiser. The crew was equipped with power hammers, pry bars, hydraulic rams, and even two cutting torches. May the gods help if a torch was used on a missile!

Montgomery told Kat, "Bay Two's launch racks did not power up. It's all up to your team, Kat."

The first two big missiles dropped clean. Then, the next missile on the right rack dropped clean however the one in the left rack jammed. Cici and her crew were responsible for the left rack; they all leaped forward. As Cici jammed the pry bar in above the missile she saw Light hit the rack with a power hammer. Suddenly the rack broke and the missile dropped free. A long piece of the broken rack cut the suit of Ronda Canfield wide open. She was just too close, trying to free the missile. Ronda exploded out of the wide cut as blood and guts sprayed Cici and Light. A bone with meat attached bounced off of Light's helmet. It was over in seconds. The vacuum of space ripped the poor girl apart.

Kat told himself, *Shane Kat Jang stand steady!*

He told the team, "Steady team, we have more missiles to launch. Captain Montgomery will block the left rack, everyone to the right-side rack."

Two more missiles dropped from the right rack and their plasma engines fired and then it was over. Gunson launched no more missiles.

Minutes earlier, when the first missiles launched, Tracey tackled the two pirate heavy cruisers. On her screen, she watched as the pirate cruisers blasted three of five missiles before they reached either ship. Tracey saw one of *the Lady's* large missiles slam into the closer cruiser mid ships, it was a good hit. The heavy cruiser began to breakup. The last and fifth big missile missed and raced toward the sun.

The pirate opened up with her rail-guns. The rail-guns in the Lady's turrets began to fire. Seconds later Tracey heard an explosion as a rail-gun projectile from the remaining pirate cruise ripped through deck three of the Lady. The blue light flashed on her screen. Sergeant Baryic yelled, "Fire, fire!" Tracey locked the guns on target and fired. The first shot missed. She tracked her second shot and within seconds it hit. It almost missed but struck the aft most engineering area and destroyed the tubes for the plasma and dark matter engines. The second pirate cruiser was disabled. Sergeant Chahill yelled, "Nice hit! We got the scum!"

On the Control Deck, Peter could not understand what in the hells was wrong with Demitrianna otherwise called the Black Widow. She was screaming her head off. They had destroyed one major pirate ship and disabled the other. On top of that, two of the three small pirate ships were disabled and the other one was sending a surrender signal. *What could she be so pissed off about?* Peter thought. Before he could stop himself, Peter shouted out, "Are you totally nuts Widow? We got the kills."

Chapter Sixteen
– The Battlecruiser Lady Delapasse Docked at Pangergar's Station 02-07-518

The Battlecruiser was docked at the Pangerbar space station. The crew completed transforming the main mess hall of *Lady* into a room for the ceremony. General Bridgeford and senior offices sat on a raised platform which filled one end of the room. Just below the platform were the seats for Kat and twenty other offices and crew. At the other end of the room were chairs for the audience. The Vid cameras were on and transmitting to all ships of Green Fleet and to the station. The Vid would then be transferred to the city below and finally be shipped home to the League by fast courier.

As Kat sat awaiting the Board of Inquirer, he would soon hear his and the other's fate. Kat thought, *was it only seven days ago that Green Fleet won an impressive victory? How can I once more be before a Board? How did I go wrong? The board was called three days ago. Witness after witness testified, painting each of us as either incompetent, or as criminals. Captain Demitrianna Constantine twisted the facts and drove home our so-called crimes at every point in the inquirer.*

Colonel Chung began to read the list of verdicts starting with the lowest ranks.

"Ivan Zimmerman, Crewmember – You are found guilty of incompetence in Missile Bay One. You are discharged from the Free Space Force."

"Fidelity Stone, Crewmember – You are found guilty of incompetence in Missile Bay One. You are discharged from the Free Space Force."

And so, it went for the next seven crew members until he reached the last four of Kat's missile bay crew.

The colonel read the verdicts for the remaining four team members.

"Shadow Freeman, Crewmember –You are found guilty of incompetence in Missile Bay One. You are discharged from the Free Space Force."

"Light Freeman, Crewmember -. You are found guilty of negligence causing the death of a fellow crew member. You are discharged from the Free Space Force."

"Cici De Santis, Chief Sergeant - You are found guilty of negligence causing the death of a fellow crew member. You are discharged from the Free Space Force."

"Shane Kat Jang, Fleet Officer 2nd Class - You are found guilty of negligence and failure to lead, causing the death of a fellow crew member. You are discharged from the Free Space Force."

I am next, thought Nirabella. *What in the hells did I do wrong? The boy from Deck Three had a massive head injury. No one could have saved him.*

They continued, but now Demitrianna Constantine stepped forward and read the remaining verdicts.

"Nirabella Freestar, Fleet Assistant Physician 1st Class - You are found guilty of negligent in the medical care fellow crew member and causing his death. You are discharged from the Free Space Force."

"Erica Nguyen, Crewmember – You are found guilty of incompetence in the backup control station of turret five. You are discharged from the Free Space Force."

Three more crew member's names followed with the same outcome of being discharged. Then the last three names were read.

"Baryic Chahill, Chief Sergeant - You are found guilty of incompetence in the backup control station of turret five. You are discharged from the Free Space Force."

Tracey Mills-Watkins, Lieutenant 3rd Class PO - You are found guilty of firing the rail-guns of turret five without your superior's authorization. You are discharged from the Free Space Force."

Tracey's mind raced, *'Damn you, Black Widow you slime sucking bitch. Why the whole team? By the way, you evil bitch, we did disable a pirate heavy cruiser! I know I saw that blue light flash.'*

Tracey noted a small smile creep across Demitrianna's face as she read the final name.

"Peter Guderian, Lieutenant 3rd Class PO – The charges against you are numerous and serious. However, insubordination while in combat is enough. You are discharged from the Free Space Force."

General Bridgeford spoke the final words. "It wounds me to the core to discharge twenty-one of our crew. However, your disgraceful actions leave me no other course but to clear the garbage from this ship."

******

Four hours after the verdicts, the discharged crew members were marched out onto the main deck of the space station. The guards turned and marched back into *the Lady*. Discharged and disgraced, they were on their own. The Pangerbar station was much larger than most expected. But, of course, as a trading center much of the business took place on the station. Why lift a cargo down to the surface only to re-lift it later?

Tracey looked over the twenty-one. She decided *we are a ragged band, each of us in civilian clothing.*

We walk down this deck stripped of Space Force uniforms and with our packs holding only a few personal possessions. One of the young crew members, Fidelity Stone did not have any civilian clothing. She was given old unmarked gray coveralls. Kat is wearing red shorts and a yellow pullover. And, look at Erica Nguyen she has a pink uni-tard and a man's shirt on. I am not much better in my hiking outfit with boots, tan shorts, and an old green top that doesn't look like much. We the ex-officers need to help the young crew as much as we can. Thank the gods they let me take the carrier for Purple Cat.'

Peter Guderian said, "Let's find an inn and get a drink and rooms."

Fidelity Stone responded, "Some of us don't even have the money for a drink much less a room."

Peter then said, "I think I can cover a round of drinks, plus rooms and food for all of us during the next few days. Fidelity, you cute little redhead, I even promise not to try to sneak into your room and ravish your beautiful body tonight."

Fidelity answered, "Peter, you ugly little half Troc, you don't need to sneak into my room. My door will be unlatched just for you. I will ravish your, not so beautiful, but sexy, body tonight and for as many nights as you wish."

Fidelity's and Peter's exchange broke the tension and all twenty-one of them laughed until tears ran down their cheeks.

After the group regained composure, Kat asked, "Does anyone know a good inn on the station?"

Cici answered, "The White Pennant is good. Not fancy but very clean and the food is decent. I stayed there two years ago. The prices are reasonable by station norms and I know the two ladies who own the place."

Tracey picked up the carrier with Purple Cat and said, "Cici lead on," and they all followed Cici down the main passageway. The walls were covered with green vines to help keep Co2 levels down.

As Nirabella walked toward the inn with Light and Shadow she asked in a quiet voice, "Do you think its love or money with Fidelity?"

Light answered first, "Its love. She has been in love with Peter since she came aboard with the new crew members. She loved him before she knew his family was rich."

Shadow then responded, "Fidelity may be short, but she has great tits, a very fine ass, and is as sexy as a Vid goddess. Who cares whether its love or money? Either way Peter is a lucky man."

"Pig" commented Light.

After a few hundred meters Cici turned and walked down a side passageway which ended in a small open square with raised boxes and pots holding flowers and lush green plants. Of course, the boxes and pots were constructed of aluminum and painted to look like wood or ceramic. Weight consideration was everything on an orbiting station. The square was flooded with sun light; the station must be on the daylight side of the Planet. There was no direct sunlight. All light was brought in by a complex system of light tubes.

An open walkway circled the square. The White Pennant was on the walkway just across the small square. The inn's tavern opened to the square. Tables and comfortable chairs lined a low fence and on the gate hung a sign that said, "Welcome". What appeared to be a real wood bar formed the back wall of the tavern. It was the middle of Second Watch and the tavern was almost empty. As soon as Cici walked through the gate what appeared to be a real woman rushed out and clasped her arms around Cici. She was thirty plus, big, blond, and loud. A delightful smile lighted her face.

She said, "Welcome back, it's been far too long! How is the bravest Sergeant in the Space Force? I often remember the night you broke up the big bar fight and saved our tavern. Welcome, double welcome, to you and to all your friends! All of you have a seat and I'll get cold beers and drinks."

Then she exclaimed, "By the gods, that's not Sergeant Baryic in your group? I didn't know you two knew each other. How are you handsome Baryic? You look as good as ever, but a lot grayer. I have not forgotten that night when you were remarkably yourself. But, these young people don't need to hear about that!"

Cici spoke, "Morgan, thank you for the wonderful welcome. None of us are any longer in the Space Force. We need to arrange food and rooms."

"I'll be damned; you are the group discharged from the battle cruiser! I heard about it, but I was working and did not see the Vids. How can the Space Force discharge people like you?" Morgan asked no one in particular.

"Cici your group will get our best rates on food and rooms, however, we don't have that many rooms open, you will need to double and triple up. Baryic can sleep with me and Sue if he likes. We won't charge him for the room." She smiled.

By this time most of group found seats and Anna, a younger version of Morgan, was serving beers and ice tea.

Morgan's partner Susan entered the tavern and gave Cici and Baryic big hugs. Sue looked about the same age as Morgan and with a splash of red hair. Sue stopped before Fidelity, "My gods you could be my daughter!" It was true she looked like Fidelity would in twenty years and with several added kilos.

After introductions, Cici, Peter, Tracey, and Kat sat with Morgan and Susan to work out the details of their stay and who bunks with whom. Sue offered to cut the cost of food if they would eat crew style, one meal at a scheduled time. After a quick discussion, Peter told her they would take that option for breakfast and dinner. For lunch, they were on their own. Peter then dispensed enough imperials from his data pack to cover four days' expense. Sue told Tracey that Purple Cat could stay, but asked if Tracey would please let her out of the carrier to hunt.

"Morgan and I run a clean inn but not everyone does. We get rats and motans from nearby food stalls and shops," Sue said. Tracey agreed to let Purple Cat hunt.

Three hours later after food and beers most of the crew had disappeared to bed. The officers and sergeants, minus Peter, sat before the artificial fireplace in the tavern talking. Peter and Fidelity had vanished with two glasses and a bottle of local wine. The team discussed various topics such as getting new clothing and the possibility of moving down to the surface. They also discussed going back to the League but everyone agreed they didn't want to go home after what happened.

Kat sipped his ice tea and asked, "Ladies and gentlemen what work can we find for ourselves and the young crew members? How do we make a living?"

Baryic, who said nothing to that point, spoke, "I believe our best course of action is to buy a warship."

"WHAT!!?" Tracey blurted spewing her drink across the table.

Chapter Seventeen
- Pangergar's Space Station 02-10-518

After a day of contentious and spirited discussions, the team decided to go with Baryic's proposal. They spent the next two days finding out as much as possible about buying a warship.

Tracey discovered it was not hard to buy a private warship out along the Green Line. Lots of money; a very large amount of money was required. Warships were sold at auction by several brokers. One broker was scheduling an auction next week.

Kat and Baryic learned that by contracting to escort merchant ships the cost of a ship could be recouped in two or three trips. The farther out along the Green Line, the better the money.

Peter reported the local banks would lend money to buy a ship if a company could come up with cash to cover a quarter of the total cost. The interest rates were outrageous but the number of ships lost in the escort business was high. The banks made money. The private ship companies took the risks.

The next day Kat, Baryic, Tracey, Peter, and Cici met with a grossly fat Troc surnamed Akvanitek. His desk was covered in model spaceships and used food containers. He wore robes of wildly colored cloth which Trocs adore. The metallic green and orange of his robes did not match his red and pink hair.

He told the five of them, "My firm Akvanitek and Smith will auction four warships next week. I believe ten million Imperials will take any of three smaller ships. I know your gang is from the League. At current exchange rates that's hundred million League Stars. If you can show us that you have sufficient funds, I can arrange an inspection before the auction. You may bring up to five inspectors for an hour per ship."

Tracey asked, "An hour per ship is not much time to inspect, how can we be sure a ship is sound?"

"You can't!" the big Troc answered. "However, for twenty thousand Stars we can provide a complete survey report for any of the ships."

"What are 'sufficient funds'?" Kat asked referring back to Akvanitek's comments about the upcoming auction.

"Proof of twenty million League Stars would give us confidence you are serious." Akvanitek continued "If your gang should win the biding, you will need at least twenty million additional Stars to put one of these ships in first class condition. Please let me know as soon as you can about the inspections."

After a pause Akvanitek added, "Peter, my sources tell me you have been talking to banks. If I were you I would use The Bank of Pangerbar. They are less picky about who they deal with. Your gang of FSF castoffs will need all the help you can get."

The final words came from Smith, a big boned woman with a round face, brown hair, and wearing greasy coveralls. She had sat in back of the office and said nothing until now.

"Your gang going pirating or contracting? I suppose you know on The Green Line there is little difference!" she asked.

Somehow over time and with determination, Peter pulled together just over twenty million Stars and a loan commitment for sixty million Stars by the end of the week. The gods only knew what Peter had done to get the money. Fidelity knew Peter sold off all rights to his Guderian inheritance, but what else he did was a mystery. The other Officers, the Sergeants, and crew stripped their personal accounts and added 450,000 Stars to the funds.

After inspections and after reading the costly survey reports, all twenty-one team members assembled.

Tracey told them, "We are ready for this auction. I believe we will be able to buy one of the two Imperial built fast escorts. We'd like everyone's final vote on this plan to buy a ship. Please vote 'yes' for the plan or vote 'no' to drop the plan."

Peter counted the votes and enthusiastically announced, "We have twenty-one 'yes' votes!"

Chapter Eighteen
- Pleasant Valley Pangerbar 02-15-518

The day following the ship auction, a lifter sat down in Pangerbar City. It was near dawn on a crisp autumn day. Nirabella, Light, Shadow, and Fidelity walked across the immense plastio-cement landing field. The gravity pulled at them after experiencing the low gravity of the Space Station. Like the Space Station, the landing field was totally dedicated to trade. Warehouses lined the edge of the field for kilometers and fifty lifters waited for the next loads. To the North was the city proper, clean and beautiful. To the South the land dropped off into a shallow valley. Slum dwellings polluted the valley. The poor who worked at hard labor and menial jobs on the landing field lived in the slum. Nirabella and her companions came to this landing field to undertake a specific plan in this slum.

At the modest passenger terminal, the first six electro-van drivers refused their fare as soon as Nirabella gave them the location of their destination. Finally, a driver with a battered electro-van said he would take them for twice the standard rate. As they got in, the driver set a large rocket pistol on the seat next to him.

"My name is Marsborn. The gun is just in case." he said.

Nirabella reviewed the plan in her mind as they drove. *All four of us are armed. The twins carry knifes and rocket pistols. Fidelity and I carry knifes and compact pistols. We have two packs of gifts. How bad can this slum ironically called Pleasant Valley be? My gods look outside; it's the worst slum I have seen. Those three children are roasting a dead dog over a scrap plastic fire. The little one is missing both arms and turning the spit using one foot and balancing on the other. How does the city government allow humans to live like this? Can we find the kids? They had won the bid on one of the warships. Now they need to fill out the crew. The innkeeper Morgan had given a letter and told them where they might recruit a crew. Of course, you would need to be desperate or crazy to join an unproven warship without pay. But the kids might just be who they needed.*

Marsborn commented, "This is high ground; Pleasant Valley gets worse down by the river."

Pleasant Valley, in fact got worse. The area was a morass of shacks built from every type of scrap dumped by the space port. Every corner held a crude bar or something worse. Light counted three bodies before they reached their destination.

The four got out of the van on a nameless narrow dirt street. Across the street was a large sheet metal shack. A walkway of scrap foam led a few steps up to a metal door with a single slot near the top.

Fidelity said, "Let me go up and knock, it might be less intimidating." Fidelity knocked on the door.

"Get the hells away from the door, we're not home!" a high female voice yelled.

Fidelity spoke to the closed door, "We've come to help and to offer you a way out of Pleasant Valley."

The voice behind the door angrily said, "We aren't going whoring, or selling drugs. We might kill if it's enough money."

"We have gifts of food." Fidelity said quietly.

"Push some through the slot." The voice instructed.

Shadow tossed Fidelity two packets of high energy food paste. She in turn pushed the packets into the slot.

After three very long minutes negotiating, the door slowly opened. Standing before them was a girl of no more than nineteen years. She was of mid height, with dull brown hair. Her face would have been pretty if she wasn't so thin. The thin girl wore dull gray-brown coveralls that had been washed so many times the original color was gone. In her hand was an old rocket pistol.

Fidelity told her, "Morgan at the White Pendant gave us this letter."

Suddenly Nirabella charged up the steps and pushed past Fidelity and the girl. "You have someone here with a wicked infection! I smell the wound! Let me see the infected person. It's possible I can save them."

Shocked, the girl slowly turned and walked to the back of the shack. They all followed her. A hidden vegetable garden filled the back of the shack. The roof was pushed open to the sunlight. A young man lay nude on a cot near the garden. He was gaunt and sweat covered him despite the coolness of the garden. His right leg had a deep wound from his upper leg to below the knee. As they approached the boy the stench was overpowering.

Nirabella knelt beside the boy and asked, "What's your name?"

The boy weakly rasped, "Ping."

"Ping, I am going to take a look at your leg and see what we need to do to control the pain and to heal it." She said calmly.

"Just give me a shot of drugs to kill me." He whispered.

Nirabella told Ping, "You are not going to die." But, she knew it might not be true.

Light handed Nirabella her medical kit as she asked what else she needed.

"Boil the cleanest water you can find, add two drops of the green liquid to each liter. Then bring me a bowl of the water and everyone wash with the water. Shadow, Fidelity, find all the clean cloth you can and then Shadow please guard the door and the van." She injected Ping with Imperial Pain Stop and antibiotics. She started an IV drip to give Ping nourishment and liquids. Next, she began to cut away the rotting flesh. Within minutes a stack of clean sheets and towels was handed to Light.

While Nirabella and Light worked on Ping's leg, Fidelity talked quietly to the girl.

"My name is Fidelity Stone, what's your name?" she asked.

"Rhonda Santacruz" the girl answered.

Fidelity asked Rhonda if she was alright.

"No, we're not 'alright'," Rhonda responded and then continued, "Ping is dying and we're all trapped in this hell hole."

Fidelity put her arms around Ronda. "We can help, please tell me where the other kids are."

"They are working the midnight to midday shift at the field. They will be back here in a few hours. I stayed home today so Ping would not be alone. I washed him and packed herbs into his wound. It did not help. We can't afford a doctor."

"How many of you live here?"

"If you count Ping there are twenty-three of us left."

Fidelity asked, "Please tell me your story."

Ronda nibbled a food bar and began, "We were dumb kids, so dumb you can't believe it. One year ago, back on Freehome, we all passed the first screening for the Space Force Crew. But, we were not in the final group selected. There were twenty-nine of us who were close but not selected. This con artist told us and our parents that he could get us on as Space Force Crew out on the Green Line. Our parents used their savings to pay him. He took their money and dumped us here on Pangerbar. There never were openings in Space Force, may the gods damn his soul to the deepest hell."

Without correct documents, we could not get legitimate jobs on Pangerbar. Four kids were able to sign onto commercial ships. After a month, the money ran out and those left moved to Pleasant Valley where we took any job we could get at the landing field. Two kids simply disappeared not long after we moved. A week ago, Ping's leg was deeply cut at the landing field. They do not assist slum people; we are merely expendable labor," Ronda concluded sadly.

Three hours later Nirabella was still sitting next to Ping. To remove the rot, she cut away a significant amount of flesh. Ping was weaker and she hoped to get him to hospital but their driver Marsborn dashed that hope. Even if they had the money, he told her that it would take days to get a slum kid into a hospital. Their best hope was to get him to the space station.

The twenty-one other members of the reconnaissance mission arrived in the kids' home. They learned the kids leader was a girl of sixteen named Centari Shamir. Shadow explained the reason for the trip to Pleasant Valley.

He told them, "We need a crew for a private warship. We will take all twenty-three of you. You know each other and have worked together to survive under impossible conditions. Each of you came very close to being sent to Free Space Force crew training. We believe you would fit into our crew quickly."

"Before you make any decision, here's what you're getting into," Shadow said. "First, you will serve aboard an Escort. She is an old pirate ship and needs considerable work. Secondly, the ex-officers and crew are Space Force castoffs; everyone was found guilty of charges and dismissed from the Space Force. The next issue is pay. There is no money to pay any of us. When and if we turn a profit, you will get a share but we are deeply in debt to a bank. We will see you have a clean place to live, full sets of clothing and adequate meals. However, the clean place to live will take some time because the ship is a mess.

Centari interrupted Shadow, "You don't need to say more; we accept with grateful thanks. We do have one condition. We won't leave Ping to die here, as you said we survive together. By the way, we call ourselves The Lost."

An hour later they were packed and the team and the new crew members were moving out to load the van. Twenty-seven was a hell of a load for the old van. Some would ride on top. Nirabella, Light, and four of the crew were just moving Ping out to the van when the driver, Marsborn yelled, "Everyone get out here and bring your weapons!"

When Nirabella arrived out on the road she found Marsborn, Shadow, Fidelity, Centari, and Ronda all with pistols drawn. As they stepped across the road Light drew her pistol. Coming down the road were six of the ugliest creatures Nirabella had ever seen. A man rode on the back of each beast.

"What in all the hells are they?" Nirabella asked.

Centari replied, "The beasts are Kirgiiiz. The men are the Contract Patrol. The government hires them to keep the peace in the valley. Mostly the patrol just steals all they can. Keep back from the beasts they have a two-meter tongue with a sharp claw at the tip."

As the beasts came closer Nirabella saw them clearly. She thought, *Look at them, segmented bodies over five meters long, two meters at the shoulders, six legs with claws, two front limbs with more claws and a massive head with a mouthful of teeth. They are armored with scales the color of yellow green pool slime. The men on their backs do not look any better. They are big, unkempt men wearing bits and pieces of old body armor. The three in front carry rocket pistols. The three behind them have long guns. How do we deal with this?*

The three menacing men in front slipped off their Kirgiiiz mounts. The largest man, his face covered with a tangled red beard spoke, "I see you are moving. We're here to collect the moving tax."

Centari replied, "There is no such thing as a moving tax."

The big one said, "There is a moving tax if the Patrol says so."

After a short pause, he continued, "We have a special tax deal for you. We kill all of you slowly or you give us all your money and weapons, let us rape your women and we allow you to live!"

Suddenly Light said, "You don't have to rape me, I love big men. Let's go to it."

Shock ran through everyone including the patrol men. Light pulled off her utility pullover and stood there bare breasted. Next, she kicked off her boots and her utility pants then the last of her under garments. Wearing only socks she walked toward the big man.

She said, "Let's go big guy, I don't want to wait all day."

She stepped up to him and put her arm around him and said, "Over in the van we can go at it until I faint."

Arm in arm they took ten or twelve steps toward the van. The attention of the other patrol men was fixed on Light's bare body. She stumbled and he pulled her up. Light kissed the big man on the cheek and drove the razor thin knife into his armpit. The big man coughed up blood and dropped like a rock. Light hit the ground using the body as a shield. Shadow fired and the head of the man on the right exploded. Fidelity shot the man on the left five times in the chest. His armor was not that good. Centari and Ronda took out the center beast with multiple hits.

As the beast on the right lashed out with its claw tipped tongue, one crewman dashed in from the side and cut its tongue off with an ax. He was slashed in the shoulder by a limb claw, but rolled away. Marsborn stepped in close and emptied his pistol into the beast's eye, it collapsed. A dozen crew members attacked the beast on the left. They rammed a sharpened five-meter steel beam into its flank. The beast lashed out, two young men at the front of the beam were cut in half. Three more of the crew fell back with serious injuries, but they had driven the beam deep within the beast.

Someone flipped Light her pistol and she hit one of the patrol men still mounted and took off his left arm. *Poor shooting,* she thought. Nirabella shot wildly killing no one but wounded the three remaining beasts convincing the remaining two patrol men that a moving tax was not needed. They disappeared in the dust as they rushed their beasts back up the road.

Light stood up and said, "Perhaps they should have checked my socks instead of ogling my body."

Halfway back to the landing field the van was rent with screams. Centari and Ronda screamed as Nirabella cried, "Ping is gone; may the gods forgive me I could not save him." She put her arms around both young women. The van was filled with sobs until they reached the landing field.

As the sun set, the lifter landed. In silence, they loaded two bodies in bags and Ping, then assisted the four wounded into the lifter. One of the kids, Mark Bittman, carried Centari and then Ronda aboard, they were beyond walking from the grief of Ping's death. Nirabella pulled Marsborn on board. There was no future for him on Pangerbar. The lifter took off with all twenty-nine on board.

Piloting the lifter Tracey asked, "Tougher than you expected?"

Light answered sarcastically, "Not exactly an autumn day's stroll."

Chapter Nineteen
– Space Near Pangergar 04-17-518

Two months later, the Escort *Outcast Lady* was accelerating at ten gravities matching her speed to the great old liner *White Star* that she escorted. Like all imperial built ships, the liner was shaped like a striker fish with a pointed nose. Two other escorts *Boomer's Girl* and *Dark Fire* were also matching speed with the great liner. As the four ships approached critical speed Commander Shane Kat Jang commanded, "Give me your final checks for time wave travel."

"First Officer Tracey Mills-Watkins reporting all ships systems are stable and fully functional."

"Weapons Officer Cici De Santis reporting all weapons locked out and safe for time wave travel."

Engineering Officer Baryic Chahill smoothly adjusted the gravity field, and stated, "Time wave engines ready."

"Chief Time Wave Navigator Peter Guderian ready!"

Commander Jang said, "You have control Mister Guderian! Initiate the Time Wave Drive whenever you wish."

Peter replied, "Thank you Commander. I have full control and I am initiating TWD on my mark - Now!"

They felt the minor disorientation as Peter sent the ship into the peak of a wave of compressed time and space.

"The *Outcast Lady* is now above light speed." Peter announced on the com system throughout the ship.

Nirabella, in an acceleration couch at the edge of the control room, smiled. Cheering rang out throughout the ship. Light, Shadow, and Centari Shamir, in the single missile bay of the small ship, halted checking missile storage and cheered Kat's announcement. On the mess deck Anna Morgan, Morgan's daughter, and Rhonda Santacruz stopped storing supplies and raised a toast with cups of hot Gubble brew. In the Engine Room Neil Marsborn and Fidelity paused from monitoring The Time Wave Drive Engine and cheered.

At that moment, Purple Cat killed a motan by driving her special center claw into the motan's single eye. C-cats have five claws on each paw. The center claw is not hooked. It is straight and via powerful muscles and special ligaments the claw can be driven forward stabbing prey with deadly force.

The motan was typical of the species; the overall size was about 10 centimeters across with a round center body and a single eye on top which could be focused in any direction. The legs were arranged in an X shape each one with a razor-sharp claw. The powerful beak on the bottom is surrounded with eight tentacles to feel food and push it into the beak. All this covered in a tough scaled skin which enabled motans to withstand attacks and to even survive the vacuum of space for as much as two standard days.

Purple Cat started killing rats and motans as soon as the crew took possession of the ship two months ago. The ship was filthy and overrun with rats and motans so the cat's hunting supply was excellent. As the cleanup and repair of the ship proceeded, hunting became more challenging. However, Purple Cat was still killing one or two vermin a day.

****

A few hours later Tracey and Kat sat at a table in the mess area.

Kat said, "It's been a hell of a demanding two months. By the gods, I never thought we could get the *Outcast Lady* ready."

Tracey replied, "What a piece of trash she was when we took possession. The gods did not favor us at the auction. "

"Tracey, it was the only ship we could afford. You were at the auction. We had only the eighty million stars. Both of the Trocnavar -built fast escorts went for more than ninety million stars. We could only afford the last of the escorts and we had to bid almost seventy million to get her." Kat reiterated.

"Kat, what did we get; an ex-pirate ship, the one that surrendered at the last battle off Pangerbar? She is a League designed and constructed, a fast escort sphere ship. She was built over seventy years ago. The ship was filthy and poorly maintained. It took us three days just to clean out the trash. We spent days in air dock for repairs and more days working on her when docked at the station. The only good thing about her was the Free Space Force had started to install a new navigation computer and a new weapons computer before they decided to sell her. Somehow we got those wired in and operational." Tracey sighed.

"Tracey, *Outcast Lady* is a good ship; all of us together have made her a good ship. The crew, both those from the *Lady Delapasse* and the ones Nirabella and her team brought back from Pangerbar, are working together effectively. Hell, even Anna Morgan chose to join the crew and run the mess deck."

"Kat, you are right, but two points. First, we have a crew of fifty-one including Anna Morgan and six people who joined off the space station. The *Outcast Lady* was designed to be operated by seventy highly trained crew members. Point two, this is our first contract and it's to escort one of the most famous ships operating on the Green Line. This voyage is deep along the Line. If *White Star* is lost, our reputation as an escort is destroyed."

"Tracey, if *White Star* is lost I believe we will all be dead in the effort to defend her!" Kat exclaimed. Kat went off to check on engineering. Tracey sat for a long time thinking about *Outcast Lady. She is not a true sphere ship,* she thought. *Somewhere in the ship's history someone added an extended mid-section giving her an egg shape. It allows for more fuel and supplies to be carried and that's good out here on the Green Line. The ship is an egg covered with hatches, antennas, sensors, and control jets. Under the surface is two hundred millimeters of plastio-cement and foam carbon armor. The aft section is the smooth black surface of a Time Wave Drive. The TWD surface is pierced by a circular hole at the aft center of the egg. Long tubes project through the hole, the nozzles for the main plasma and dark matter engines. At the center of the bow is the armored iris ten meters in diameter. Under the iris is a clear dome over the Control Center.*

Mounted around the midsection are three rail-gun turrets, placed so that all directions of fire are covered. However, the turrets don't match each other; two are single guns firing an eight-kilo projectile. The other turret is equipped with twin quick-fire rail-guns shooting four kilo projectiles. Her single missile bay has two drop racks each capable of holding eight medium F2 League or X2 Troc missiles. The pirates did leave fifteen new Troc missiles X2 in the racks.

Maybe the little war ship is all right? Yes! Tracey told herself, *the Outcast Lady is a fine pocket-sized war ship!*

Chapter Twenty
- In Orbit above the Planet Martha's Hide 05-15-518.

Martha's Hide was very small for an inhabited planet. The space station, an important link in the trade along the Green Line, was capable handling significant trade. However, the surface settlement was too small to provide the supplies and grow the food needed to support the trade. Almost everything was imported.

It was a strange place of haunting beauty with only a thin atmosphere. Mesas and mountains rose up from dry and dusty plains. The planet's two settlements were each built at the foot of mountain ranges where a limited amount of liquid water runoff could be found underground. The settlements are constructed below surface with clear covers to let in light and with pressure systems to keep the atmosphere inside at near standard. The thin surface atmosphere was the reason for the cargo aboard *White Star*.

The liner had been converted some years ago by ripping out most of her passenger cabins and areas and installing two immense cargo holds. The holds now contained the two largest atmospheric and water concentrators ever built. These would allow the settlements to expand meeting needs of the space station. The units were so complex and delicate they could not be disassembled for shipment.

The Trocnavar Commander of *White Star* issued the final order to start the surface landing on Martha's Hide. Commander Fetel Caniitack transmitted, "As each of you know a surface landing is complex and difficult with even with a small space ship. With a ship the size of *White Star,* landing is near madness. However, we are all being paid splendidly to take this risk. Two of the escorts *Boomers Girl* and *Dark Fire* will remain in orbit to protect us from pirate attack. As planned, the third escort *Outcast Lady* will act as the pathfinder to the surface. May the Imperial Gods and the Human Gods keep us safe. Begin when ready, Commander Jang!"

Kat double checked to ensure all crew members were in spacesuits and strapped into seats. Kat then issued the command to begin decent. "Ms. Mill-Watkins you have pilot control, fly her down." In his mind Kat said, *Damn I hope all those hours she logged in gliders and lifters pays off.*

Tracey thought, *I damn well will get White Star down safe.* She knew the liner would be just two minutes behind the *Outcast Lady* and would base her flight plan on the information Tracey and the crew sent back to the old liner. It was critical they get correct information back to Caniitack and his crew.

Tracey began the descent. The ship was turned such that she would enter the atmosphere stern first.

Tracey fired the plasma engine and *Outcast Lady* began to slow. Before starting descent, the crew had done several things. The armored iris was closed to protect the Control Center. The dark matter engine tube was withdrawn into the hull. Finally, the lifter was fully manned with Cici as pilot.

"Mr. Chahill, give us all the lift you can from the gravity system. Cici, please go to full power from the lifter engine," Tracey instructed.

Both these actions reduced their apparent weight. As soon as the plasma engine fired Tracey began to battle the buffeting. She danced the maneuvering jets to stabilize the *Outcast Lady*. At one hundred eighty kilos from the surface the atmosphere began to create serious drag. Tracey increased power to the plasma engine slowing their airspeed. At a hundred thirty kilometers, the ship hit a massive wind shear.

Tracey fought to save the ship. *My gods she is going to tumble! I need to flip the control vanes on plasma engine plus use all control jets. By the gods, I think she is stable, won't over react and send us into an opposite tumble!*

Peter, who monitored communications with *White Star*, checked to ensure the info was received and flashed a signal to Tracey's console. He watched as minutes later the big ship rode through the wind shear more or less smoothly.

Tracey continued to dance *Outcast Lady* down balanced on the plasma engine. The sand storm struck at ninety kilos. She went to sensor control only, finding the best course within the storm for the liner behind her.

At seventy kilometers, the ground control picked her up. "This is the Control Captain, we have your signals. The course down looks acceptable for both of you. Expect severe turbulence at thirty kilos."

Tracey's mind raced. *Find the best path you can in the turbulence. Our little ship will bounce around more than the big liner. White Star should be safe even if the Outcast Lady is damaged.*

She kept the ship balanced on her plasma engine until three thousand meters. Then the plasma engine failed.

Tracey ordered, "NOW, Kat, NOW!!"

It was the command Kat hoped to never hear. He flipped the cover on four switches which had not been used in seventy some years and tripped all four. Kat thought, *I hope by the gods of Far Star this works.* Then he heard the detonation of exploding charges and blasts as four hatches round the outside of the nose blew open. Large yellow bags flew into the slip stream around the ship. After long years in storage the four gigantic emergency parachutes opened fully above the *Outcast Lady* slowing her descent.

"Thank you engineers and builders of long ago, the damn things still work, THANK YOU" Tracey whispered fervently.

Chahill extended the landing legs as the *Outcast Lady* rushed toward the landing area.

It was an incredibly hard landing. The scream of bending metal sounded as the four legs were crushed but somehow did not collapse. The tube of the plasma engine was driven into the engine's retraction housing in the hull. Within seconds Marsborn, Fidelity, and the rest of engine room crew sprayed air seal over the leaks in the damaged housing. Kat announced, "We're down and the hull integrity is holding. All sections check in. Great job everyone."

Minutes later they all watched their screens as *White Star* majestically set down in the cradle prepared for her. A great cheer arose throughout the *Outcast Lady*.

Within ten minutes Cici De Santis led a team cutting away the lines for the parachutes. High winds often developed on Martha's Hide. The parachutes would drag the ship over if high winds arose. Working in spacesuits was not easy. The work was going slowly, skin tight suits, light helmets, and a compact air source still inhibited them. Shadow, working on top of the ship, looked up from cutting lines and saw pirates attacking the *White Star*.

Chapter Twenty-One
- A Planet Called Nothing #1 02-13-518

Three months before and many light years away from the *White Star* landing, the sun rose on an island on a planet called Nothing #1. At first light a Trocnavar named Artystaar Tiigano awoke on a leaf bed. The arm of a male Human lay across her bare breasts. She was totally nude. Warm tropical air drifted through the windows. She looked to her right, as expected he was no one she knew. She looked to her left; a human woman lay next to her. Doubly good, she barely knew her. The smell of stale yellow spiced liquor and sex mixed with the tropical air.

Gods be damn, she loved this life; the mindless sex, wild drinking, the battles in space, the screams of the victims, and most of all the killing. It was the close face-to-face killing she relished. Boarding a ship and taking it was pure ecstasy. For a standard year Artystaar had been part of a pirate crew called the Blood Fire. It was the life she had been born for. Recently she was made a team leader by the crew. Of course, her noble Trocnavar family was light years beyond horrified. And they only knew a small part of the life she now lived.

Born into a noble household the third of three daughters, she was trouble from start. When she was five she drowned her sister's c-cat. During her eighth year Artystaar tried twice to kill her big sister, once with hot cooking oil. At ten standard years, she told her parents she wanted no part of the family business.

Her father exploded, "What do you mean you want to be an Imperial Space Force officer? You want to serve in the Blue Fleets! Are you insane? This family has traded in bound labors for hundreds of years! We are nobles! By the gods, the Tiigano clan has resources and we don't need to send our children to the Blue Fleets!"

The Imperial Space Force consisted of the outer fleets, The Empress's Fleets or Blue Fleets and Inner Fleets Emperor's Fleets or Orange Fleets. The Orange Fleet guarded the core of the Empire and protected about ninety of the one hundred fifty or so inhabited planets in the Trocnavar Empire. All officers were nobles, or high noble Trocs, some even members of Emperor's clan. Of course, the best and newest ships went to the Orange Fleets.

The Blue Fleets protected outer edges of the Empire. It was a less imposing force. They were equipped with rebuilt older ships and second class ships. The Blue Fleets were an expendable shield for the Empire. The Blue Fleets were also charged with crushing the frequent rebellions by the outer planets. The officers consisted of poor nobles, common Trocs, and even some humans. Rules and regulations were far less formal in the Blue Fleets, which was just fine with Artystaar.

Artystaar never made it through Blue Fleet Officer Training. At the end of the first year she killed her lover while drunk. Her current lover had objected to her adding another male for the night. Because she was a Troc, claimed self-defense and the boy was human, she was simply dismissed from the Blue Fleets. Several months of wandering later she found the pirates.

She took stock of herself. She had the looks of a young Trocnavar Vid star; a short, stocky, strong body, with the smooth curves and the large breasts typical of Troc beauties. Her round face was captivating by both Troc and human standards. Her wide set eyes were deep orange. Artystaar's blue and gold hair was space cut close to her head. A dyed red streak on the left side of her head marked her as member of the Blood Fire.

Artystaar recalled last night's activities. *The man was good, perhaps even very good, but the woman was something special. She was older but with a fine figure and trim body. Her breasts were still high. Blonde hair framed a face with a straight nose and cold gray eyes. The lady's smile was wickedly beautiful. Her skills at sex were extraordinary. Best of all she had three red Kill Dots tattooed on her right arm just below her shoulder.*

I have ten kill dots on my arm. She thought. *Only two are red -the rest are black or green.*

Artystaar and the woman met at a tavern called The End of Space. Her name was Sandy and she worked behind the bar. A man at the bar told Artystaar that Sandy had been a passenger on a small trader which pirate raiders captured. During the attack, Sandy seriously wounded two pirates and killed three. The pirate commander was so impressed he let her live. She got her red Kill Dots for the dead pirates. Also during the fighting, she got a raw scar down the left side of her back. After fighting and earning Kill Dots Sandy's next stop was a job at the tavern.

After several more months of seasoning working in the tavern, Artystaar decided that Sandy would be a suitable addition to the Blood Fire.

Chapter Twenty Two –
Main Landing Field on Martha's Hide 04-15-518.

Months later on Martha's Hide, Shadow stared in shock. It took a moment for Shadow to understand what he was seeing. It was difficult to see the hangers, warehouses, and the field control building across the landing field. The *Outcast Lady* landed over a kilo from the buildings. Halfway between the *Outcast Lady* and the base buildings the *White Star* rested in the cradle built for her. The *White Star* blocked most of his field of view.

Two massive mechanical carriers sat near the hangers ready to move out to the *White Star*. Already moving were six electro-trucks loaded with equipment for the atmospheric and water concentrators. As they drew closer to *White Star*, Shadow sensed something was wrong with the trucks; instantly Shadow knew! The gun mounts on the trucks were all manned. No one ever manned guns in a peaceful space port.

Shadow instantly signaled "attack" to the *Outcast Lady's* Control Center. He then signaled the team clearing parachute lines to get off the ship's nose. Shadow thought, *you have to admire the bastards! It's very clever! Attack on the ground where we never expected it. How did they get control of the trucks?*

Within seconds of receiving Shadow's alarm, Kat declared a full battle alert and issued a series of commands.

"Tracey and Cici man the lifter pilot and gunner slots. Baryic, Nirabella, plus all trained warriors and me to the lifter! Everyone get into suits with full combat weapons!" Kat ordered.

"Peter, you have control. Man, the turrets and see if you can shoot without hitting the W*hite Star.* Notify Commander Caniitack that help is on its way!" Kat continued.

"Shadow, are there any flags, symbols, or markings on our attackers?" Kat asked.

Shadow responded, "No identification that I can see."

"Peter, find out who in all the hells we are fighting." Kat commanded. "We leave for *White Star* in five minutes. Victory, Honor, Ship!"

Piloting the lifter, Tracey surveyed the situation. The big ship lay ahead of them like a beached giant fish. The plan was to find an air lock door on this side and unload Kat and his troops. Once inside they would attack those boarding the ship on the other side. Tracey, Cici and a rear gunner, would then fly around the big ship and destroy as many of trucks as possible.

Tracy found the airlock and flew the lifter up to it. The door was twenty-five meters off the ground. Turning the lifter, she locked the transfer tube from the rear to the airlock. Kat was first into the airlock's outer chamber followed by Baryic. Within a minute all twenty-eight were in the chamber.

Just as Tracey began to disengage from the airlock rocket projectiles ripped through the lifter. One of the trucks had driven around the *White Star's* cradle. Bits and pieces flew everywhere as the unknown gunner hit them with a second blast. Cici whipped around the quad rocket gun turret and destroyed the truck. But it was too late to save the lifter. Cici and Tracey scrambled for the transfer tube. As they passed the rear gunner, Cici said, "Don't stop he's dead." Cici made it into outer airlock chamber, but just as Tracey reached the tube the damaged lifter fell free. Tracey jumped; one hand grabbed the edge of door. She thought *this is it! I die on this gods cursed little planet!* Then a strong hand seized a strap on the front of her spacesuit. Cici smiled as she pulled Tracey in.

On other side of the airlock Kat's team was greeted by Mark Bourey, a White Star officer.
"First, thanks for coming to our aid. We are fighting to hold the engine room and control center. The control center is the key. The attackers have at least one hundred troops for the assault. Follow me forward toward the center." As they ran forward Mark said, "The space suits are great; we may lose air pressure at any time.

114

Kat asked Mark, "With the lifter crew, there are twenty-nine of us. What is your plan?"

"It would be best if we attack from the rear while they are assaulting the area around the Control Center. On Deck B two parallel passageways run forward, first to the officers' quarters then the Control Center. The attackers are using both passageways to reach the Control Center. If we send our main force into the right-hand passageway and send a much smaller force into the left-hand passageway as a diversion, we should break the assault," Mark explained.

Kat responded "Mark, we'll go with your plan! Baryic, you take five of the team and fake an assault on the left side. I will strike the right side with the balance of the team."

It didn't go exactly as planned. Kat's team almost immediately got hit by a group of attackers hiding in a cross passageway. One of the team was killed outright. Two others of Kat's team were seriously wounded. Only their spacesuits saved them. The tough fabric slowed the shrapnel turning a certain death into "a maybe." Nirabella stripped the spacesuit off the wounded crew to begin medical treatment.

Gods protect them if this ship loses air pressure. In the thin air of Martha's Hide, they won't last two minutes, Nirabella thought.

Kat killed one attacker then reloaded his rocket pistol. Cici killed another. A dozen attackers held the passage in the officers' quarters just outside the Control Center.

Nirabella looked up from her patient and screamed, "Stop Kat! You're hit in the leg!"

Kat complied immediately with Nirabella's warning. With Cici's help Kat kept limping forward.

Peter's voice broke into Kat's ear plug.

Kat responded, "How in all the worlds did you get an open com link?"

"Kat just listen!" Peter warned. "You are fighting Tri-Star Republic Shock Troops, a very tough and disciplined force. At least a hundred boarded the *White Star*. Six more trucks full of troops are on their way!"

On the left side of the ship, Baryic and Tracey were making progress. Light, who was with them, found two large metal storage units on wheels and were rolling the units down the passage in front of themselves. So far, they had encountered only three of the Tri-Star Troops. Ahead of them loomed the bulkhead door into the officers' quarters just outside the Control Room. Tracey quickly keyed in the code Mark the *White Star* officer had given her and the door opened.

Kat reversed the plan. He left Marsborn, Shadow and a handful of troops to hold the passageway on the right and brought most of his forces back through the cross passageway to support Tracey and Baryic. The only hope of stopping the attack was to drive the Tri-Troops out of the officers' quarters before their reinforcements arrived.

At that same moment, Peter decided to launch missiles. Out of the few crew members left on board the *Outcast Lady,* Fidelity clobbered together a missile bay crew. Somehow, they got two missiles ready to launch.

"Peter, this is Fidelity, we are ready to launch. Are you sure this will work? I have never heard of a missile launch while docked on a planet's surface."

"Neither have I. Fidelity, get your crew clear of the racks, I launch in thirty seconds." Peter advised.

The missiles shot free of the bay and hung in the air for milliseconds before the engines fired. It was just quick enough so the missiles did not hit the ground. Peter's program sent them away from the *Outcast Lady* and the *White Star.* For a moment, Fidelity believed the launch was a failure. The missiles turned upward for a kilo. Next, they turned and flew over the *White Star.* The two missiles then turned downward. Peter's program sent them in a complete five-kilometer loop and targeted the six new trucks.

Unfortunately, both missed. The first missile hit a hundred meters behind the truck convoy causing some damage. The seconded one did a bit better. It hit less than ten meters behind the last three trucks. The shrapnel cut through the three trucks ripping them apart. The other three trucks were heavily damaged halting them to a stop. If the air had been denser on Martha's Hide, the dying shock troops' screams might be heard.

The spirit of the Tri-Star Troops was broken with the missile attack and with Kat's teams' strong effort to save the Control Room. With their reinforcements gone, the Tri-Star Troops began withdrawing from the *White Star*. Within minutes the remaining shock troops were fleeing to only where the gods knew. There were not many places to hide on the barren surface of Martha's Hide. Over the next few days the local militia would hunt them down.

Kat called for everyone to check in. The first called was Marsborn. "Marsborn, what is your team's status?" Kat asked.

There was no response.

Shadow softly said, "Commander, Marsborn found peace with the gods. He died holding this passageway. He was one brave bastard. Nirabella did her best to save him."

Kat open com to the crew and somberly said, "Two brave crew members died today. May Neil

Marsborn's and Ivan Zimmerman's spirits find a fair passage to Far Star. Commander Jang out."

****

Four days after the battle, the *White Star* rested on her landing cradle. Tracey walked down the liner's main hall toward to the premier class dining room. The fading glory of the great old liner was apparent. The sheets of polished stone in the bright colors that the Trocs love covered the floors and walls. However, Tracy could see that in places the repairs were done in sheets of plastic. The ship was well maintained but old, very old.

Tracey walked arm in arm with Kat. He leaned on his cane. Behind them was Peter with Fidelity on his arm. Behind them was Baryic with Cici and Nirabella each on an arm. Cici's arm was, of course, in a sling and a living cast. Finally, came Light and Shadow. If one looked closely one could see Shadow's shoulder bandaged under his uniform. The officers and crew members of the *Outcast Lady* wore what passed for dress uniforms; washed, cleaned and pressed dark green utilities with their badges of rank in place. The officers of the *White Star* and the owner's envoy awaited them in the dining room.

The room was elegant. A formal dinner was set on a long table. Commander Fetel Caniitack and his officers stood awaiting them. Tracey thought, *Red and pink table cloths, fine porcelain dishes, and titanium ware. Fresh flowers covering the table, only the gods knew what they cost here on Martha's Hide. The stewards are in nicer uniforms than we are. The*

Troc officers are in full color robes, the human officers in formal dress white uniforms.

Caniitack greeted them, "Welcome my friends it's a great honor to have each of you share our simple dinner. Commander Jang without your efforts we would have lost the *White Star* and the concentrators to the forces of the Tri-Star Republic. I know both your team and my crew suffered serious loses. I cannot bring back those people. White Star Company can insure the resources to put the *Outcast Lady* back in space.

"The White Star Company will make every effort to repair and upgrade the *Outcast Lady.* One of our cargo ships has arrived with all the essential parts and a team of expert repair personnel. It is our gift to you. Please find your seats and we will begin. Allow me to introduce my officers and two guests. Our owner's envoy, Kiiirtan Seliicarr, you know my first officer Mark Bourey." On it went.

Tracey's mind drifted until the last person was introduced. A lady stepped out of the darkness as Caniitack said, "May I present Captain Demitrianna Constantine formally of the Free Space Force."

Tracey thought *make a note to myself to gut shoot the bitch after the sweets are served!*

Demitrianna said to the group, "Hello, I have a proposition you will want to hear."

"Not fucking likely -Black Widow!" Kat responded.

Undeterred, Demitrianna, using Kat's first name of Shane replied, "Shane and most of all Light, and Shadow should hear the proposition."

Chapter Twenty-Three
– Planet Nothing #2 –05-20-518

Light years from Martha's Hide on a planet called Nothing #2, cold air cut like a hand of ice down the passageway to the main docking area. The space station was not much, just two ancient hulks attached to each other. The station orbited the equator of a nameless planet of frozen ice and rock. Artystaar sat in a tavern just off the main docking area called the Tavern Boy's Home. It was not like any home she had seen but at least it was almost warm inside.

As the old man at the bar spun out his tales, Artystaar thought, *something has changed. Why are the pirates getting Troc ships? Why are we allowed, in violation of every treaty made between The League and Empire, to sell free humans back into the Empire as bound laborers? Why is the Tri-Star Republic on the move? What can they gain?*

At Troc Officers School one of the instructors had told her, "There are four things to remember about the Tri-Star Republic. First, it is not a republic. Secondly, it's a horrible place to live. Third, the military is tough, disciplined, ruthless, and is killed when they do not achieve victory. Finally, the Superior-Star Leader is completely and totally insane."

Sandy sat next to Artystaar listening intently to the old human. She was now a member of the Blood

Fire. They were to be crew on the *Dark Song,* an ex-imperial escort. The ship was less than sixty years old, fast and well-armed. She had been sold to the pirates just a month ago and given her new name. The Blood Fire team was waiting for an armed merchant to pick them up for the trip to the new ship.

Artystaar told Sandy, "We are going along an unknown branch off The Green Line. The branch was charted by pirate ships years ago. The branch does not go near Green's Star. This string of planets bends back to several planets all called 'Nothing'. This branch allows the pirate's refuges while raiding the length of the Green Line. Ships, personnel and supplies are hidden along the branch. This is without the knowledge of the League of Free Stars, the Tri-Star Republic or any of independent planets along the Green Line. Nor, are the Troc ships trading on the Line aware of the branch."

Sandy asked, "*Dark Song* sounds like an excellent war ship. Why by all the gods is the Trocnavar Blue Fleet selling this ship?"

"I have no idea. But, damn, it will be good to crew on a real war ship," Artystaar admitted.

"One more question, how did the Trocs get the ship out here undetected?" Sandy asked.

Chapter Twenty- Four
– Main Landing Field on Martha's Hide 05-19-518

Dinner would have to wait. Tracey, Kat, Peter, Fidelity, Baryic, Cici, Nirabella, Light, and Shadow were all shown to a small private conference room. They were quickly joined by Demitrianna and Commander Caniitack. Tracey checked her right boot for her compact pistol.

Kat yelled, "Demitrianna you have five minutes to present your proposal. Proceed."

The woman otherwise known as 'Spider' started, "I can understand why each of you hates me and the Free Space Force. I am no longer a member of the Free Space Force. However, I come to you with a private request from the Ax, General Bridgeford." Demitrianna waited for a response. There was none. She continued, "You all know pirates are threatening trade along the Green Line. They now strike with significantly larger and better armed ships. The Troc Empire may be supplying the pirates with these ships. It could even be that the Tri Star attack is somehow related to the pirate's actions. In order to find out exactly what the pirates are planning, the Free Space Force sent an agent to discover what is occurring. The agent was able to make their way deep into the pirate gangs." Once again, she waited for a response. Once again there was none; only the sound of crew restlessly shifting in their seats.

She said, "Several reports were received by FSF Intelligence. Then they lost contact with the agent. Green Fleet can't send ships blasting in to rescue the agent. We don't even know where the agent is. Ax believes a small ship with a brave and daring crew and without ties to the Free Space Force may have the best chance of finding the agent. He would like to contract the *Outcast Lady* to find her and bring her out safely. The agent is Major Tara Vasta Freeborn of FSF Intelligence, known to some of you as Auntie Tara." This time someone gasped.

Kat raised his hand to stop her. "Demitrianna, I personally would accept the assignment in a flash; however, the officers must vote on the contract. The crew must also accept it."

Tracey spoke, "Kat you don't need a vote. We all know who Major Freeborn is and we are with you."

Fidelity added, "All the crew members will accept the assignment; we are also with you!"

Kat then said, "Thank you all! Demitrianna continue. Tell us why Ax selected us for this task. Also, what is your role in all this?"

"Ax's reasons are simple," she said. "First, he believes you operate outside of normal bounds. Rules, protocols, rank and chain of command are meaningless to you. Second, you Shane, Shadow and Light would do whatever it takes to save Auntie Tara.

Finally, Ax thinks you have somehow assembled a damn good crew. My role is clear; I will take over as Special Advisor and as Chief Time Wave Navigator. Based on my skills and abilities, I am the only possible choice!"

Tracey was first to speak. "We sure as all the hells do not need a Special Advisor and we have an excellent Chief Time Wave Navigator! MS. CONSTANTINE, YOU ARE UTTERLY CRAZY IF YOU THINK YOU ARE IT!!!!"

Kat once more raised his hand for quiet. "Demitrianna CTWN is not quite the role we see you in."

Demitrianna replied, "Kat the resources I will bring with the contract are crucial. No Demitrianna, no funds."

Commander Caniitack, who had not previously spoken interrupted, "White Star Lines will ensure Commander Jang has all the resources needed. It will be done quietly, very quietly."

Kat said, "As Tracey told you, we have an excellent CTWN. Peter has the confidence of the whole crew. He has been outstanding. Erica Nguyen has done a fine job of backing him up and is our 2nd TWN. We do have a critical need for a 3rd TWN. We might offer you the slot, if you agree to all our conditions. As the first condition, download all the information in your data pack to our packs, starting now."

Chapter Twenty- Five
–In Space Riding the Wave - 06-23-518

A month later the rebuilt *Outcast Lady* rode a wave of compressed time and space. The ship was outward bound on a course set by Kat and Peter. Fidelity lay curled up in Peter's arms on the large bunk in his cabin. As Chief Time Wave Navigator Peter rated a cabin equal to the ship's Commander. They had spent the 2nd watch making love. Fidelity asked, "Peter tell me about your childhood. I have never known a half Troc. Where were you born?"

"Fidelity, first let me check the monitors and see how our new 3rd TWN is doing." After two minutes Peter said, "We are solidly on the peak of the wave, she is doing a satisfactory job. Are you sure you want to know my story?"

"Yes, my love I want to know everything about you." Fidelity cooed.

Peter began his tale, "I was not born a Guderian. I was not born at all; I was grown in a medical module. My existence is the result of extensive Trocnavar genetic manipulation. Trocs and humans cannot interbreed. The two races developed separately and are far too different genetically. However, a small number of half Trocs have been created in genetic labs. As you must know from the Vids, Trocs often keep both male and female human bound laborers as lovers. Trocs and humans are close enough physically to make sex possible- even pleasurable. My mother was just such a concubine. A Troc merchant and noble named Count Kiikt Diiionejj bought her as a child and raised her with his daughters. The Count was a wealthy and powerful merchant on the Imperial Core Planet Kaiii-var. He imported and exported goods from and to the League of Free Stars.

My mother Victoria grew into a great beauty by Troc criteria. By sixteen standard years she developed the soft full curves that Trocs love. She also had a pretty oval face, flaxen hair, and blue eyes. When she turned seventeen, the count took her for his pleasure. My mother was extremely bright and realized her best hope for escape lay in becoming his favorite.

Over the next few years she did just that. She knew his every need both in and out of bed and saw that they were met. By the end of three years mother was his hostess for celebrations and business meetings. If the Count wanted an orgy she arranged it and joined the other girls. She was occasionally asked to have sex with visiting nobles and merchants. Several times she spent the night with a human merchant named Richard Guderian.

Eventually the Count fell in love with her. He kept her just for himself. Then the very worst happened; the Count decided they should have a child. In private my mother screamed and cried her eyes out. She knew what that meant. The next day the laboratory doctors came and took eggs from her.

The process was very costly and an incredibly complex genetic manipulation to create a half Troc half human child. The process was known to fail about two thirds of the time. About one third of the embryos die in the medical modules. Another third is eliminated at end of their first year. The surviving babies are given to their mothers for the first year. At the end of the first-year doctors evaluate each baby. The ones with defects were terminated. I had several major defects.

As I approached my first-year mark, Mom knew I was doomed. With the help of Count Diiionejj's daughters she escaped with me in her arms. Mom ran to the Guderian Trading Company warehouse. She knew Richard Guderian from his dealings with the count. Mom, Victoria, threw herself on Richard's mercy. He remembered her and loving golden haired beauties, decided to save us. Within an hour, Mom and I were on a Guderian lifter headed for one of Richards' merchant ships in orbit. We were hundreds of thousands of kilos away racing toward light speed before the Count realized we were gone. He never found out how we escaped.

A year later, Richard Guderian formed a dual marriage with my mother and adopted me. He is the only father I have known. The Guderians did their best make me feel a part of the family. Over the next few years Richard spent a small fortune correcting my defects," Peter sighed.

Fidelity looked at Peter and said "My love" as a tear ran down her cheek.

Chapter Twenty-Six
– The Planet Nothing #2 – 07-01-518

A few days later and light years away, the Blood Fire gang was planet-side of Nothing #2. Artystaar was leading the gang on a run because they needed exercise. Her pirates had to keep in shape. They were about ten clicks out and she had just started to push hard. As they were running on a high ridge, Artystaar looked around Nothing #2 and saw immense rolling plains of grass swept out to distant snowcapped mountains. The beauty of the area was beyond description. In this hemisphere of the planet, spring was in season and the lush green grass was so deep one could fall into it. Unfamiliar blue and green trees filled the river valleys but Artystaar hated every damn square meter. She wanted to be in space!

The gang was awaiting their new ship. They shipped down to the surface for full gravity physical training. Pirates who were out of shape did not survive. Artystaar pushed the gang to their limit; she wanted them in first-rate shape when they went back into space. Artystaar looked to her right and saw Sandy running effortlessly. *She must be twice my age and running like a Weldon Lion hunting fast prey,* Artystaar observed.

Chapter Twenty-Seven

The Green Line was not truly a line of stars. It was more like a dusting of stars resembling an arm reaching out into space. There were plenty of stars off the main trade routes, some with habitable planets. For the most part, the planets were colonized by people who would prefer not to be found. These planets became places where smugglers or other marginal operators gathered. One such planet, Schwaigerland was selected as the place to begin their search.

Outcast Lady was holding in orbit near the space station. The station was not much; just three old League sphere ships hulked. They were joined together in a three-dimensional triangle. The six docks were filled with as a bizarre group of merchant ships and warships as Cici had ever seen.

Cici thought, *On the other hand, we don't look much different than the ships docked here. Commander Caniitack was true to his word. White Star Line rebuilt the Outcast Lady. The inner hull was rebuilt. New dual plasma engines were installed. No more crashing due to an engine failure. The Time Wave Drive was reconstructed and is fully operational. The rail-guns, and missile bays, were overhauled piece by piece so that they looked just like the original weapons but functioned as new. A new twenty-man lifter and a new six-man min-lifter were delivered. They added new environmental systems. And, of course four new parachutes were installed. Inside she is a gem but outside still an old battered warship.*

The officers and sergeants sat at the Ward Room table. Empty coffee cups and cold gubble brew mugs were scattered over the table. Purple Cat lay cured up on the table next to Tracey. It had been a long planning session. Kat began to outline the final version of the plan.

"We need information," Kat said. "Somehow, we must find a link to the pirates. Our cover is delivering documents, vids and data to several planets. The plan here on Schwaigerland is to send the min-lifter over to the space station with a team of Demitrianna, Cici, myself and Centari as pilot. As Commander, I will formally present our documents. Then we attempt to locate one of the contacts Spider, I mean Demitrianna, was given. We will also see what we can learn from ship crews and station personnel."

Demitrianna interrupted, "Use my nick name. I have gotten quite comfortable with 'Spider' during the long voyage from Martha's Hide. I know everyone uses it."

Kat nodding to Spider's request continued, "At the same time, we will send a larger party in the big lifter down to the space port on the surface. The second team will consist of Tracey, Light, Shadow,

Nirabella, Peter and Baryic as pilot. We will also send one of the crew to guard the lifter. You will deliver new vids, docs, etc. and data to key traders. Then you will order supplies. The team will be given several days of surface time in which you will spend in taverns and other establishments. Hopefully you can make contact with pirates or smugglers, directly or indirectly."

Kat thought, *the presence of a Half Troc may open certain doors for you. Nirabella's medical skills could unlock other doors for the team. The gods know Shadow and Light can find their way round a space port.*

Kat closed the briefing saying, "Fidelity and Erica Nguyen will hold the Outcast *Lady.* May the gods of Far Star be with us all!"

Four hours later Kat, Cici and Demitrianna found themselves in the offices of Sun Transaction Trading just off the main deck of the space station. A young man with the striking good looks of a vid actor ushered them into the inner office. Cici chose to stay with the young man.

The office was small but superbly furnished. Deep maroon carpets covered the floor and rich red Diike Wood panels covered the walls. Three real oak chairs were arranged in front of the desk. The antique aluminum desk was taken from some ancient space ship. It reflected the fine glow of aluminum worn by use of a thousand hands. Demitrianna said to herself, *you could buy a small ship for what that desk cost.*

****

In the port city of Schwaigerland, Tracey was standing at the bar ordering a Beer and Blue, a mixture of beer and blue grain alcohol. The tavern named 'Stars to Dust' was just a block from the space port. It filled up with thirsty customers as second watch ended. Someone slapped her ass. Normally she would break a couple of fingers. This time she turned and said, "Hello, handsome, what ship are you off of?"

The tall young man replied, "I am Eric an Engineering Sergeant formerly of the Ms. Weldon VIII. Up to a few weeks ago she was the finest contract escort along the Green Line. Would you like to join us at my table in back?"

Tracey grabbed her Beer and Blue and followed Eric toward the table. In Tracey's view, he was a fine-looking man with an athletic body, short brown hair, and a strong face. Tracey motioned for Light and Peter to join her. Eric introduced them to the other female person at the table.

She's interesting, Tracey thought. She's *definitely human but trying to look like a Troc.*

Tracey observed that she was stocky with blue and magenta hair. Her face, which might have been

138

attractive, was marred by a long scar down her right cheek. She did not give her name or station. Both Eric and the woman appeared to be shocked to see Peter.

****

The man behind the desk motioned Kat and Demitrianna to sit in the oak chairs. He offered them ice tea which the young man from the outer office served. He also asked the young man to make sure Cici was served tea and had a clear view of the entry way. He then looked at Kat and Demitrianna for a minute and said, "No need to introduce yourselves; I know who Shane, Kat, Jang and Demitrianna Constantine are. But let introduce myself. I am Ivan Sun the number two at this concern. My mother Juliana asked me to help if possible."

Kat took stock of the man. Ivan was mid-height, no more than twenty-five standard years, with a finely cut face and his blonde hair was short. *He does not have the look of a ship's officer. His whole presence screams rich ship owner,* Kat thought.

Ivan began, "I believe you may be trying to contact pirates. Why not just shoot yourselves now and save a lot of trouble? These are incredibly nasty people. Do you know what a kill dot is? No? -- You and your crew are likely to end up as kill dots. If pirates don't slaughter you, you will pray to every god you know that they had."

"If you can't find pirates," Ivan continued, "I suspect your plan is to contact smugglers. That's where I may be able to help you. There is a planet called 'Horizon' about ten light years from here. My company sometimes ships high value cargo to Horizon in armed war ships."

An hour later Kat, Cici and Demitrianna sat in a tavern which opened on to the main passageway. Cici and Demitrianna shared a half liter of wine; Kat sipped a Gubble brew letting the rich warm bubbles vaporize just under his nose. Kat asked Cici, "What did you find out from pretty boy?"

"I learned 'don't trust Ivan or his mother and stay away from Horizon'." Cici replied.

****

Kat, Cici and Spider met Tracy at the space port on the surface a few hours later. Tracey, Light and Peter were accompanied by a female and a human male. Tracey spoke first. "I would like you to meet Czajka and Eric; they have some information which may be helpful. However, Czajka wants to trade the information for something we have."

"Czajka what do want for the information? Just how valuable is it?" Kat asked.

Czajka replied, "Meeting one of your crew was not luck. I knew an officer or sergeant would show up at 'Stars to Dust' eventually. Our speculation was confirmed when Officer Watkins showed as quickly as your ship made orbit delivering vids, data and documents to traders. The fact that you, the Commander, would send officers to a tavern in the first hour on the surface, told me worlds. A warship like yours is far too costly to operate on what you can make hauling vids, data and documents."

"I believe you plan to solve the problem and make bags full of Imperials as a smuggler," Czajka continued. "Tracey was looking for information on trade routes, types of ships, and sorts of cargo. My best guess is you will head for Cats Claw, Star Island, Tanaka's Rock or even Horizon. The both of us have contacts on all four. Plus, we know the smuggler's trade. This much I will tell you: do not trust any trader on the station or on the surface. All of them would sell their mothers for half a League Star."

Spider asked, "Is there someplace we can talk in private?"

Chapter Twenty-Eight
- Planet Schwaigerland - 07-10 -518.

Nirabella, Shadow, and Baryic walked into the warehouse office of the Schwaigerland Trading Company. Nirabella's data pack was filled with bills of lading and a long list of needed supplies. This was the third trading company they had visited. Over twenty companies traded near the landing field. Schwaiger's reputation of was one of the best. The two clerks in the outer office greeted them.

"How may we help you?" the young woman asked. "Hello" was only greeting of the older, large and very fit man.

The office was clean but well-worn. Nirabella quickly explained that they were there to arrange delivery of fifty cases of documents and vids. She downloaded the bills of lading from her data pack to the office system. After a quick review of the bills, the female clerk led Nirabella and Baryic into a conference room. It was simple but elegant and new. Shadow remained in the front office. He took a seat with his back to the inner wall and facing the entrance with a clear view outside.

A thin, tall, woman of more than sixty standard years greeted Nirabella and Baryic. She held a copy of their bills of lading in her hand.

"Good morning," she greeted. "I am North Schwaiger-Smith. Thank you for delivering the cases. We will send lifters to pick up the shipment during next watch." The young woman brought in a tray of sweet breads and hot Martheain Herb Tea. The lavender color of the tea deepened as the small tea bugs gave the color and the spicy distinctive flavor to the tea.

Nirabella thanked North, "Martheain Tea is a rare and costly treat. The euphoric effect is delightful. One additional item –we must resupply our ship. I am downloading the list of needed supplies to your system."

North scanned the list, "We can fill your order for supplies quickly, including the dark matter you need. Our bid should be the lowest on Schwaigerland."

"The list is not out for bid. We would like the resupply to be completed quietly, with as little notice as possible. I have just downloaded your firm enough Imperials to cover 20% of the cost. We will pay the balance on delivery." Nirabella said.

Baryic then asked, "Please tell us about trade in this area of space."

North replied, "That, my handsome friend is a complex issue. There is fair amount of legitimate trade between these fringe planets and major Green Line planets. There is also smuggling of every type out here on the fringe. Most of the smuggling is done simply to avoid duties and taxes imposed by the main trade planets. However, a fair amount of it is with the pirates."

"Yes, the pirates do attack our ships," North affirmed before the question could be asked. "They kill and capture our people and ships and devastate trade. We fight them, kill them and destroy their ships, but if the profits are large enough, we damn well trade with them."

Nirabella asked, "Where does the trade with pirates take place?"

"The choicest planets for trading with pirates are Cat's Claw, Star Island, and Tanaka's Rock. They all have governments controlled by traders. At least minimum protection is offered the ships that trade with them. A war ship such as *Outcast Lady* should be safe. On the planets' surfaces a semblance of order is maintained by contract troops hired by the traders. If you can deal with some risk, profits can be substantial."

"The other planet, Horizon is used for trading with pirates," North continued. "I don't recommend going near it. The corrupt government is run by a gang of pirate commanders. Your ship could be attacked while in orbit. The streets of the port city are wild and death comes easily. Trading on Horizon is not for the weak. Every trade is racked with fraud and deception. But, profits can be tremendous."

Nirabella thanked North for the information. She told North to let herself or Baryic know when she would start shipping supplies up to the *Outcast Lady.*

Nirabella, Shadow, and Baryic were drinking cold beers at a table in the back of a tavern called The Red Gunneran hour later.

Baryic asked Shadow, "Tell us what you found out."

"The clerks think North is a sharp trader but a decent boss. The big clerk is some type of bodyguard. While protecting North he lost an eye on a planet called Horizon. She paid a pile of Imperials for a replacement eye. The gods know that's more than most traders would do," Shadow concluded.

****

Nirabella, Shadow, and Baryic met Kat heading back to the lifter as he guided them to a Tavern on the edge of Landing Field. The 'Wave Peak' was a decent tavern catering to officers and sergeants. They found the other two parties and two strangers in a private room in the basement. Peter was checking the room for any type of listening devices. Peter crushed a tiny device then dropped it into a water glass and added salt. He finally wrote on a cardboard sign --- *Now looks clean, we can resume our talks.*

Kat said, "Ladies and Gentlemen, our two guests Czajka and Eric would like to speak."

The female began, "We believe you plan to take this ship smuggling. I am Czajka; yes, it's my full name. I was the Weapons Officer on the Ms. Weldon and Eric was an Engineering Sergeant. We shall dispense detailed information within a day or two that would otherwise take you a year to find. It will cost you just 1,000 Imperials."

"It's blood price!" Kat exclaimed. After he regained his composure he instructed, "Go ahead tell your tail. We will pay if and when know the info is good."

Czajka began to talk.

Chapter Twenty-Nine
High Orbit Above the Planet Nothing #7 08-01 -518.

Not too many light years away from Schwaigerland, the pirate ship *Dark Song* rode a high orbit above the planet called Nothing #7. On board a tough young Trocnavar Commander Niikia Kaiii-var announced, "Artystaar Tiigano will be First Officer."

Artystaar walked to front of the mess deck on the *Dark Song* and joined Niikia Kaiii-var as their new Commander. Artystaar reflected: *When we arrived at the station here, where ever 'here' is, we found Dark Song waiting for us. There was small crew on board, however, and Niikia did not take command. Apparently, the Blood Fire gang would make up the majority of the crew. True to pirate tradition, Niikia called for a vote to select a Commander. Niikia Kaiii-var reputation for blood thirsty attacks, great prizes, and a fair share for her crews, made the vote a no contest. Certainly, her twenty-two Kill Dots did not hurt. Most of them were black. What surprised me was when she called for the crew to vote for me as First Officer.*

Artystaar evaluated their new Commander. Niikia was tall for a Troc, about mid height for a human. Her face and body looked as if it was carved from stone; square jaw, flat nose and deep gold eyes. Her hair was black and silver which is very unusual for a Troc. There was something about her that said,

"Trocnavar Fleet Officer, not pirate". But her kill dots said 'pirate'. Most of her dots were black. Red kill dots were awarded for killing fellow pirates, green dots awarded for killing civilians and black dots were for killing military. Killing crew in Trocnavar Blue Fleets, Tri-Star Republic, Free Space Force, contract ship, or any other military, did not matter. Killing someone in face-to-face combat resulted in a black dot honor.

Artystaar's heart raced when she first saw *Dark Song* floating docked at the station. *Dark Song* was an ex- imperial escort. The ship was less than sixty years old, fast and well-armed. The Empire built ships long and lean. The *Song* was 100 meters long and shaped like the classic striker fish. The Control Center was on the "upper" side. The center was shaped like a half tear drop and set into the hull twenty meters from the nose. It was covered with view ports, antenna, and sensors and retractable during combat.

Aft of the control center was a section twenty plus meters in diameter with four turrets in a circle around the hull. Each turret was equipped with a single rail gun. The guns could fire in all directions except directly aft. The section also held a drop bay for midsized missiles. It was the 'extra section' which made the *Song* a perfect pirate ship. Extra fuel, water, supplies, rail projectiles, and missiles were stored in this section held in the lifter bay.

The aft section of the hull held engineering. Arranged around the hull, in a three pointed star configuration, were three structures. On "top" was the communications tower. Shaped like a fishes' fin, it bristled with sensors and antenna. A fifth rail gun was at the rear edge of the com-tower to protect from attacks from astern. In order to save weight, the gun was in an open mount. The other two structures were Time Wave Drive pods built on massive fins. The rear surfaces of the pods were domes with a smooth black surface. The tubes of the plasma drive and the dark matter drive protruded from the fishes' tail.

Dark Song was docked at the station orbiting Nameless #7 which was mostly cold rock and frozen waste. However, a livable zone existed around the equator. Blue seas, factory cities, and agricultural estates filled the narrow livable zone.

The crew was loading the last of the supplies. As they watched, Artystaar and Sandy discussed the station and the planet.

Sandy asked, "Why is the station so large? I counted twenty pirate ships and two Trocnavar merchant ships. There are full repair facilities with a large air dock and two smaller ones. Is that an old battle cruiser in the big air dock?"

"Let's just say things are changing," Artystaar said.

Sandy continued, "What about the planet? It appears the green zone is settled and the factories and estate farms are delivering all types of supplies and materials. Who is the labor force for such widespread development?"

"Sandy, sometimes you ask too many questions," Artystaar winked and continued. "The captured Free Humans provides much of the labor. Out here there is no need to meet the terms of The Grand Treaty III. Who will know if we recycle Free Humans back to be bound laborers on a nameless planet?"

"Let's see if our new commander has plans to sleep on 3rd watch," Sandy replied ignoring Artystaar's rhetorical question.

Chapter Thirty
- The Planet Horizon - 08-15-518.

Two months in space later, the *Outcast Lady* neared Horizon. It was a strange planet with only one small moon and no tilt to the planet's axis. No tides and seasons existed. Either tropics or deserts covered the equatorial islands. Endless temperate zone islands covered the area halfway to the poles and large arctic zones enveloped the poles. Circulating ocean currents kept the planet from becoming uninhabitable. Currents transferred vast amounts of heated water to the poles and cold water to the equator. Only a handful of the tropical islands held pirate bases. Horizon's capital, 'Friendly' was located at the mouth of a river system on the largest tropical island.

As the *Lady* neared orbit, Tracey used the optical systems to scan the city. She reported, "The name must be a joke. Large areas of forest have been cut with no sign of replanting. Factories and warehouses line the river which flows through the city. The road system has no pattern; it looks as if wild animal tracks were paved. Giant piles of trash can be seen from orbit. Smoke fills the air. A dark scum clouds the river where it reaches the bay and extends kilos out to sea."

"The Space Port appears disorganized, poorly laid out, and lifters are scattered around the field," Tracey continued. "I can see two old space ships which crashed while attempting surface landings. Long ago the ships were pushed to the edge of the landing area. In spite of its poor condition, the Space Port is defended by an array of the up-to-date weapons. The Capital is a slum, the Space Port a mess. But, the estates, along the golden beach nineteen kilos south of the city, are beautifully kept. These estates are also defended by the modern weapons," Tracey concluded.

"Thanks Tracey," Kat said. "Sounds like what we are seeking." Kat continued on an open com line, "This is Commander Jang of the ship *Outcast Lady* requesting an orbit position."

The reply came back, "This is Horizon Space Station Control; I don't give a damn where you park that junk pile. Just stay clear of satellites or other ships. Your orbit tariff is two hundred Imperials, transmit the funds now. What is your purpose on Horizon?"

Kat responded, "We are delivering a shipment to Sun Transaction Trading. We request a space station docking port for our lifter. We will be docking in one hour."

The station consisted of the hulks of two large Imperial merchants attached to a spherical center section. With half of the lifter docking ports unused, there should be no problem with Kat's request.

"Attack plans would already be underway if Station Control knew the shipment contained a thousand cases of live Martheain Herb Tea Bugs. The bloody damn bugs are worth more than the whole damn station," Czajka, their guide, commented. She was acting as an agent for the *Lady*.

****

The Space Station reeked of sweat, cooking vegetables and burned out lifter motors. Half of the plants used to clear CO_2 were dead. Strangely the station was clean with swept decks, clean walls and no trash. Tracey, Kat and Czajka walked down the main passageway. Shadow followed a few steps behind, his eyes scanning the foot traffic around them.

A lean young man suddenly came running out of the crowd in front of them. A second assailant lurked in the background. The young man pushed Kat to the deck and cut free Kat's data pack with the speed and fluidity of a skilled Field Ball Player. He tossed the data pack to the second assailant. She caught it and began to run. As the young man raced past Tracey, she drew her compact pistol, turned and shot the man in the back of the head with the speed and fluidity of a skilled Field Ball Player. A fine mist of blood and brains exploded from his forehead. Three seconds later Czajka's dagger plunged in his left lung via his back.

Six steps farther back, Shadow sliced the throat of the accomplice who had been waiting for the handoff. The girl looked no more than seventeen standard years. She had been drawing her rocket pistol when Shadow cut her down. Shadow thought, *by the gods, how sad, she is my age and a pretty one!*

Regaining his feet Kat said, "Thanks damn thanks! It looks as if someone wants to know about us, the ship, or our cargo."

Tracey recovered the data pack from the corpse lying on the ground and handed it to Kat.

A few bystanders gathered around the bodies. No one appeared concerned over two dead bodies lying in the station's main passage way. A tall kid with a pock marked face, yelled, "Nice shooting Blondie!"

Shadow and Czajka carefully sliced open both of the female corpse eyes. Czajka withdrew a lens from inside the girl's right eye.

"What have you got, Czajka?" Kat asked.

"It's a lens doc from her eye. It's likely to have a letter of intent engraved into it stating the price to be paid for your data pack. Perhaps we can find who sent these young people." She smiled and said, "Thanks to First Officer Watkins, I don't think we will find out much from the boy's eyes."

The first official to arrive was a structural inspector whose only concern was to ascertain the ability of the station to hold atmosphere. She was gone as soon as she determined that there was no damage to the outer wall which could cause a latent failure.

After the structural inspector's departure, a security officer arrived. He was a human with dark hair and carried twenty-five kilos too much weight. He took statements from each of the group and also from couple of witnesses. He then confiscated the dead girl's rocket pistol, worth ten plus Imperials on the gray market. Within a half hour he called in a cleanup crew, accepted a small bribe and told everyone at the scene that they were free to go. No one had said anything about the lens doc.

Tracey asked, "We just killed two people on a crowded open passageway and it generated less fuss than shooting a dog would back home. Is this customary?" She was incredulous.

"Welcome to Horizon," Czajka replied. "By the way Tracey, both you and Shadow have earned a kill dot. The tattoo shops will have a copy of the security report within an hour. You can get your tats today. I would not delay; the value of kill dots when dealing with smugglers and pirates cannot be overestimated."

"Shouldn't you also receive a kill dot?" Tracey asked.

"No. The thief was dead before my dagger broke his skin." Czajka replied.

Chapter Thirty-One
- Planet Horizon - 08-07-518.

A few days later, the big lifter from *Outcast Lady* dropped toward the Horizon's surface. Shadow and Light sat together talking. Light asked, "What is it like getting a tat?"

Shadow told her, "At the meeting with Sun Transaction Trading, the Vice Director Sam Yazdan showed more interest in Tracey's and my kills than in our cargo. After the meeting, he insisted we use a talented tattoo artist named Benjamin Jing Hoe. Once we located Ben's shop, we began the process. Ben had a copy of the security report. He told us we were getting black dots based the fact that both the boy and girl assailants were trained thieves and known killers. Black dots are used for kills of the military, but also extended to smugglers, thieves and anyone else trained in hand to hand combat. "

"Each dot is twelve millimeters in diameter," explained Shadow. "The dots are not just solid color. Each dot is an intricate design. A two-millimeter outer ring of color is followed by a two-millimeter band of information. Sometimes just the date of the kill is within the band. Sometimes the victim's initials or name and the location of the kill are added. The center is a four-millimeter circle of nearly solid complex design."

Shadow continued, "Tracey and I chose to add the date and the names of our kills in the band. We thought their names would go unrecorded otherwise. Completing the tattoo took only twenty-five minutes."

Light said, "You two were good to add their names. Their bodies are unclaimed and will be burned with the trash. No one will remember them on Horizon."

Light looked around the 20-person lifter. Each of them wore a new dress uniform of light tan with a black pullover. The jackets were waist length. The uniforms, typical of contract officers and sergeants, were tailored in the last few days on Horizon Station. Shadow, Fidelity and she wore sergeant's uniforms with dark green four pointed stars pinned on over the heart and the same star embroidered on the pullover.

Tracey as pilot and Cici, as gunner were both dressed in the officer's version of the new uniform with six pointed Stars. As Commander and as Chief Time Wave Navigator Kat and Peter also wore the officer's version of the tan dress uniform. Both had pinned on dark green seven pointed stars.

Tracey flew northward toward the verdant green islands of the temperate zone islands. Purple Cat was curled up in an empty seat just behind Tracey. Before they left, Czajka had insisted Tracey bring Purple Cat because it was customary that Horizon women of the pirate aristocracy carried their c-cats to all social gatherings.

As they flew, Cici looked out from gunner's bubble and saw the lush green islands changing. Palm- like trees were replaced by near-oaks, near-pines, and giikotr like trees. She saw no sign of estates or farms. On a few islands, herds of Vraciek were grazing in the open grasslands. The Vraciek were not native to Horizon, someone had to place them on the islands. In the lush endless summer, the Vraciek would grow quickly and face no winter starvation. But they would need to be herded to new grass areas every few weeks. The Vraciek were too dumb to move themselves to new pastures. Someone must herd them and live on these islands.

Cici remembered, *my father loved the Vraciek that we raised at home on Craig-Land. They looked somewhat like a cross between a large sheep and small cow covered in blue fur. The Vraciek are not as smart as sheep. Imperial geneticists bred them to be docile and easily handled. They just want to eat and breed. It took people with my family's love of the land and passion for ranching to protect and raise them. The fact that the meat, milk, and wool they produced were all excellent allowing us to live very comfortable lives. Nevertheless, when herding at night, I remember lying out on green hill tops, staring up at the stars, and wondering what is life like up there?*

Cici snapped back to full alert as two armed lifters closed on them from the north. The lifters swung a wide circle and took positions on either side of their lifter about 100 meters out. One of lifters sent a tight beam command, "This is Commander Contreras, follow us in and do not, I repeat do not deviate from our course."

Tracey responded, "Commander understood. We are locking on to your course."

They flew over the surf line of a large island within two hours. After a half hour more, the lifters continued north into a gap in a range of mountains over the coastal plain. Kat, who stood behind Tracey's seat said, "By the gods what a view!" They flew over a ridge covered with near-pines. Opening before them was a high valley. A clear river flowed down the center then through a gap in the ridge that they had just passed over and fell 300 meters into the mist of the plain below. On either side, forest covered mountains rose up. Between the mountains was a wide grass covered valley. The far end of the valley opened into a view of a distant snow covered mountain range. In the center of the range rising above the clouds was a volcano. Kat thought, *the mother of all volcanoes; it formed this island.*

The armed lifters began their descent and Tracey followed them down. Below was a plastio-cement landing field. Four other armed lifters were parked on the field. Encircled in trees at edge of field were two buildings; one a flight control center and one a modest warehouse. Camouflaged air defense weapons arrays were located at the north and south ends of the field.

As Tracey landed an electro-van drove out from the Flight Control Center. An officer walked over from the armed lifter which landed to their right. A human officer was dressed in blue dress uniform pants with a bright orange pullover. Pinned on his chest was the black seven pointed star of a Captain. The opening in the right sleeve of his pullover exposed four Kill Dots; two green, one black and one red.

He hailed them, "I am Sanjay Contreras. Please follow me to the van." The party loaded into the van and it started up a dirt road toward a low hill covered with trees at the north end of the valley. Unaware of the importance of this meeting, Purple Cat slept contentedly in the carry bag on Tracey's right shoulder.

After a somewhat bumpy ride, the van stopped at the foot of a set of carved stone steps which led into the trees on the hill. Kat looked around as they walked forward and topped the stone steps.

It's the biggest camping building I have ever seen, he observed. *The structure spread out along ridge of the hill, plastio-carbon posts six meters high supported a flat roof over 50 meters long. The walls are fabric in some areas open in others. In the center of the camp, banners of orange fabric few from poles on either side of the plastio-carbon doors, why the doors? Guards, dressed in orange utilities and with rocket long guns, are opening the doors for us.*

Once inside Captain Contreras led the group into the main entrance hall. The far wall opened into a view of a valley covered with a dense mass of trees. In the distance the mountain range rose up with the great volcano emerging from mists of the valley floor.

Kat said to no one specific, "And I thought the view from flying in on the lifter was something special."

A small old man in the grey uniform of a bound human laborer greeted them. Tracey let out a "Damn" on the occasion of the first time she was face to face with a bound laborer. She had seen them in vids, but seeing one face to face was different. The old man appeared thin and fragile and Tracey was not sure he could walk much further.

The man smiled and, as if reading her thoughts said, "Miss, you will get used to us if you spend much time on Horizon. All of you please follow me. There is a room on the right where you can rest and relax until it's time. The other servants and I will bring refreshments." He then turned and added, "Captain Contreras will rejoin you later." It sounded almost like a whisper. "Oh, yes you will need to leave all your weapons here with the guards"

They rested in a room just off the entrance hall. One wall was open to the view of the snowcapped mountains. The room was furnished with comfortable camping furniture and equipped with all the facilities needed. True to his word, the old man and three ladies, as old and frail as himself, served cold drinks and hot gubble brew. All of the ladies were in bound laborer grey. During the next hour, the old man asked each of the crew if they were comfortable and inquired if they needed anything. One of the ladies even brought bowls of water and food for the c-cat.

After refreshments, the old man and one the women returned to the room dragging two large folding tables. The two of them were barely able to move the tables. Kat and Tracey jumped up to help with one table. Peter and Fidelity grabbed the other. Cici and Light took heavy trays of food from the other two old women. Shadow moved the camp chairs to the side to open a space for the tables and helped set them up.

The old man announced, "My apologies for the delay. We will be serving you a light meal." The 'light' meal was very generous and tasty and served in many courses.

Upon completion of the meal the old man said, "Please follow me to the sovereignty room." They were searched one more time for weapons by armed guards posted at the doorway. The Sovereignty Room opened on one side to the view. At the far end was a platform raised a single step up. Two guards flanked the platform. Three humans were seated on the platform. In front of the platform two dozen chairs were arranged in three rows. Captain Contreras was seated in the last row but otherwise the seats were empty.

Tracey and the others walked toward the platform. The old man motioned them to the chairs.

The man in the center must be the grand leader on Horizon. He's over two meters tall, black hair cut short; scars on his face, right arm covered Kill Dots, one ugly bastard, Tracey thought.

The 'ugly bastard 'arose, walked to edge of the platform and said, "I am Garman Rayyan Warlord of Horizon and Pirate Fleets; Lord of Death and Destruction. We are not pleased with your existence."

Tracey thought, *is he going to kill us now or after dinner? Perhaps he will wait until dawn. If that's the case, I will not sleep alone this night.*

At that point, the old man stepped on to the platform and said, "Thank you General Rayyan, I will
take it from here."

****

Centari Shamir was the leader of the group of young people called the 'Lost' who were recruited for the crew on Pangerbar. Centari was tracing the source of the lens-doc previously cut from the dead girl who was neutralized in an altercation earlier in the day. Sam Yazdan, the Vice Director from Sun Transaction Trading, gave Nirabella and Spider a list of people to interview regarding the incident. Spider enlisted Centari to help.

Centari sat in the office of an information broker, Yazdan the Fat and a distant cousin of Sam Yazdan. The office overlooked the sweltering main road of Friendly. The road between the city center and space port was filled with taverns, whore houses, weapons shops and drug dens. Yazdan's office was on second story of an establishment which appeared to be housing all four.

Fat looked across his desk with sweat dripping off his face and said, "Gorgeous, rip off your clothes and join me on the couch and any information I have is yours. Otherwise my fee is a hundred imperials and that's a discount because Sam sent you."

Centari calmly sipped the ice-cold beer just served to her and responded, "Fifty total, half of it upfront and half if the information is good. You can keep your damn couch for the whores down stairs." She licked the foam off of her upper lip.

"Done," Fat replied starring at her tongue and lips.

Centari sat her beer on the table and plugged in her data pack and transferred the funds to Fat's data pack. Next, she transferred two groups of pictures to Fat's data pack. The first was enlargements of the lens doc from the girl's eye with the letter of intent engraved into it. The second was several pictures of Auntie Tara and information on dates that she may have been at Horizon.

Nirabella and Spider sat waiting for Fat's information as he sipped a fresh cold beer and began.

"Rarkiikar Clovis hired the young assassins to get Commander Jang's data pack. Why I don't know but they offered good money for the pack."

"Who is Rarkiikar Clovis?" Nirabella asked.

"Not 'who', but 'what' is the question," Fat corrected. "Is the term 'Rarkiikar' unfamiliar to you? Rarkiikars are independent operations within the Empire who provide information, security, mercenaries, and assassins and, only the gods know what else, to the few who can afford them. They are ancient and secretive groups. Rarkiikar Clovis is one of the few headed by a human. I have no idea why they wanted your Commander's data pack. I place my life at risk by telling you even this much."

"Thank you for the information," responded Nirabella, "What did you find about the lady that was in the photos?"

"My source in Station Records found a lady very much like your pictures who arrived during the 5th month as a passenger on a transport named *Running Dog*. The lady's docs gave the name Jane Star, which is a rather common name. She rented rooms for a week with a woman called Jennifer Wolf and then she disappeared. The records show Jennifer listed her profession as Special Heath Therapist. I think you know what that means. Let me give you the location where Jennifer works if she is still on Horizon."

****

Tracey expected the guards or the General himself to kill the old man. However, they showed him great diffidence and helped him to the center chair.

After sitting down the old man continued, "Commander Jang you, your officers and crew are a major disappointment. Commander, I had great hopes for you based on the fact you reached Horizon at all, much less, with a costly live cargo intact. Also, the kills Ms. Watkins and Sergeant Freeborn made on the space station were impressive. I expected to recruit the *Outcast Lady* for our pirate fleets. Reports of your crew's kills on Pangerbar –which was nice work by Light Freeborn - and the defense of the *White Star* on Martha's Hide, - Kat's wild counter-attack and Peter's brilliant missile launch - lead me to believe the crew of *Outcast Lady* was the stuff of pirates."

"However, your actions here at camp totally disqualify you from consideration," the old man continued. "Each of you treated myself and the other bound laborers with respect and kindness. No one who shows such humanity to the old and frail is fit to serve in my fleets. I talked to each of you and your main concerns were not money, power, killing and sex, but rather the mission of the ship, the safety of the cargo and your crewmates.   You are UNFIT! Totally and completely UNFIT!"

The guard on the right exclaimed. "Lord Erasmus Sunstar, Prime Minister of Horizon, God of the Fleets, and Lord of Wealth and Power has spoken!"

Kat appealed, "High Lord Sunstar I ask that--". He was cut off when the lady to the left of Lord Sunstar raised her hand. She was small, dark haired, with a heart shaped face and of an indeterminate age. She was human but dressed in the traditional flowing blue and orange Trocnavar robes. Two black and gold striped c-cats sat at her feet.

"Commander Jang, do not make things worse by speaking." The woman instructed.

Warlord Garman Rayyan rose and spoke, "Tomorrow at high mid-day, two of your crew will fight my son Major Karrack Rayyan. He is bigger, quicker and stronger than me and is called the 'Hand of Death' by his troops. You will be transported to the volcano crater. The battle will take place on an ancient stone arena at the edge of the crater. You will fight unarmed. If two of you can push Karrack into the volcano, victory is yours. By first light you will state which of your crew will fight. Should one or more of you survive; the Lady here will talk to you about the future. The gods have given Major Rayyan victory nine times; the gods will give him more!"

Welcome to Horizon. Nice really nice, how can we be so damn lucky? Cici thought. That thought passed quickly and she then volunteered to fight.

As soon as they were locked in quarters, Peter said, "I am the strongest here, I volunteer to fight."

Light and Shadow each said, "We should fight we're quick and have killed in the streets."

Tracey then said, "I am both quick and strong I should be one of our fighters."

Kat, as the Commander declared that he should fight. And so, it went, all of them volunteering to fight Karrack Rayyan in the volcano. The debate lasted two hours.

****

Nirabella, Spider and Centari found themselves not in some sullied slum but at an elegant club on the golden beach kilos south of the city. The *Sea Goddess Club* was tucked in among the private estates that lined the beach. The club offered both women and men to those clients who could afford the prices.

Nirabella, Spider and Centari were looking for a whore named Jennifer. All three were heavily armed, or as heavily armed as one could be in beachwear. Nirabella was dressed in a light summer rap. Spider and Centari wore string bikinis but carried oversized beach bags.

They landed in the mini-lifter which ensured a certain dazzle; not everyone arrived in their own lifter. With thoughts of Imperial coin as tips, the club staff rushed to help Nirabella and her companions. A 'guide' began showing them the facilities and the available merchandise. The guide's name was Dean. He was tall, fit, with striking black hair. After the tour and sitting in the bar on the beach Dean asked, "What are you ladies looking for? We have everything, even specialists in Nu-terriia fur orbs."

Nirabella replied, "We have heard one of your ladies; Jennifer Wolf is exceptional."

"You want only one lady for all three of you? Are you a triple?" Dean asked.

"Yes, and perhaps," Nirabella coyly replied.

Dean called over one of the bar girls and told her to go find Jennifer. As they waited Nirabella studied the patrons in the beach bar. It was filled with traders, bankers, and estate holders, both male and female in swimwear designed to cover bodies past their prime. There were male and female officers, mercenary commanders, pirate leaders and contract killers showing off hard bodies and Kill Dots. The final group of customers was composed of couples of various ages and body types wearing less than they should. Four tables away a fat man was holding his female's hand while they were serviced under the table.

Welcome to Horizon, Nirabella thought.

Jennifer casually sauntered up to their table. She was not what Spider expected. Jennifer was tall with a full figure and legs which seemed to go on forever. Short brown space cut hair framed a handsome face with eyes hazel resembling storm tossed seas. Spider thought, *older than expected, mid-thirties. Good looking but no great beauty. She must be damn good in bed for this club to keep her.*

"Why don't you join us?" Nirabella asked enticingly while offering Jennifer a chair. Within a few social pleasantries, Nirabella had arranged for Jennifer's time during the afternoon and Spider ordered a private beach cabana.

171

The cabana opened on one side to the ocean. The 'ladies' sat comfortably in the pillow lined cabana and talked about 'lady' subjects. Centari was on guard, however feeling uncomfortable with the setting and seemingly mindless conversation. Jennifer asked numerous questions from the other three and Nirabella and Spider answered many of the questions. At an appropriate time when all the ladies appeared relaxed, Nirabella showed Jennifer the pictures of Auntie Tara and asked, "Do you know her? Do you know where she is?"

Jennifer sipped her drink and sat for a long time appearing lost in thought. Finally, she said with no regard to answering the question, "Let's strip off our suits, walk out into the water and enjoy the sunset out there." The ladies were not self-conscious as they stripped off their suits, under garments and shoes and ran down to the water's edge.

The four of them waded into the low surf. Jennifer turned to them and said, "I believe sea water is very hard on electronic devices. Also, the noise of waves makes it difficult to pick up sound. Do I have your assurance while you are on Horizon or the space station that you will never discusses or reveal what I tell you?"

Each in turn said, "Yes, you have my pledge."

To an unconcerned beach goer, there were just four attractive naked women frolicking in the surf.

Jennifer began her story, "Yes I know her, and yes I may have some idea of where she went. Here is what I know ---"

****

Tracey looked around her. The air was thin and ice cold on the volcano top. The platform was thirty meters square and built with finely fitted granite stone work. A large fire blazed in the center of the pit. The north side of the arena opened to the edge of crater. Wisps of smoke emerged from the hot lava below. Low stone walls defined the other three sides. Behind the walls, tiers of seats rose up. A thousand or more spectators jammed the seats yelling for the fight to begin.

Half an hour earlier they unloaded from a big lifter and marched into a holding area just behind the low wall on west side of the arena. One of the guards told them, "If your two fighters put up a good show before they die, The High Lord may let the rest of you live."

High Lord Sunstar, now resplendent in white fur, arrived carried in a sedan chair. On his left walked Warlord Rayyan, in full dress blue and orange uniform with a cape of Weldon Lion skin. To Lord Sunstar's right walked the Lady wrapped in a many colored Trocnavar feathered cloak. Her c-cats walked beside her. The three marched into arena and were seated in the raised box at the center of the south side.

Tracey handed Purple Cat to Fidelity and seated herself on top the low wall facing the east side. Kat sat beside her. Tracey scanned the arena and thought, *Major Karrack Rayyan seated across from us on west wall is bigger, taller, and uglier than his father. He is wearing only a pair of orange utility pants and soft boots. The muscles of his arms and torso ripple with power. Like his father, his right arm is covered in Kill Dots. He is one very big ugly bastard.*

The deep tone of the tube bell rang out and Tracey and Kat easily scampered over the wall. Tracey ran toward Karrack as a flash of purple passed her.

My gods thought Tracey as she ran forward; *Purple Cat is going to attack him. Where is Kat? There is Kat to my right frozen; a dark stain of piss growing on his pants. What the hell! Damn Tracy! Hit Karrack with everything you have.*

Purple Cat hit Karrack first driving her special claws into his left kneecap. He kicked Purple Cat across the arena but her effort was enough to leave him open to Tracey's first blows. He staggered back, recovered and delivered a massive blow knocking her flat. Within seconds he was on his knees above her and drove his fist toward her face. Tracey dodged the first blow. He was quick but she was quicker. The second blow missed to the left. The third blow glanced off the side of her face as four teeth exploded from her mouth. She heard Karrack say, "Have you first bitch". *I'm going to die,* Tracey thought as thousands of stars filled her vision.

Tracey heard a scream – the sound of deep agony and of extreme pain – it came from Karrack. He whipped his head to the left as Kat drove the red-hot end of the burning branch into Karrack's right eye. It was not stars Tracey had seen but rather actually sparks from Kat's first blow to Karrack's neck. Karrack rose to his feet and Kat struck him once more in the chest. Tracey, still on the ground, tackled Karrack and he fell down backward. The back of his head slammed into the stone deck. Kat shoved the end of the branch into Karrack's mouth and then broke off the hot coal inside. The screaming signaled agonizing and searing pain.

Tracey regained her feet and then Kat and she began pushing, kicking, rolling and prodding with the burning branch to maneuver Karrack toward the edge. It seemed to take forever before they forced him over the brink. He screamed the entire way down.

"Die you bastard, die!" Kat screamed and flung the burning branch with one end wrapped in his piss soaked pants into the void. It was only then Tracey realized what Kat had done; his hands were a mass of blisters and blacken skin hung from his fingers. The wet pants gave Kat the only imperfect protection from the searing fire.

The audience sat in stunned silence as the great tube bell rang four times for Karrack's death.

Tracey looked at Kat and said, "Thank you for my life. It is an honor to fight beside you. Damn, you should have told me your plan."

"What plan?" he responded with a sly smile. "I just needed to piss."

Chapter Thirty-Two
– The *Outcast Lady* in Space - 08-19-518.

Outcast Lady rode a narrow and high wave of time and space. The narrower and the higher the wave the faster is the passage. Three days ago, Kat chose the fastest passage away from Horizon. After accelerating at high Gs for two days and reaching the minimum five percent of light speed, Peter initiated the Time Wave Drive and sent the ship into the wave. However, a narrow high wave was extremely difficult to maintain. Ships were known to disappear if they fell out of a wave. Some of the time wave mathematicians thought that the lost ships fell into another universe. Others thought the ships simply blew apart and were lost in deep space between planets. Each year several ships were lost. The highest losses were among the fast courier ships which rode the highest waves.

After one watch, Peter was exhausted. Spider took over and found how challenging riding a high wave could be.

I will not show weakness. I will complete a full watch. Careful -- too close to the edge of the wave, don't lose the wave; hold your line. Back on the crest, damn that was first-rate work. Only eight hours to go, Spider thought.

Just below the Control Room in the Ward Room an informal meeting of the officers and sergeants was underway. Many crew members jammed into the room to form an audience. Kat sat at the end of table with both hands wrapped in living medi packs. He lost the little finger on his right hand. The doctors budded on a new finger but it would take months to grow within the protective shell covering the bud. Tattooed on Kat's right shoulder was a new red Kill Dot.

By the traditions of the Free Space Force, Tracey as First Officer sat at the other end of the table. Her right jaw was a mass of purple with medi strips that closed the slash and shells covered the new buds for her missing teeth. Tracey's right shoulder held a new red Kill Dot next the black one. Tracey and Kat were both awarded kill dots for neutralizing Karrack. It was most unusual for both to gain a dot for one kill.

Kat a held a cup of Gubble brew in a mitten- like medi pack, took a sip and said, "Nirabella thank you for your account of the lens doc and what you found out about Auntie Tara. Cici, please fill in everyone on events up north after we killed Karrack. Our current plan and direction is driven by those two episodes."

Cici began her account, "Their guards were so stunned that we able to overpower them and grab their weapons. I remember breaking a guard's arm, grabbing his rocket carbine and going over the arena wall behind Peter. Just behind us were Light, Shadow and Fidelity all armed with long guns or pistols. The twins grabbed up the ammo packs before jumping over the wall. We formed a ring around you and

Tracey thinking the Warlord would have you killed. Nothing could have prepared us for what happen next."

Cici continued, "Two dozen troops, not wearing the orange and blue of the Warlord but in winter camo of blue, white and gray, poured into the arena forming a ring round us; not facing us but facing outward to protect us. Then I saw a woman in reptilian skin armor standing over Purple Cat. With her was a pink male c-cat. The woman gently picked up Purple Cat, walked though ring of troops and handed Purple Cat to Fidelity. She then joined the ring protecting us."

Everyone in the Ward Room looked at Purple Cat asleep on the table next to Tracey. Her right front paw was in a cast and clumps of fur were missing from her coat but otherwise she appeared ok.

Cici continued, "The troops were led by Captain Contreras who now had changed out of the Warlord's orange and blue and into winter camo. The Lady walked through a gate in center of the south wall and out to where we stood. She walked up to Kat and Tracey and said, 'We better get all of us out of here as soon as possible. You two just gave Horizon the shock of the century. The Captain and the troops in winter camo are my household troops. I have a 60 man lifter waiting just outside. The shock will last only so long, so please move out.' The woman in reptilian skin armor said, 'Yes we move out now.

Many will be enraged over my stupid brother's death.'"

Cici thought, *such love. It must be an exceptionally close family."* She continued with her narrative.

"As we boarded, the medical team on the lifter began treating Kat's burns and Tracey's wounds. Several hours later we docked with the hulk of an old transport in orbit above Horizon. The ship was a large ancient sphere ship being used for a storage warehouse. We docked at an enclosed lifter bay. As soon as the bay doors closed all appearance of being a hulk vanished. A second set of inner doors opened revealing first class docking ports for four lifters. Our lifter from the *Outcast Lady* was already docked at one of the ports.

Kat and Tracey were sent off to the medical facility." The crew and audience were in rapt silence. Next, Lady gathered the others into the meeting room and proceeded with a quick update.

Lady began, "Welcome to my home. You will be safe here. As you can see by the exterior, anyone picking up or dropping off supplies at two main docking stations will see only a poorly maintained dock and a disorderly warehouse. However, you will find the interior is a modern and organized base of operations for Sun Transaction Trading. Please join me for a meal, then you can cleanup and get some sleep. We will talk more on first watch."

"Thanks for your summary Cici. Thank you, too, Lady," Kat said. Kat continued, "A day later Baryic ensured that all the damn Martheain Herb Tea Bugs was off loaded to Sun TT. Two days later we had a contract with Sun TT to transport one hundred sealed cases to an unnamed planet. Later that watch, we were back aboard the *Outcast Lady*. Supplies, fuel, dark matter flasks and new small arms arrived in short order. We will be smuggling our cargo past Green Fleet and Tri-Star-Republic patrols. Also pirate attacks will be an ongoing danger."

Chapter Thirty Three–
In Space - 08-15-518.

Light years away and days earlier the *Dark Song* had dropped out of the space time wave and began to decelerate. Ahead of her was a tramp liner, *Express Girl*, also decelerating on an orbit toward the planet Valley Myers. When they were within 12,000 kilometers of *Express Girl*, the commander of *Dark Song* ordered battle alert. The tough young Trocnavar Commander Niikia Kaiii-var directed Artystaar Tiigano, her First Officer to prepare to fire missiles.

Artystaar ordered the weapons officer Quinn, "Target her light wave drive, open missile bay doors, and prepare to drop missiles."

"Doors open, missiles live, target locked!" Quinn called two minutes later.

"Drop two missiles on my mark --- Now!" Artystaar ordered.

Quinn called out, "Two precision target missiles away."

****

Commander Niikia directed Artystaar to slow and match the speed of the crippled liner. The two Trocs watched as their ship *Dark Song* closed on the helpless liner. Hours earlier they shot out the liner's LWD engine. The ship was a small mixed cargo and passenger liner. *Express Girl* was a contract ship not registered to any planet. She was imperial built of an old class called Summer Fish. On board was a crew of seventy or so and perhaps 200 passengers.

Commander Niikia now sent the following message, "Commander Jensen your LWD is destroyed. In normal space your liner cannot out run or out maneuver a fast war ship. There is no escape. We will match our speed to your ship, the *Express Girl,* and deploy a transfer tube. If you should resist in any way, we will fire our rail guns directly into your hull. The depressurization will kill most of you. The few in space suits we will hunt down and kill."

Commander Jensen responded, "You black hearted bastards spare the civilians and their children. We will comply with your request."

Artystaar and Sandy pulled themselves across the zero-gravity transfer tube. Forty officers and crew of the Dark Song were behind them. The air lock doors were open and they landed on the deck as the artificial gravity of the ship pulled them down. Minutes later, shots rang out as they reached the main deck. A dozen or more troops opened fire on the pirates. Artystaar thought, *So much for an easy assault. You can never trust the word of humans. Niikia can't fire on the liner now with forty-two of us on board. By the God of Death, I love killing, let the fighting begin.*

Artystaar motioned for two of her pirate gang to move forward. The two pirates she first ordered forward were killed. Artystaar got in a shot and dropped one of the troopers who showed himself. Sandy shot one and Bald Xiggott shot another. Artystaar shouted, "Three down, let's get the rest!" and led the pirate gang forward. As she stepped over the defender's body she saw that he was a contract Shock Trooper.

Artystaar, Sandy, Xiggott and four other pirates dashed forward into the main dining room and took cover behind overturned tables. The defending troopers unleashed a mass of gunfire. The pirates began to return the trooper's fire. More pirates rushed into the room.

What in all the hells are Shock Troopers doing defending a tramp liner like Express Girl? Artystaar asked herself.

The fire fight went on for an hour. In the end, all twelve Shock Troopers were dead including any crew members and passengers who joined the defense. Six pirates were dead and two were so badly wounded that they would be sent to the gods.

The remaining crew and passengers were now herded into the main dining room. Some would live to be sold as bound laborers, some would not. The better-looking ones were being dragged off to cabins. Artystaar and Sandy walked up to a handsome family, a man, his mate and two teenage girls. The man began begging, "Please don't take me, by the love of the Dark Goddess take my mate and my daughters. Do anything you wish with them, use them, kill them, or sell them. My mate is skilled at satisfying. Please! Please take her and the girls, let me live and not be sold! I will do anything; I will make them do anything."

Sandy look into his eyes and gut shot him. She whispered, "Die slowly weakling scum! I placed the wound so it's going to be a very long night." Sandy then turned to Xiggott who was guarding the group of prisoners and said, "Lock the women away in a cabin. I will keep them myself to sell. Leave the weakling here to die. Xiggott, I know you will see that the guards do not ease his way out."

"As you request, with pleasure," Xiggott responded.

As the three women were marched away, the mother raised a trembling hand and stopped. She walked over to where her mate lay and spit is his face. Then she intertwined her arm in Xiggott's hairy arm and walked away.

Artystaar commented, "I would have taken pretty boy to bed before I shot him. The woman and girls are beautiful; you will get a fine price. Shall we go and execute Commander Jenson?"

****

Several weeks later in the evening dusk, Artystaar, Sandy and their commander Niikia walked through the streets of Awful-Landing, the only real city on the Planet Stoneland. They had been drinking. A thief and three of his gang followed them, planning robbery and darker actions. But when the women stopped under a light any thought Rocket might have about taking advantage of the woman disappeared with a quick count of kill dots. He stopped counting at thirty and slipped back into the darkness.

Earlier in the day, Sandy sold the woman and girls captured on *Express Girl*. A rich trader from Blue Port purchased all three, the woman for himself and the two girls for his two sons. The auction price was higher than expected and Sandy bought several rounds of drinks at a local tavern to celebrate her good fortune. As night fell they headed back to the inn where they were staying.

As they walked Niikia said, "Sandy the crew voted you in as Crew Sergeant. Xiggott put your name up. The crew admired the way you fought and then gut shot that weakling and took his women. Also, you added kill dots for hand to hand kills on the *Express Girl*. There is going to be a pirate operation which will change Green Line forever. I will count on Artystaar as my First Officer and you Sandy as my Crew Sergeant."

Niikia continued, "Tonight we drink with the sweet tavern boys who are working the inn. We leave here at first watch tomorrow."

Chapter Thirty-Four
Near a Red Dwarf - 09-01-518.

Commander Kiitay sent a tight beam to Commander Jang. "If you sub-human warriors can manage it, match our orbit and we will come over to talk. See that the meeting is in a shipshape room. The last human contract warship I was aboard was a filthy junk pile."

The two ships orbited a cold airless rock of a planet. It was the only planet in the system and a far distance from the Red Dwarf star at the center. Kat and Peter were unable to find any record of the system. Given that the *Outcast Lady* was equipped, due to a fluke at time of sale, with the latest Free Space Force navigation computer, the star system must be unknown. At least the planet was unknown to the Free Space Force or any Green Line trader or warship. The system location was provided by Sun Transaction Trading in the contract to deliver the sealed cases.

Ninety clicks ahead of them was an imperial built ship, a mixed cargo and passenger liner. Not just any imperial ship but a newly built Fat Fish class merchant ship. Kat thought, *how did a trader operating on the edge of known space acquire a new first rate ship? She is a superb one; three times the length of Outcast Lady. Someone must really want these boxes, someone high-ranking in the Empire. How do they plan to get their cargo back to the Empire? It a long way back to Green's Star and then*

189

even further back to the Empire. Why such a long voyage?

Kat announced to the control room, "Ladies and Gentlemen, just ahead of us is the liner *Ice Queen*. They are sending over representatives. Please show the representatives every consideration during their visit. In addition, prepare to off load our cargo within the hour. Ms. Watkins, Mr. Guderian, and Ms. Czajka will handle the meeting."

As soon as the lifter from *Ice Queen* was inside, the bay doors closed and atmosphere retuned, out strode three officers. They were not wearing the dress whites of commercial officer's uniforms but were in tailored utilities in the bright colors so favored by Trocs. The commander was Trocnavar and the two others human. Tracey greeted them on the dock and escorted them to the Ward Room. The look of shock could not be hidden by the officers as they stepped in. Peter and Czajka rose and saluted the three. Tracey introduced them, "Mr. Guderian, our Chief Time Wave Navigator and Ms. Czajka our trade agent."

Commander Kiitay managed to introduce the two other officers; a Lieutenant named Harveston and another Lieutenant, a female named De Lunes. Kiitay said, "I never expected to ----" and trailed off into silence.

Tracey continued, "Shall we prepare Martheain Herb Bug Tea? The bugs are from a recent shipment." At that moment Anna Morgan, chief of the mess deck, rolled in a cart with a formal tea service on it. Anna began to prepare the tea.

As Anna served the tea Peter quietly said, "You seem confused Commander Kiitay. May we help in some way?"

"You are a half Trocnavar, we did not expect that. First Officer Watkins has a red and a black Kill Dot." He glanced at the bare shoulder of Tracey's utilities and said, "We did not expect that either. To our sensors, your ship appears to be a battered old war ship but inside the equipment is first rate and the crew and the ship are as sharp as any ship in our commercial fleet. Next you serve us tea that costs a month's wages. Who are you people?" asked Kiitay.

"We are simple traders hoping to turn a profit. Our plan is to off load our cargo and fulfill our contract," replied Czajka as Tracey thought, *perhaps we over-played the tea.*

Tracey's thoughts continued, *and who are you Commander? Why is the Ice Queen operating out on the edge of known space? Surly a ship like yours could find work closer to home. How could you possibly get back to the Empire in less than two years? Do you know anything about a mixed cargo and passenger liner called Fast Lady? When did she reach port at Blue Port? Is Jane Star - Major Tara Freeborn? Was Jane Star a passenger on the Fast Lady? There are so many unanswered questions.*

Tracey asked, "Commander Kiitay what do know about a ship called the *Fast Lady?"*

"Only that the ship did not make Blue Port on schedule. We don't have time to waste. Can we start loading our cargo now?"

Tracey watched as the last of the sealed cases were loaded on to the *Ice Queen's* lifter. At that moment, one of *Queen's* officers carelessly revealed a key bit of information.

De Lunes said, "Thank the gods that this is finished. We should have the cases safely delivered in four weeks."

They sure aren't going back to the Empire, Tracey thought and then asked, "Where are the cases going?"

De Lunes replied, "The Viceroy likes his staff to have only the best." She then stepped into the lifter as it powered up. Tracey walked off the lifter dock as the doors prepared to open to space.

Sometime later Kat, Peter and Tracey sat talking. Kat outlined what they now knew. "The Trocs have a major operation out here on the fringe of the Green Line. They are operating new first class ships here on the fringe. We do not know the location of their bases but it appears one is within four weeks' travel time. Auntie Tara was trying to find what the Empire doing out here when she disappeared. If we can believe

Jennifer Wolf, Auntie Tara left Horizon on a ship called *Fast Lady* during the first month of the year. The *Fast Lady* was headed for a planet called Blue Port but never arrived. Peter, set in a course for Blue Port, we leave in one hour."

Chapter Thirty-Five
–The Planet Blue Port- 09-30-518.

"*Fast Lady* never arrived here at Blue Port," The Station Master Amy Bradshaw declared. "But, many believe the ship was taken by pirates. How many times do I have to tell you that the ship did not reach Blue Port? I damn well run this station, and, as you know, it is the only space station for Blue Port. I would know if *Fast Lady* arrived here," Amy Bradshaw indignantly concluded.

After a month's long voyage, Tracey and Kat sat in the office of the Station Master. The blue ball below filled the side window of the office. Water covered ninety percent of the planet. The ridges of mountain ranges formed islands, many lush and green. The planet was on the outer fringe of the Green Line. Out here Blue Port was an island semi-civilization amid a sea of barbarianism.

Amy Bradshaw commented, "Commander Shane you really should consider a game of Field Ball. Ms. Watkins, I understand you play an excellent soft bat forward."

Kat started to say, "Are you crazy?" but Tracey's hand on his arm stopped him.

Tracey replied, "Thank you for the suggestion. I believe we can put together a creditable team. Please tell us more."

And Amy Bradshaw did just that.

****

Later during on board watch the *Outcast Lady,* Kat and Tracey gathered the officers and crew on the mess deck. Kat began, "For reasons I cannot explain at this time we need to put together a Field Ball Team. In the next three days, our team must be ready to play in a tournament and, if possible, win at least our first two games. Our participation in the tournament is critical; the impact is far beyond Field Ball."

"The teams will come from pirate ships, trading cargo ships, contract warships such as us. In addition, teams will come from trading houses, schools, government agencies and the military here on Blue Port. This tournament takes place every two standard years. It is major event our here on the fringe."

"As many of you know, First Officer Watkins was a star player at Officer Training School. Tracey it's all yours," Kat concluded.

Tracey took over, "The officers and sergeants of *Outcast Lady* are challenged to play in Blue Port Field Ball Tournament. We need a coach and nine players plus subs for the team. A practice field is reserved on Boca Island where dawn will be breaking in an hour. All officers and sergeants who played either on upper school or advanced school teams or as a professional be on the lifter when it leaves in half an hour. We begin training as soon as we land. If you have gear you like, bring it, if not we will get you gear."

"I know several of the crew are outstanding players, please see me. For of a couple of you we can arrange a promotion to Acting Sergeant. I don't think we can bend the rules for more than two." Tracey finished.

Two hours later they came in over the leeward side of Boca Island. A wide plain of green farm land filled this protected side of the island. A river meandered snake-like to the ocean. At the river's mouth a town spread out. Light identified three Field Ball circles on an open plain just south of the town. She watched as a flashing signal was turned on to mark the landing field. *We're expected,* she thought.

Light watched as they closed on the Field Ball field. Three rings were laid out near a school. Only one was a full regulation hundred-meter ring. A level circle of grass enclosed by two tracks half a meter apart formed the field. The black and white goals were up and on their tracks. The black goal ran on the outside track. The white goal ran on inside track. The goals rotated on the tracks in opposite directions. They were complex mechanisms, three meters high with a two-meter aperture. The goal aperture changed size at random times from two meters to half a meter. As the goals rotated around the field they change speed at random. It was not an easy task to knock a ball through a goal. Below, someone was testing the moving goal operation.

As the lifter landed at the school, a short wiry man greeted them. "Welcome to Boca Upper School! I am Robin the second coach here. Station Master Amy Bradshaw asked us to provide you with whatever you need. I believe we have everything you require. First, our local sports shop is sending out a van full of equipment. You will be able to purchase anything you require. Secondly, the main field here is fully staffed and is yours to use for as long as you wish. The local inn, Jill's Place, will provide food and accommodations. You will be our guests. Finally, the B team from school and I will be on hand as a practice team. Our first coach and our A team are in the capital for the school pre-tournament."

Kat said, "Thanks Coach, we need all the help we can get. This is Tracey Mills-Watkins our team leader. As soon as we have our equipment, we will take the field and play a practice game with your team."

Equipment arrival did not take long. Field Ball requires a complex field, but the equipment is simple; knee pads, elbow pads, a light helmet, good shoes, gloves for Goal Guards and the bats. The hard bats were one-meter-long made of solid aluminum bars three centimeters in diameter; flattened on one end to provide a flat area for hitting the ball. The other end was dipped in soft plasticine to give a solid grip. Soft bats use the same aluminum bar but not flattened on one end. The soft bats, except for grip area, were covered with plasticine foam. The rules stated that you can hit another player with a soft bat but when hitting the ball, the range is limited. You cannot hit a player with a hard bat. However, the range is much greater.

The first practice game was a disaster. They lost nine to one. Tracey rationalized telling the team, "We have not played together and it shows. We'll complete two hours of drills and then we will play a second practice game."

Tracey and Kat continued to drive the team and themselves through cycles of play and drills until they were playing under the lights. Finally, Nirabella told Kat to call a halt before they killed someone. Kat thanked Coach Shinn and the B team students who seemed disappointed to stop. The *Outcast Lady* team was damned glad to stop, get a shower, hot meal, and some sleep.

Following a dinner of Aki-Aki stuffed with local greens and grilled red fish steaks, Kat and Tracey sat on the veranda of Jill's Place. As the warm evening air drifted in, they reviewed the team lists compiled during the day. After half an hour of discussion they settled on a final roster.

Kat began, "One of the crewmen we appointed to Acting Sergeant, Mark Bittman, looks like our best bet as 1st Goal Guard. He was a first-rate upper school player."

Tracey continued, "Cici is the best choice for 2nd Goal Guard. She is strong and quick although out practice. Light and Shadow are a must as our 1st and 2nd Runner. – I don't know where they played, but both are damn good."

Kat added, "The second Acting Sergeant, Brittany Diamond, is a natural as Throw. Great arm! Tracey, you must be our 1st Soft Bat Forward. You are a star player." Tracey nodded. Kat continued, "I would like Spider as 2nd Soft Bat Forward. She played "B team" at OTS and did well today. Also, Baryic Chahill played a strong 1st Hard Bat Back today. The old man can still play."

Kat said "I think we must use Peter as 2nd Hard Bat Back. He is as strong as a Kirgiiiz Beast. For myself I played "A team" at OTS and can coach and be a substitute. I can't play a full game because my hands are still healing."

.

Tracey added the last names, "Fidelity, Czajka, and Centari Shamir can sub; all are decent players. Of course, Nirabella will be the Team Doctor."

Purple Cat, snoozed curled up at Tracey's feet. Earlier, for dinner, she killed a fat motan in the vegetable field behind the tavern. She did not comment on player selection; c-cats have little interest in the lists human are always writing.

Tracey awoke Light and the rest of the team at dawn. The next two days' activities were a blur for Light. As night fell on final day of training; she stood on edge of the field thinking. *I can't remember much except games and then endless drills. I must admit we are better now by all the hells. I can't imagine why Kat wants to stop looking for Auntie Tara and play this tournament. He says we must win our first two games, what in all the planets is that about? Watching Mark Bittman play is astonishing. He is a handsome one, taller than Kat, with his black eyes, dark hair, tan, chisel cut features and a body of stone. He is one of the kids we rescued on Pangerbar and is growing up fast. Someday I may give him a tumble, but now is not the time.*

After a quick breakfast, everyone loaded into the lifter for the trip west to the capital.

****

The contrast between the pastoral calm of Boca Island and the capital city of Harland's River could not have been greater. The capital was also located on the lee side of an island. The city was split by the river and sat on a large bay that held water ships of all kinds. The city docks were filled with fishing boats, cargo ships both big and small, passenger ships and a couple of water-warships. Tracey flew the lifter in over the city. Brightly colored flags and banners flew from all along the main road of the city. The road curved along the quayside at midpoint and an

200

arched bridge spanned the river. Every tavern and inn flew flags and banners marking the teams who stayed there. Beyond the city was an open field with six Field Ball fields. Each field was encircled by bleachers. Surrounding all six was a mass of brightly colored tents and wagons forming an open fair.

Tracey landed at the space port on the other side of the city. A young man from the Station Master's office greeted them. "My name is Diego and I will be your guide. By tradition each team parades though the city and out to the game fields to officially sign in. We will use an open topped electro van. The flags on the van I had sewn with the tan and black colors of your dress uniforms. I added the bright yellow to keep it festive."

Tan flags with wide black and yellow diagonal strips flew from the van. People cheered them as they slowly made progress across the city.

Along the waterfront, they passed an inn called the Seabird built out over the water. The tan, black, and bright yellow flags flew from the high points on the roof. Diego told them, "This is the inn where you will stay. It's a good clean inn. My uncle owns it," he said proudly.

****

The Outcasts were losing the third-round game to local team called the Trade Winds. The score was four to one in the final period. Light thought, *the two sisters are superb players --- both great runners. The*

201

four boys playing with them are also excellent. I think they must be bothers. Unless I miss my bet the other three players are semi-professionals. No wonder we are getting our asses kicked!

Just then one of the judges called time out. The younger girl came to a stop beside Light. She slipped a tiny plasticine tube into Light's hand and said, "I knew you were the one; hide this and give it to your commander when you are off the field." She was gone before Light could say a word. Peter scored another goal but the Outcasts lost four to two. The game ended and Light walked over to Kat and told him about the tube. Kat thanked Light and said, "I will take it as soon as we are back at the Seabird. Guard it with care until then."

Kat and Tracey gathered the team and he told them, "This third round is the end the of our tournament run. You played well and Tracey and I are proud of each one of you. A fine dinner and celebration awaits us at the Seabird." As they were leaving the field Kat pulled Tracey aside and asked her to be on guard until the team returned to their ship. "Ensure Light is safe," she said.

The excellent seafood dinner served at the Seabird included a dozen types of fish, shell fish, sea insects and the superb wines of Blue Port. With the exception of Tracey and Kat, the team drank and danced until dawn began to break. After dinner Tracey and Kat had slipped off to Kat's room. What the team members assumed was happening in Kat's room was quite wrong.

After Guide Diego said "goodbye" later the next morning, they were ready to lift for the *Outcast Lady* in orbit. Four of the Seabird tavern girls had an emotional time saying goodbye to Baryic and Mark Bittman. Diego gave Cici a kiss goodbye with a sparkle in his eyes. Tracey thought, *by all the hells, the party last night was a damn fine one! Too bad I missed it.* Cici walked over to her and said, "Nice going Tracey! Did you two have your own private party?"

Chapter Thirty-Six
– *Outcast Lady* in Orbit Above Blue Port - 09-38 -518

Back on board the *Outcast Lady*, Light, Kat, Peter and Tracey met in Kat's office. Light told them what occurred on the field and Tracey handed him the object in question.

"I haven't seen one of these since I was twelve," Kat said as he snapped the tube in half. Inside was a rolled sheet of plasticine. As Kat unrolled the sheet he observed random letters covered one side. On the other side was a chart. Kat continued, "Let me show you something." Taking a knife out from his desk drawer he cut open the end of tube. Flame flashed out of the broken middle of the tube. Anyone trying to open the tube at either end would destroy the message inside.

"Light, please go to my cabin and bring us the book <u>Death of the Empire.</u> You will find it in the drawer next to my bunk. The information on this sheet is encoded. The book is the key to decode this message. Decoding the note will take a while."Minutes later Light returned holding an ancient book with paper pages. "Thanks, please ask Morgan to bring us hot Gubble brew and tea," Kat instructed.

Kat explained, "The old book was written three hundred years ago by General Thomas Freeborn

Jang. It outlines a plan to collapse the Trocnavar Empire. At that time, the League of Free Stars possessed none of the resources needed to accomplish that goal and the book was soon forgotten. A few family members kept copies and handed them down for generations. The Freeborns developed a series of codes using the book. Let us begin decoding the message."

Light, Tracey and Peter offered to help. Kat told Tracey, "Grab a pad and write down the numbers and letters I call out." He then said to Peter, "See if you and Spider can understand the chart." Next, he asked Light be their runner. He then asked her, "Ask Spider to join us. Then fetch a copy machine, the best one on board. "

By the end of third watch Tracey had looked over ten pages of notes and estimated the decoding was 70% complete. Peter and Spider had a rough idea of what the chart showed. Kat told them, "My thanks to each of you. Light, please have all the officers and sergeants meet in the Ward Room. After the meeting, no further work by this team will be done during first watch. I mean what I said about sleep and rest. We need to get some sleep and clear our minds for the task to come. On second watch, we will start planning the operation. As a head start, I will ask Baryic to go over to the space station and quietly find out who is the best junk dealer in the system."

****

Blue-Port was surrounded by nine moons of which Moon 9 was the farthest out which was just fine with James "Motan" Smithson. James acquired his middle name while becoming the biggest dealer in old space ships, used parts, and space junk in the Blue-Port system. James looked across at Kat and Tracey and wondered *who in all the hells are these people?*

Looking at him Tracey thought, *how does one get nick- named after a life form like Motans? The small vicious beasts spread from their home planet to almost all of the planets in the Empire and the League of Free Stars. They love both Troc and human blood. So, far no one has stopped them from spreading to ships throughout known space.*

The low life James looked back at Kat and Tracey and said, "I can supply your requirements. Can you meet the price?

Chapter Thirty-Seven
– The Planet called Nothing #8 - 10-01-518.

The lifter dropped through heavy clouds as rain pounded. Sandy knew the planet on which they were landing was beyond the fringe of the Green Line, not at the far end of Green Line, but on a side branch folding back toward the Empire. It was nearly a thousand light years back to the Empire. Riding a high and narrow wave of time and space, cargo ships could make the passage in 500 days, give or take a few. Fast warships could make the run in close to 400 standard days. However, it was still a voyage of one standard year. One would need a least five planets or comets as a source of water for reaction mass. Every star chart and computer model Sandy looked at showed empty space between here and the Empire.

A fast courier ship, riding the highest possible wave might cut the time to close to three hundred days. But that was still almost a standard year. To make the voyage that long, four excellent time wave navigators were needed; one for each watch plus a backup. One of the new Imperial Super Flash couriers fitted with extra dark matter flasks and reaction mass tanks would also be required. Yet the Empire was bringing over warships, cargo ships, and supplies. Sandy was sure the battle cruiser that she saw in dock at the planet called 'Four' was sent out along a hidden route linking back to the empire. *Dark Song* must have also come over the hidden route. Imperial Blue Fleet is sending out ships, supplies, and crucial personnel.

Sandy reflected, *the time span of the operation was impressive. The Emperor must have given the Imperial Space Force approval years ago. Niikia Kaiii-var, our commander, is here for the final briefing on the plan.*

Chapter Thirty-Eight –
The Moon X9 of Blue-Port - 10-05-518.

It is going to be a very complex operation, Kat thought as he and Tracey slowly worked their way along the right wing. The remainder of the team was spread out over the wings, tail surfaces and nose cone. Every square centimeter of the leading edges needed inspection. An unrepaired crack or chip in the ceramic foam could kill them.

In spacesuits, Kat and Tracey floated along the glider's right wing. Tracey held an optical inspection unit and moved along the wing edge while Kat pushed a repair unit for the wing edge. The glider was docked in orbit above Moon X9 along with two other gliders, a dozen outmoded ships and junked space assemblies. Motan James, the scrap trader, told them this glider was the best of the lot. So far, he appeared to be correct.

Peter and Fidelity floated out on the left wing. Fidelity looked over the glider. The body was a box with rounded edges twenty meters long with three wide with a rounded nose flowing back to the cockpit bubble for a crew of two side by side. The body ended in a cargo ramp. Above it was a 'T' shaped tail five meters tall. The swept back wings spanned twenty-five meters. Fidelity asked Peter, "Tell me about Colonial Cargo Gliders. I have only seen them in the vids."

"They are gliders designed for a one-way trip down to a new colony," Peter said. "The glider carries cargo to the surface and is cargo itself. You grew up on a planet in center of the League. You never see one on the central planets of the League. They are used on the periphery of the League when new colonies are founded."

Fidelity asked, "Why are there so few of them?"

Peter continued, "Thousands have been built. However, the reason why so few exist is simple. The gliders are built of low cost materials, carbon micro tube reinforced plastio-ceramics, cheap plastics and only a few parts of steel, or aluminum. In order to prevent burning up during flight down, the nose cone and leading edges of the wing and tail are covered with ceramic foam over the plastio-ceramics."

"The glider can be broken down into assemblies and used by the colonist during the first years of the new colony. The body can be cut into homes; the wings make excellent roofs for barns or workshops and the tails and nose cones are used for walls and small buildings. In addition, the gliders are stuffed with supplies and equipment for the first year. We are fortunate; this one was built for an aborted colonization and never used."

"Peter, why don't the colonists use lifters?" Fidelity asked.

"Cost and the gravity bending technology of lift engines makes them expensive," Peter responded. "The FSF uses lifters without thought of cost. However, lift engines are costly for a private operation. It's not cheap to operate lift engines or maintain lifters. Small Cargo Gliders Type-17, like this one, can haul 12,000 kilograms of cargo and salvageable assemblies to the surface. The only extra cost is the assembly of the glider. Normally a crew of two is on board. The pilots and co-pilots are trained for a single flight. It can be dangerous, about one in two hundred is lost on way down. Most colonists ride lifters down to the surface. Only the poorest colonists ride the gliders down. The important thing for our mission is we create no lift engine gravity abnormalities. Consequently, the gravity instruments scanning the sky can't find us."

Fidelity said, "And twelve of us are going to ride this unpowered antique down to the surface unnoticed, land on water at night, make our way across several kilometers of a wilderness lake, infiltrate a hidden Imperial base, find Auntie Tara, capture one or more senior Troc officers, and then, in the confusion, hope a lifter can get down undetected to pick us up? You, Tracey and Kat are out of your minds if you think this operation can succeed! And don't think filling the area under the cabin floor with flotation foam is going to save the ship on the lake."

Peter asked, "Then you're not going to volunteer?"

211

"By the Dark Goddess, miss all this madness? Of course, I am going to volunteer!" Fidelity answered enthusiastically as they continued inspecting the wing.

Before the *Outcast Lady* left the Moon 9, all of the crew had volunteered.

Chapter Thirty-Nine –
In Orbit above the Planet Nothing #8 - 11-3-
518

A month later the *Outcast Lady* dropped out of the wave near a planet simply called Nothing #8. The planet was fifteen light years from Blue Port. As soon the ship was clear of the wave, Peter called out, "TWD off line, you have ship control Commander Jang. We are eighteen light minutes out. Our speed is 15,860 kilometers per second."

Kat issued as series of orders. "Ms. Watkins, begin deceleration, power down all ships systems except life support, the gravity controls, plasma drives and the dark matter drive. Ms. De Santis, do not power up any weapons. Mr. Chahill, match gravity power to our deceleration rate. Spider, cut power to our sensors unless they are needed to track the Troc base and ships. We are going to drift into orbit running dark."

Tracey responded, "Using limited power to the dark matter drive. We will slip in as quietly as possible."

Three small moons orbited #8. Closer in, two rings circled the planet. The two rings were composed of millions of asteroids ranging in size from dust to the size of a planetoid. Some of the asteroids were comprised of metal, iron, some rock, and some ice. The plan was to use a group of large metal asteroids in the inner ring to hide the *Outcast Lady*.

Days later, the *Outcast Lady* was in an orbit inside the inner ring of the planet. The ship was running dark and hiding deep inside the ring. Seven spaceships orbited further out from the planet. There was no space station. Six ships were Trocnavar built. Five of those ships displayed various pirate devices and colors. The exception was a new Trocnavar light cruiser. The cruiser was without markings and painted dark gray. The final ship was an armed troop carrier. It was a sphere ship built in the ship yards of the League of Free Stars but now in the purple and white colors of the Tri-Star Republic.

Kat admitted, *this is going to be tougher than I thought. We never planned for seven ships in orbit around #8.Thank the gods they are all in high orbit beyond the third moon. Too much risk of an asteroid hit in low orbit. It will be difficult to find us inside the inner ring.*

On the hull Cici, Baryic, Shadow, Light and another dozen crew members worked to release the glider from the cradle mounting her to the side of the *Lady*. Next, they would reinstall the wings which were folded for the journey and then attached a transfer tube.

A watch later, the Assault Group gathered on the main deck near the transfer tube. Each one was dressed in camo uniforms of purple, red, yellow, blue and black. The planet below was covered with brightly colored trees and foliage. This was very likely one of reasons the Trocs selected Nothing #8 for their base. The colorful plants reminded the Trocs of their home world.

Each of the group was armed with a rocket pistol and carried either a second rocket pistol or a compact pistol. Each had numerous clips of ammo. Cici, Peter, and Mark carried hand axes while the twins, Tracey, Fidelity, Nirabella and Spider also had combat knives. Baryic and Centari carried machetes on their belts. Finally, Kat had a curved FSF officer's sword of two hundred years ago strapped to his back. The long weapons and explosives were packed with the three inflatable boats.

As they floated via the transfer tube, Cici checked the names on the list. No gravity generators were on the glider so they kept floating. The weapons and supplies came aboard with them. Within minutes all the gear was stored and each of the assault group strapped into their seats. Cici called each one out, including herself. "Cici De Santis loadmaster and warrior, Tracey Mills-Watkins pilot and First Officer, Shadow Freeborn warrior, Light Freeborn warrior, Spider Constantine copilot, Centari Shamir warrior, Peter Guderian heavy weapons, Mark Bittman heavy weapons, Baryic Chahill demolition, Fidelity Stone communication, Nirabella Freestar medical, and finally Kat Jang Commander."

The big lifter, piloted by Czajka with Anna Morgan riding gunner, locked on to the glider. Czajka, the ship's business agent, turned out to be fair lifter pilot. She would use the lifter to slow the orbital speed of the gilder and keep it from burning up. She would drop the glider and return to the *Outcast Lady* hidden in the inner ring. To the Troc ships in orbit and the base on the surface, the gravity abnormalities created by their unpowered glider would look like a meteor dropping from the inner ring field.

They needed to enter the atmosphere at an exact time and point. Tracey watched the instruments and called out, "Five, four, three, two, one, launch." The lifter and glider floated free of the *Outcast Lady.* Czajka began slowing their speed and they dropped toward the planet below. Minutes later Tracey told Czajka, "Drop us on my mark; five, four, three, two, one - Now!"Anna's final words, "Victory, Honor, Ship, my friends!" rang out as the gilder dropped clear of the lifter.

Tracey flew the beast toward the surface. Spider began calling out air speed, altitude, and distance to the landing zone. Tracey fought the controls, the CG-17 had only limited power boost for the controls making the descent a test of strength. Soon Spider was working the controls with her, matching her moves. It was an exotic dance where Tracey was leading with Spider matching every move. Sitting just behind them, Kat took over calling out air speed, altitude, and distance. He thought, *by all the gods, the ladies are dancing with our lives. I told everyone the mission was high risk. That was a hell of an understatement. I striped the Lady of the key officers and crew to staff this team. If we fail will Erica Nguyen, the only time wave navigator left be able to get the Outcast Lady back to Blue Port?*

Minutes later they passed through an opening in a mountain range. Tracey flew over the storm below. The storm raged just as predicted over the hill country. Turbulence tore at the old glider as Tracey hoped the wings would hold together.

Soon they were over the forest covered hills. Holes in the clouds reveled flashes of lighting illuminating the brightly colored plant life. *The colored camo uniforms were perfect*, Tracey thought.

Kat called out, "Fifty clicks to our landing zone."

Tracey saw only storm clouds around them and nothing of the lake fifty kicks out. *I hope we make a smooth landing,* she thought."Strap down for landing," Tracey instructed.

Cici yelled, "Damn Tracey! You had this crew all strapped down a long way back!"

Spider asked, "Flaps?"

Tracey responded, "One quarter down". By lowering the flaps (movable sections on the back edge of the wing) lift increased and allowed the glider to fly at lower speeds for landing.

At twenty-five clicks out Tracey called for flaps half down. The CG17 glider hit major turbulence as they passed through the front of the thunder storms. Tracey and Spider fought to control the ship in a five-hundred-meter freefall. They stabilized the ship in the calm air in front of the storms.

Kat calmly said, "Ten clicks out."

Tracey found the lake ahead of them; a wedge of shinning silver surrounded by the darkness of the forest at nightfall. None of the bright colors showed in the gloom. "Spider, give us 3/4 flaps at five clicks and full flaps half a click out," Tracey instructed.

Tracey focused for the landing. *Ok, here we go. Good job Spider on the flaps. Now, four clicks out. Speed and altitude dropping and I see more of the lake. Looks good, water is calm with the storm a half an hour behind us, should be time to unload and get us into the boats before the storm hits. Final approach, focus on the landing. Two hundred meters' altitude, bring her nose up a little and ease her down. CG 17 was never designed for a water landing. Down and skimming across the water. What in the hells? DAMN NO!"*

At 150 clicks an hour they hit a submerged log as big as the gilder. They went airborne and then nose first into the lake, flipping the gilder on its back. The screams of ripping reinforced plastio-ceramics and breaking metal fill the air. Those noises were soon replaced by the sound of water rushing in.

Chapter– Forty
- Trocnavar Base on the Planet Nameless #8 -
11-07-518

The main hall was round, built with stone walls and a high dome of timber. Officers and other leaders gathered within the inner circle on rings of comfortable chairs. The separation from the outer stone wall was formed by a stone ring pieced by archways. At each archway stood a sergeant facing outward whose sole function was to ensure the total isolation and safety of those within. Gathered within the hall was a mixture of Trocs and humans dressed in wildly assorted robes and uniforms. Imperial officers dressed in color splashed robes, Tri-Star officers in purple and white dress uniforms and humans in every kind of uniform or pirate dress.

Sandy stood with a rocket carbine at port arms facing outward from arch number thirty-seven. A thin old man and his party moved toward her. Glittering in white robes, he arrived carried in a sedan chair. A tall woman in reptilian skin armor flashed their pass cards. Sandy stepped aside and the party entered. She watched the Troc commanding officer greet the old man. *Who in all the hells was the old man?*

Before she turned back to her guard position, Sandy glanced at Artystaar and Niikia Kaiii-var seated in the front ring. Both rose to greet the old man. *Strange, very strange*, she thought.

The Troc commander Count-Viceroy-Colonel Bifusss Markiii rose to address the group. Sandy listened as he spoke.

"We are here to launch a plan which will drive the Free Space Force from the Green Line," Markiii said. "The Empire has spent years getting resources in place. Now is time for action. The Empire will take control all of the trade along the Green Line and you, our partners, will no longer be pirates and mercenaries living on the fringe. You will rule the Green Line for the Empire." Markiii waited a moment before continuing.

"We shall begin with an intelligence report on our enemies. As most of you know, Rarkiikars are independent organizations, who provide information, security, and assassinations. We have engaged Rarkiikar Clovis to provide all these services. It is headed by a human with great insight. Death Lord Clovis, you may begin."

Sandy could hear the noise of speakers changing places but with her back turned she had no idea what Lord Clovis looked like. *What did matter?* She thought. *The Count says we are going to be rich. Well, that just might matter.*

Lord Clovis began his presentation, "Rarkiikar Clovis has agents in place throughout the Green Line and the League of Free Stars. I shall present an overview of Free Space Force's Green Fleet and any contract warships that might support them. We will review my team's efforts within League's Parliament to limit support and funds to Ax Bridgeford and his little fleet. Finally, I will describe the political climate of the major trading planets along the Green Line."

"The fleet consists of the battle cruiser *Lady Delapasse* and the heavy cruiser *Republican Lady;* both are Imperial built," Lord Clovis said. "The *Republican Lady* returned to the fleet with a complete refit. We stopped Bridgeford from getting a second battle cruiser via influence in their Parliament. Those fools in their Parliament don't know eleven of the members are ours." Lord Clovis waited to observe the reaction of those present. Seeing none, he continued, "The fleet also has two light cruisers called the *Sea Goddess* and *Lady Montoya* both of which are League sphere ships. The other ships of Green Fleet are four destroyers and four fast escorts; a mixture of League and Imperial built ships. The destroyer *Fire Dancer is* a League built sphere ship and the fast escort *Summer Storm,* an Imperial built ship, is typical of this group of ships. Finally, the fleet is supported by only one armed supply ship named *Bighorn Bull.* Once more, we were able to drive funding cuts in Parliament for a second one. Not much of a fleet to cover the entire Green Line," Lord Clovis surmised.

"The two things we have not been able to impact are the readiness and morale of the fleet. We have lost several agents within Green fleet. Bridgeford's

Executive Officer, Colonel Harrison Chung appears to be particularly skilled at hunting down our agents. Our success with contract warships has been much better. We assassinated two key commanders who supported Bridgeford. Bribes and rumors dulled the enthusiasm of many others. My estimate is less than half a dozen will sign on to fight beside Green Fleet. Many of those will run at the first sign of a real battle. My estimates are seldom wrong," He concluded.

Sandy glanced over her shoulder and watched as the old man quietly arose and spoke, "I believe you are wrong about the skill, courage and commitment of the contract commanders and crews. I recently lost a fine officer to such a crew. I believe Rarkiikar Clovis may have also seen an example when you lost two agents on Horizon." The old man sat down. The room went quiet. Whoever the old man was, he held the respect of many in the room.

Sandy thought, *is the bastard right about contract ships or is the old man, right?*

Lord Clovis was thrown off balance by the old man's statement but quickly recovered and continued, "Thank you for your observations High Lord. I will review your concerns with my organization."

After droning on about the details of the political climate of the major trading planets and showing many projections Clovis concluded saying, "A complete and detailed report will be downloaded to your data packs at the close of this meeting."

Count-Viceroy Markiii stepped quickly to the speaker's platform. "Lord Clovis, thank you for the fine work of Rarkiikar Clovis. Let us proceed to the plan of war."

It's about time, only the gods know what the Empire paid Clovis. Sandy reflected and added an afterthought; *only two planets appear to matter in this plan.*

"Our plan is a simple one," Markiii said. "The attack will be focused on only one planet. However, we shall appear to attack the other key planet light years apart. General Bridgeford cannot defend the two locations with his handful of ships. The war plan is as follows ----"

Chapter Forty-One –
Lake West of Trocnavar Base- 11-07-519.

The gilder lay upside down and sinking nose first as water rushed in through the shattered front window. Tracey found herself strapped into the pilot's seat with her upper body under water. She quickly unstrapped herself and flipped right side up. As her head broke the surface she sucked in air. She knew she had to get out immediately. Someone flashed on a light and then she heard the rear door being blown open. *Good job Cici,* Tracey thought. Most of the team would get out via the rear door. She started swimming out the open window and as she turned she realized Spider was still strapped upside down in her seat and not moving. For a moment, Tracey considered abandoning her and swimming to safety.

In the dim lighting, Tracey swam down to release Spider's harness. She fumbled with harness and was unable to open it. Returning to surface she took another breath and dove down once more to try to free Spider. She still could not release the harness. Something had been damaged during the crash. Once more she surfaced for air as her mind spun. *How can I get Spider free?* Tracey thought. The water grew deeper as Tracey made another dive. Wrestling with the harness one more time, her hand slid along Spider's leg, by the gods, of course, Spider's knife was strapped to her leg. Tracey pulled the knife and quickly cut Spider out of the harness. She dragged

Spider free and swam out the window pulling Spider to the surface outside.

In the darkness, strong hands pulled Spider and then Tracey into one of the boats. As she was pulled over into the soft side of the inflatable boat, she thought, *Thank the gods; Cici got the boats out the rear door.* Lying flat on floor of the boat, Tracey heard the sound of the gilder slipping below the surface. Peter, who just pulled them the out of the water, was administering artificial respiration to Spider. The dull red glow of a combat light illuminated scene. Tracey raised her head and saw that Mark Bittman was deploying the storm shell. The shell was a water proof cover with supports. It would keep out most of rain. Tracey wondered how close the storm was. Just then she heard a sputtering sound and then gasping breaths. Peter yelled, "Breathe, you crazy bitch - breathe!" Spider was alive!

Tracey pulled herself into a sitting position with her back resting on the tube which formed the left side of the boat. The first thing she saw was Peter pulling Spider into a sitting position alongside her. Tracey looked over at Spider, saw her head wound, and asked, "You O.K.?" Spider gave a weak smile and turned her thumb up. She then mouthed, "Thank you". It was the first-time Tracey ever heard Spider thank anyone. Tracey said, "I wasn't going lose my copilot".

Tracey looked around the boat. The two of them and Peter sat near the bow. As she looked back toward the stern, her heart sank. Nirabella was working on one of the team. She could not see who it was because the cargo box in the center of the boat blocked her view. Tracey raised herself slowly to standing. Her head hit the storm shell before she was fully erect. Stooped, she made her way past the cargo box aft to Nirabella. Baryic lay on floor with Nirabella working on him. He was severely injured.

Baryic was badly busted up; there was something wrong with whole right side. His leg was twisted strangely and his hip and rib cage did not look right. Nirabella had cut away his utilities and applied three medi-packs. These living organisms were loading him with antibiotics, Imperial pain-stop, and drugs to control bleeding. *Let it be enough to get the old man through this night,* Tracey prayed as she touched Nirabella's shoulder. Nirabella turned to Tracey and whispered, "No". Tracey knelt and placed her hand on Baryic's good arm. There was no response. All she could hear was his shallow breathing. After a minute, Tracey knew she must move on. She was in command of this boat and much needed to be done.

The boats were ten meters long inflated. The storm shell covered the first eight meters. Tracey moved to the stern of the boat. The last two meters was open with a control console in the center of the opening. Mark, the big crewman, was standing at the control console. He said, "Ma'm the helm is yours. The commander would like a word with you." Tracey had not seen Kat on board. They were operating under signal silence. *Where in all the hells was Kat?* She thought.

A voice called out, "Over here Tracey." She turned and saw Kat standing in the stern of the second boat. Cici manned the control console next to him. The two boats were tied together. Kat asked the status of the boat. She replied, "Boat is undamaged, cargo box is intact. Six of us are on board. Baryic has massive injuries; Spider has a head wound but she should be alright. The rest of us are Ok. What is your status?"

"Boat and cargo are intact. We also have six on board. Fidelity's forearm is broken. Light is setting it using a medi-pack. The arm is useless, otherwise she is alright. The rest of us are good."

Tracey asked, "Where is the third boat?"

"The third boat broke loose inside the glider during the landing. It caused serious damage when it hit Baryic and Fidelity. Shadow, Cici and I tried to pull it out but it was jammed in. It sank along with the gilder and a cargo box. A third of our arms and equipment are gone. Peter and Light got Baryic and Fidelity out."

"Tracey, if we going hide inside the storm as it moves toward the Troc base, we need to get moving. The storm is only ten minutes out." Kat instructed.

"Understood, we are powering up the electro-motors. As soon as you cut the line we can be underway," Tracey said.

She turned to Mark and said, "Mister Bittman set in our planned course. Keep Kat's boat in site if possible." She picked up the com mike, "Peter, get the automatic rocket rifle into the bow mount. Keep it under the storm cover for now."

"It's already mounted," Peter replied.

The rain and wind overtook them eight minutes later.

****

Sandy checked the time for her nightly walk along the lake wall. It was mid third watch. *It would be difficult tonight* she surmised. Niikia, Artystaar and she were engaged in an orgy with two bound bed boys and Lord Markiii, the son of Count-Viceroy Markiii. They were all high on drugs and liquor. His Lordship was not picky about the sex of his partners. He was enjoying each of them in turn. The bastard also wanted to watch as they did each other.

Sandy considered, *tonight it will be impossible. We have been here a month. I carefully cultivated the routine of mid third watch walks along the lake wall.*

Now this damn orgy has made a mess of things. I will miss my walk this night and it could be THE night. I must trust Emmelyn to keep her word. Now dive back in and smile at the slimy bastard.

****

The two rescue boats raced across the lake under cover of the storm. Rain pounded down as waves swept over the boats and lightning strikes darted across the sky. They reconfigured the storm covers so that the only space for two of the crew and the control console was open to the storm. Much of the water was being kept out. The twin pumps kept the deck dry. The pounding of the boat made the trip a hell for Baryic. Tracey could only hope the painkillers kept him sedated.

In her mind, Tracey reviewed the layout of the Trocnavar base. *It is built at the tip of a peninsular of land jutting southward into the Lake. The Troc base is a great walled circle a kilometer in diameter. The harbor is a quarter kilometer bite taken out of the south side of the circle. Next to the docks is a landing field for lifters. Around the landing area are warehouses. The center building is headquarters and officers' living quarters. We are coming in from the west; a wall ten meters high runs along the west side with a walkway on the top. The wall drops directly into the lake. It should be lightly guarded if the information we gained with our probe is correct. We land in the center of the wall, at a point called Alpha.*

Two hours later both rescue boats were half a click off the west wall of the Troc base. The storm still raged around them. The team gathered in Kat's boat except Nirabella who cared for Baryic in the other boat. Kat reviewed the reworked plan. "Peter, Cici, Mark and Spider will take this boat around to the harbor side. Set explosives on the largest boats in the harbor that are closest to you. If you can't get close to a boat then set the explosives in the harbor wall. As soon as you get my signal, blow the explosives and begin firing the auto rocket rifles into boats and the lifters parked on the harbor docks. Within minutes your team should head for the point Beta and wait for the lifter."

"Centari, Nirabella and Fidelity will crew the other boat and care for Baryic," Kat continued. "You will drop the rest of us at point 'Alpha' on the lake wall. Then you will pull back and setup half a click out with the last auto rocket rifle and await my signal to come in and pick us up. If you don't get a signal within two hours, head for point Beta."

"Tracey, the twins and I will scale the lake wall and see if we can make contact with the major, extract her and head back for pick up at point Alpha. If she is not there we will improvise a new strategy. Is everyone alright with the plan?" Kat asked.

"Victory, Honor, Ship" all responded.

Kat found it strange they would use the Battle Cry of the Free Space Force after the treatment the crew received at the hands of the FSF.

Chapter Forty-Two –
The Trocnavar Base- 11-08-519

In the driving rain, Tracey pulled herself over the lake wall and dropped a meter onto the walkway behind it. With no one in sight, she signaled the others. Within a minute Light, Shadow and Kat joined her on the walkway. They pulled up their ropes, hooks and coiled and hid them as best could along inside of the lake wall. There was still no sign of anyone. They could see the fort wall on other side of the walkway. Doors and windows pierced the wall in a few places. All were dark. Shadow pointed to an alcove twenty meters to the south. He signaled them to wait and crossed the walkway toward the alcove. There was a muted thump and Shadow motioned the three of them forward.

The guard lay dead at Shadow's feet, shot at close range with a compact pistol. The special low power ammo was quiet, hence the muted report. A voice in the darkness said, "It's about time you killed him! We don't have all night." It was not Major Freeborn speaking. They turned and saw a small figure in dark rain gear. The voice was female and human. She instructed, "Dump the body over the lake wall." As soon as Kat and Tracey shoved the dead guard over the wall, the figure motioned the four of them into an unlit doorway ten meters further along the inner wall.

Inside the door, they walk a few meters down a hallway. The woman opened the second door and inside was a room fitted out as a guard station. *That door on the other side of the room must lead deeper into the Troc base,* Tracey surmised. The mysterious woman pulled off her rain gear revealing a small thin body perhaps thirty standard years old with short dark red hair. Her large green eyes sparkled with an inner fire.

She began quickly "My name is Emmelyn. We have very little time but first an agreement. I will help you get Sergeant Sandy out of the base. In return, when you leave here you will take my two children with you."

Kat responded, "The dangers will be extreme. Your children will likely be killed along with us."

"How stupid do think I am? Of course, they will probably die! But there is small chance they could make it to freedom. Would you rather live as an Imperial Bound Laborer or risk your life to be free? Do we have a deal; yes or no?" Emmelyn asked.

"Yes," Kat stated.

"Tell me your names," Emmelyn instructed.

She opened a large gray bag and began pulling out an assortment of items. Out came scarves and arm bands in bright colors, a power razor, power scissors, and then spray cans of hair dye in vivid colors. "Let's begin with you," Emmelyn told Light. "Strip off your top, good a black bra, keep the rocket pistol on your belt and hide your other weapons in your utility pants. Next, tie this orange scarf around your left arm." Within minutes she had two arm bands added to Light's outfit and right side of her head shaved and dyed orange.

"You're next," she told Shadow and cut away his right and left sleeves. "Excellent; a black kill dot! This may work. The colored utilities you all wear will blend in adequately." Emmelyn then added blue and green arm bands to his left arm. Finally, she shaved the right side of his head and dyed it blue before moving on to Kat she told Shadow to keep one pistol on his hip and hide the other pistols and the knives.

"Kat, strip off your top. By the gods, look at those scars on your chest and a red kill dot. You are almost perfect. I will add two black arm bands to your left arm and tie this yellow scarf around your neck. Then I will dye the right side of your head yellow. Keep the sword on your back. Damn, you will look the part."

Minutes later she turned to Tracey. "Aren't you the tall one? We need to show those legs and your midriff. Get out of your utilities. I will cut them down." Tracey stripped off the uniform. "By the gods, lady you have a red and a black kill dot!" Emmelyn cut the right arm off the utility top then proceeded to cut off the bottom of the top. Tracey thought it was just long enough to cover her. Emmalyn next cut her pants into shorts. She added green arm bands and gave Tracey a green scarf for her neck. Finally, she shaved and dyed green the right side of Tracey head. "Keep the carbine slung on your back" she instructed and then she turned to the whole group.

She took out two bottles of cheap clear liquor and told them to pour it over their heads and take a drink. They all took a drink. Tracey noted that Kat swirled the liquor in his mouth then spit it out. Emmelyn outlined Sandy's plan. "You are now a group of drunken pirates, act drunk. Today the Trocs revealed the final war plan. There are celebrations throughout the base tonight. Drunken pirates and imperials will be as common as motans in a meat market."

"I am going guide you into the central fort. Keep your weapons stored until we have to kill. Here is how we are going into the base. --- "

****

The boat ran south toward the tip of the peninsula until one of the harbor towers at the entrance appeared on the left. The other tower on the far side of harbor entrance lay hidden in rain. Peter and Cici rode in the bow with automatic rocket rifles. Spider was back with Mark at the helm. In a low voice, she was reading directions and depths out to the com unit. The heavy rain made it difficult for guards in the towers to see anything. It also made it hard to find the harbor entrance. Their boat was four hundred meters out from the shore. Spider noted the depth dropped off and then began to rise. *This must be a dredged main channel,* she thought. Then she said, "Mark, turn to port and follow the deep channel toward the entrance."

Mark made the turn to port, slowed the electro-motors and followed the course that Spider whispered. Within minutes they passed the two towers and were inside the harbor. In the rain, Peter and Cici scanned the harbor for targets. They could only see thirty or forty meters. Peter caught site of a shape ahead of them and whispered into the com system, "Something dead ahead. Slow the boat, let's see what it is." A half sunken lake freighter appeared out of the rain. "It's here to block the center of the harbor forcing ships entering close to the harbor sides. We can't go around it. We will be seen by one of the guards on the breakwater. Move in closer, we will see if anyone is on board," Peter said.

Mark slowly brought to boat up to the side of the wrecked ship. The top of the railing was three meters above the boat. Moments later Cici tossed a soft hook over the railing and began to pull herself up the attached rope. Peter, Spider, and Mark watched as she disappeared into the rain. Minutes later she called to them, "No one is on board but she is overrun by motans. Watch out when coming on board."

Peter told Mark, "Up you go, drop a rope and we will send up the explosives; then one of the automatic rocket rifles with the ammo. Spider, you go next and I will follow you."

They were soon gathered in the rotting plasticine deck house. Cici reported, "The rain slowed and I saw what appears to be large military lake ship anchored 300 meters inside the harbor. Only a few lights are showing. I can't see if anyone is on deck. Maybe the rain is keeping them inside. There are other ships in the harbor but the military ship is the closest. Blowing it up would cause the maximum distraction for Kat and his team. What's the plan Peter?"

Peter squashed a motan who made the error of biting his boot and said, "Cici, Mark and I will swim over to the military ship and set explosives at the water line near the Motor Room and the magazine. Well, at least where we think they are."

Mark interrupted, "I know where they are. I spent a summer on military boats back on Freehome before they duped us into going to Pangerbar."

Peter continued, "Good, Mark. Spider set up the auto rifle in position and if anything goes wrong, blast the ships and lifters hidden by the rain on the dock."

Spider looked at Peter and said, "May your children be born without color." The comment was the worst possible Trocnavar curse; however, Spider said it in Noble Trocnavar -a language only the two of them spoke. In Common Com, she said, "I will have you covered." She crushed a motan into the deck. She wanted to be with the action and not a backup.

A hundred meters out Peter realized how cold the water was. His envirosuit was not keeping the cold out. The heat his body generated by dragging kilos of explosives toward the target kept him from freezing. *Keep on swimming, keep on swimming,* his mind chanted as he pushed forward. He saw Mark and Cici swimming on his left keeping pace with him. The swim distance was daunting in the cold; two hundred meters out, then three hundred back to the hulked lake freighter. *Ax told you he chose you for Green fleet because you never give up. Keep on swimming,* Peter thought as he pressed on.

Minutes later they were floating at the water line alongside of the military ship with no sign of a guard on deck. Whoever was supposed to be the deck guard had better hope he or she was killed in the blast. If they lived, the Trocs would turn their life into ten living hells. Mark signaled them to plant two explosive charges where he thought the engine room was and one charge near the magazine. Each of charges was attached to the hull with a plastic adhesive which was also an explosive. The remote-control detonators were set deep in charge.

Duty completed, it was time to go. As they turned to swim back Peter saw that both Cici and Mark were worn out and suffering from the cold. On the return swim, a hundred meters from the military ship, Mark passed out. He was overcome by the cold. Cici reached Mark and inflated his safety vest. He was now floating with his body only partly submerged. Peter thought the risk of being seen in the rain was at minimum. He looked at Cici. Her beautiful dark eyes were beginning to glaze over. "Inflate your vest and hang on to Mark and I will pull you both," Peter said. He wondered how much trouble were they in. Both Cici and Mark were extremely fit. If the three of them was in major trouble and might not reach the boat, Spider had a remote-control detonator and she would ignite the charges on Kat's signal.

As he pulled Cici and Mark toward the wrecked ship he kept chanting in his mind, *never give up, never give up, never give up.*

****

Shadow made an excellent drunk pirate. He danced his way down a main hallway and swilled beer from a plasticine squeeze bag. They passed a larger group of pirates of which two of the wildest women tried to drag Shadow off with them. Shadow kissed them both and sent them on their way. The team walked with Shadow in front and the three others in a group behind him. As a servant, Emmelyn walked just behind carrying as case of clear liquor in a back sling. She whispered directions to Kat. So far there had been no trouble. As one of many groups of drunken pirates, they passed through three pirate check points. The check points were poorly manned and the guards half-drunk themselves. This night a bottle of liquor was the best pass card.

Down the hallway, Tracey saw a check point manned by Tri-Star Republic shock troops. As the group staggered forward, they could see the details of the shock troops. There were four guards, a big blonde sergeant and three others.

Fifty paces later, the group was face to face with the guards. They were not that drunk. The big blonde asked for their pass cards. Kat told him, "We traded the cards for this case of liquor. It's a party night, you motan brained fool. Here, have a drink." He pulled Emmelyn close to take a bottle from the case on her back. She said, "Two bottles sir?"

Kat said, "Yes, two bottles" The sergeant looked at him started to draw his pistol but stopped. He then reached out and took the two bottles.

"Leave the tall woman and short cute boy," the sergeant instructed.

"Ok, but they're running the Queen's Black Drip," Kat said.

"NO! By the gods, we don't want diseased filth. Move on and don't come back this way, scum!"

As soon as they were safely down hall, Kat said, "People, we need to move. How much further is it, Emmelyn?"

"Three hundred and fifty meters or more," Emmelyn responded and added," the corridor turns several times. His personnel troops will guard the door."

As they jogged ahead, Tracey looked at Kat and asked, "What in the god's wide space is the 'Queen's Black Drip'?"

"You don't want to know," Kat replied.

Minutes later, they faced five guards in Trocnavar uniforms at the ornate doors of a suite. "Three bottles, sir?" Emmelyn asked. The question was the signal for the kill or be killed action. Tracey slipped the carbine off her back and shot the Troc officer in the neck where his armor thinned between his helmet and body armor. The shock drove him back. Tracey stepped forward and placed carbine's muzzle to his neck and fired again. Dark red Troc blood spattered outward.

Tracey caught the flash of Kat's sword as it split the helmetless head of the human sergeant. Light and Shadow drew rocket pistols and shot two of the other guards in the faceplate cracking their helmets and knocking the two guards unconscious. Two more shots each to their faceplates sent the guards to the gods. However, the delay for three shots was too long. A third guard raised his carbine and fired. Light screamed and was blown to floor. Shadow emptied his pistol into the man's face. Emmelyn drove a wire knife into his neck. The battle was over in seconds.

Light desperately tried to focus. *I am shot. Where is the wound? My left leg feels wet, it's the left leg. Damn, lucky the guard wasn't able to fully raise his carbine. I can't feel arterial blood pumping out--- still blood loss. I need to do something. Get medipack and --- everything is turning to mist.*

Tracey realized she just killed a Troc face to face. In the past, she had killed humans face to face. In addition, there were those who died on the pirate cruiser when she fired the rail gun. She killed at least three during the fight on the great liner *White Star.* She had seen her own people die, Marsborn and others. Yet, Light's wounding shocked her to her core. The twins were special to Tracey. In that moment, she dedicated herself to getting Light out alive.

The flash grenade tumbled through the double doors into the suite. The flash came seconds later as Kat, Shadow and Tracey dived into the room. In a small space the shock blasted the room. Red and gold curtains ripped open revealing a second room furnished in blue, orange and lavender sparkle fabrics. It was, if possible, more ornately furnished than first room. The room was circular and ten meters from side to side. In the center of the room a pool of bubbled hot water was driven by air jets. The air was warm and moist. A massive bed ringed the back half of the pool. Two young men and two Troc females lay on the bed. All were nude. Just as the flash grenade went off, Kat thought he saw two heads disappearing underwater in the pool.

The two young men looked up with panic in their eyes. They both froze in place. In contrast, the two Troc females were moving fast. One was tall for a Troc. Her face and body looked as if carved from stone with deep gold eyes and black and silver hair. She quickly pulled a rocket pistol out from under the bed covers. Shadow shot her before she could raise the pistol. She fell behind the bed.

The other young female Troc with a bright splash of red hair went for a gun case stacked on the right side of the bed. Tracey shot her as she dove behind the bed.

A moment later two figures emerged from the pool. One was a human female who held a cord twisted around the neck of a small princely Troc. Both were nude.

"My I present Lord Markiii the son of Count-Viceroy Markiii commander of all the Troc forces," were the first words out of Auntie Tara's mouth. "Don't let me kill the slimy bastard. His head holds a full set of the Troc battle plans. Don't just stand there; help me get him out of the pool," she ordered. They could all see the hatred in Auntie Tara's eyes.

Back in the blue room, Emmelyn reached Light in seconds. She pulled a knife and a medipack from her pack. She cut away Light's pants and slapped the medipack over the wound in the front of her thigh. Next, she placed a second medipack over the large exit wound on the back of Light's leg. She found a third medipack and wrapped it around Light's head, hoping the living medipack could deal with Light's unconscious state. She then carried Light from the hallway into the outer blue room and placed her on a couch.

In the inner room, Kat sheath his sword, looked at Auntie Tara and said, "Get them out of the pool; keep the short Troc away from Major Freeborn!"

The major added, "Get out the Markiii's data pack. It also contains battle plans."

Within minutes Auntie Tara was in her pirate utilities and Lord Markiii was in gray utilities that Shadow had found in a locker at the guard station. His mouth and hands were taped. Tracey gathered up the guard's weapons and distributed them.

Emmelyn sat beside Light as Shadow came back into the blue room and knelt beside Light. "You ok, sis?" he asked. "We will get you out of here."

She replied, "Get Auntie Tara and her prisoner out of here. I am all right. Don't worry about the lime green Vraciek you are riding." But Light was not alright.

Emmelyn said, "Blood loss and drugs are clouding her mind. I don't think the bone is broken so we can move her."

Kat called out, "Then let's move! We won't have much time after this."

Shadow then picked up Light and placed her over his shoulder.

Just before walking out Auntie Tara said, "We need to kill the bed boys; they saw too much." She walked back into the pool room. The two young men were still frozen in terror. Auntie Tara raised her pistol. The dark haired one said, "No, Sandy we were together an hour ago! Please, No Sandy, No!" She took them both with clean head shots. A cold chill ran down Auntie Tara's back as she came to terms with what she had done.

The group headed out of the suite. Kat pushed the button sending the signal to Peter's team.

Fifty meters later, Tracey took Light from Shadow. They would switch carrying Light back and forth for the return to guard room.

****

Kat's signal reached Spider just as she saw Peter towing Cici and Mark. She held the remote detonator control. She would detonate the charges as soon as she got them out the water. She and Peter dragged the other two on to the deck of the derelict. She turned

246

slamming detonator button. Within seconds the military ship's waterline ripped open. The whole hull rose out of water on a wall of fire and then dropped back into the water sinking to its deck line. People could be seen running on deck. Several crew men were on fire.

Peter plugged Cici's, Mark's and his own envirosuit into the aux power unit. He felt warmth spreading. Spider launched the first shoulder missile into the lifter landing area then a second and third. Four or five lifters on dock were soon engulfed in flame.

Peter grabbed the auto rifle gun and began raking the dock area. Two other lifters attempted to lift off. One came directly at them. Peter sprayed fire across it as it closed on them. It fell from the sky burning. The second lifter rose from the field as they watched it fly north away from battle and the harbor. There was no hero in that one.

Peter continued to rake the dock and small boats in the harbor. Spider's next missile hit the stone dock doing no damage. Spider launched another missile at a large freighter tied up along the dock. It did not explode but within a minute, flames were spreading from the damaged hull. "Only one missile left! I' m going keep it for our grand exit!" Spider shouted to Peter.

Bullets hit the hull of the derelict. One of the troops on the dock must have figured out were the fire was coming from. It would soon be time to go. Peter checked Mark and Cici. Cici was conscious and sitting up. Mark appeared to have just opened his eyes. Peter hand signaled to Cici to get Mark into the boat and stand by. He hoped she plugged them into the boat's aux power. He then turned back to the fight.

More troops were reaching the harbor and dock area. Even with the confusion of the rain more shots were hitting the derelict. Someone in the left side guard tower fired on them. Peter knew fire from the guard tower would cut them to pieces as they exited the harbor. He swung the big auto rifle around and blasted the top of the tower. Spider, who was firing her carbine at the docks, grabbed Peter by the shoulder and pointed. A military boat was racing out from the docks directly toward them. Peter pointed to the missile launcher and yelled, "Time to go!" Spider shouldered the launcher and fired.

Minutes later, Peter went into full power racing out of the harbor with the four of them safe on board. Spider laid in a course through the delta to the South where the lake flowed into the sea.

****

Kat and the group reached the guard room where they started the night. They heard the noise like the buzzing of thousands of insects. Emmelyn pushed open the door. Tracey gasped; thirty or more children and a score of adults jammed the room. Boys and girls from three to mid-teens stood by the walls, sat on tables, under tables and filled every chair. Two girls found sitting space on top of the cabinets. One boy and girl ran to Emmelyn and hugged her. They said nothing to each other.

Two adults armed with a few rocket carbines and pistols stood guarding the door that was just breached. Some adults were armed with pitch forks and axes. Two were wounded. All were bound labor and would be killed if found with a weapon.

Grabbing Emmelyn's shoulder Kat yelled, "You said two kids! "A tall dark haired man stepped forward and put his arm around Emmelyn.

"I am Owen, Emmelyn's mate," the dark-haired man said. "People found out and nothing will stop a parent from saving their child from life as Troc bound labor. We ask only that you take the children, we adults will stay. Already nine died getting these children here. For the mercy of the gods take them." Tears streamed down his face."

Kat stood in the doorway. "We can't take them all. Our boat is designed to hold no more than twenty. There are eight of us plus the prisoner; at best, we might be able to take fifteen. Some of the children are small."

"We stole a boat. Six parents died stealing it. We plan to go with you to your pickup point. Once the children are safe we will head to the Great South Forest."

"There is still a problem," Kat said. "Our lifter is a twenty-person ship. It is designed to lift twenty troops with combat gear. There will be thirteen of us including our prisoner plus a crew of two. Even if we count one and a half kids for each adult and overload the lifter to the max it's still short. We might be able to take twenty children. Maybe a few more," Kat said.

"The risk is nothing!" Emmelyn and Owen replied together.

Tara slammed the butt of her carbine on the heavy table in center of the room. "Call in your boat, Kat. Emmelyn, start loading kids into the stolen boat. Tracey and I will ride with you. Load the rest of the kids into Kat's boat then we will head for the pickup point. From the sounds of destruction in the harbor, I believe the second team has completed their attack. The faster we move the better chance both teams have of escaping. My deepest thanks to each for what you have done tonight. Now Move!"

Chapter Forty-Three–
Some Where Far to the South - 11-10-518.

Two days of travel brought them far to the South. Here the sea became shallow and hundreds of islands filled an archipelago. On one small island three boats were pulled up on a wide sand beach. The island, in the shape of a crescent moon, was formed by the edge of sunken volcano crater. The walls of the volcano protected the sand beach which ran along the inside of the wall. It was late afternoon and no sign of the lifter.

A tarp on poles created a temporary med station. Inside Nirabella worked on Light's wound. She replaced the medipacks with fresh ones then attached two IVs, one plasma and one saline solution. She hoped that would hold until they could get her up to the *Outcast Lady.* Shadow knelt on the other side of Light holding her hand. "Sis, we will get out of here, you are going to be fine."

"I know. How is Baryic? Damn Shadow! Your face gives that one away. Go and help take care of him," Light softly said.

Nirabella looked over at makeshift cot on which Baryic lay. Last night she hooked Baryic to her main med unit in the boat as they awaited Kat's team. She hoped med unit IVs and the fresh medipacks that she applied an hour ago were stopping the pain and controlling the hemorrhaging. She could do no more.

Tara sat on a box beside Baryic. She placed her hand gently on Baryic's left arm. "Sorry old friend I didn't expect to see you like this. Colonel, you did wonderfully with this task. We have the information that Ax needs. We can get it to Green Fleet. Rest my brave Colonel, you can rest now." Baryic griped her hand and smiled faintly.

Cici, on watch at top the volcano rim, saw the first flash of sunlight on the lifter as it dropped from the sky. She clicked a tight beam signal to the beach below. *This was going to be difficult, thirty-nine children. We surly we can't take them all. Tracey, as your expert lifter pilot, would have to make impossible choices.*

As the lifter dropped from the sky, Tracey stood near the landing area and once more ran the numbers on her data pack. *By the gods, we can't take them all. The ship was designed to lift twenty fully equipped troops at max. If I over loaded twenty-five percent beyond max, I might lift off fourteen adults, without equipment and thirty-three children. Six children left behind. There must be a way. Out of scrap bits Fidelity has built a scale. Could it help?*

Auntie Tara and Kay walked up to Tracey as the lifter settled on to the sand. Auntie Tara spoke, "Tracey, we can't allow the lifter to be overloaded beyond ten percent of max. The prisoner and the information we are taking back can save hundreds of thousands of lives and keep Green Line trade open to the League. We can't risk that to save a handful of children. We must get up to the *Outcast Lady* and get the information to General Bridgeford. I am deeply sorry but we have no choice."

Tracey quickly redid the numbers in her head. Twelve children would not be going.

Peter, Fidelity and parents were organizing children. Tracey walked over to tell them but was stopped by Spider and Cici who had just come down off the volcano. Spider told Centari to grab Fidelity's scale. Spider and Cici jumped on to the lifter. Centari set the scale on the sand outside lifter. Seat cushions, emergency ration, water and spare parts began flying out door. Centari weight each item.

When the last item was weighed, Tracey was down to six children left behind.

Minutes later Mark Bittman and one of the parents carried Baryic from the med station. Nirabella walked alongside him. They stopped where Auntie Tara, Kat and Tracey stood by the lifter. Auntie Tara said, "We are going load you now old friend."

In moment of clarity Baryic replied "Don't think so. How many not going? Truth?"

Tracey answered, "Six."

Baryic said, "Take more. Not me, I will not live. Nirabella send me to the gods." Then in a clear strong voice he said, "By the gods, now!"

Nirabella, Auntie Tara and Kat looked at each other. They knew in their hearts that Baryic would never make the voyage back. All three nodded "yes". Nirabella took the 'Kiss of the Gods' from her pack and placed it on back of Baryic's neck. The heard a soft puff. Nirabella knew she was giving Baryic a way to peace. Auntie Tara held his hand until he was gone.

Tracey thought, *will I ever again see an act of heroism like this? To give your life to save children is as fine a death as a warrior could know.*

Kat asked, "How many now, Tracey?"

"Two more. In addition, if we dump our boots as we board that could mean two more," she said.

Kat said, "Hells we're going to lift off overloaded by two children! Let's get everyone on board."

Emmelyn stepped forward, "We will see that Colonel Baryic is buried with honor in the far South where the Troc scum will never find him. The Trocs will find no trace that we were ever on this island. Our deepest thanks for what you have done. May you find the speed of the gods and a fare passage home. The risk was worth it Kat, was it not?"

Kat was the last one aboard. He waited as mother said goodbye to a child who would not let go. He lifted the last child, a little girl, up to Tracey and Cici standing in the rear hatch. Tracey's heart stopped. Peering out her blouse was tiny blue and green head, a c-cat kitten. The rule was absolutely no pets. Tracey and Cici looked at each other stripped off their socks and tossed them out the hatch. Kat stepped aboard and said, "Tracey, I think that will cover the weight."

Cici closed the hatch. Tracey made her way forward through the packed cabin. Someone clapped. Then Auntie Tara stood and clapped and applause filled the cabin.

Czajka stepped out of the pilot's seat as Tracey slipped into the seat and strapped in. Spider, who was riding in the gunner position next to Tracey said, "Everything is green, lift when ready." Tracey went to full power, pulled the control back and very, very slowly they lifted off.

Chapter Forty-Four
– In Space Aboard the *Outcast Lady*- 11-11-518.

As soon as the *Outcast Lady* was underway Kat called together the crew and officers on the mess deck. "First, my thanks to each of you. You made this operation possible. It's not just the team on ground but also those who kept the ship hidden in orbit. We pulled Major Tara Freeborn out of a Troc base and captured Lord Markiii, the son of Count-Viceroy Markiii commander of the Troc forces. We also have his data pack with a full copy of their battle plans. As you know we lost Baryic, may the gods give him grace. He died a hero's death.

"We have only a single priority; get Major Freeborn and her prisoner to General Bridgeford. We are not part of Green Fleet or The Free Space Force. However, we all have family and friends back on the League planets. Without the Green Line their lives will become very difficult. The League will face an invasion from two directions. The Trocnavar will have both the main trade routes and Green Line open. I, for one, do not want to see friends and family dead or Troc bound labor."

"We are accelerating at max Gs. We will go to time wave as soon as possible and make the fastest feasible passage back to Green Four. It is the closest planet where we are sure to find Green Fleet ships. It will be a long voyage, three months riding a tight high time wave. The risks of a long run in a time wave with a high narrow wave are well known. May the gods keep us safe!"

"One final note, we will not delay to unload the children. They will be placed in safe hands when we reach Green Four. Three months with thirty-nine children onboard will challenge each of us."

Nirabella whispered to Cici, "'Challenging' is an understatement".

****

A week later Tracey, Auntie Tara and the team sat in the Ward Room. Spider was not present. Erica Nguyen and she were totally involved in keeping *Outcast Lady* on the high-speed time wave. Peter was present but in a daze and barely keeping is eyes open.

The team was reviewing the action during the rescue. Tracey outlined what happen as they burst into the inner room. "The tall Troc with black and silver hair pulled a rocket pistol. Shadow shot her before she raised her pistol. She collapsed behind the bed. The other Troc female, young with a bright splash of red hair, went for a gun case. I shot her as she dove behind the bed. Then Auntie Tara pulled Lord Markiii from the pool. We were very busy!"

Auntie Tara asked, "Did you make sure the Trocs were dead?"

"Yes, as soon as could I checked their pulses. No sign of a pulse on either one. They were dead."

Auntie Tara asked, "You put at least two more rounds into their heads?

Tracey replied, "No they were dead."

Peter, half asleep from hours of time wave navigation, raised his head, "No, No, No!"

Auntie Tara, visibly shaken asked, "No one shot them a second time?"

Kat answered, "Correct, none of us shot them a second time."

"Does the term Biikidori mean anything to anyone except Peter and me?" asked Auntie Tara. She continued, "Both Niikia Kaiii-var and Artystaar Tiigano may be alive. Some Trocnavar officers are trained in Biikidori, an ancient art of body control which allows them stop their hearts for up to half an hour. It reduces bleeding by stopping blood flow. It also allows them to appear dead when checked. I watched Niikia train Artystaar in the art. Let us hope they did not survive, the two of them are driven dark souls. The description sociopath does not do them justice. But, both are excellent leaders with great command presence. To gain their confidence, I killed the innocent; sent unarmed prisoners to slow and painful deaths, sold children as bound labors and countless other unspeakable things," Auntie Tara reflected.

"I made a horrible mistake. May the gods forgive me," Tracey sighed.

Kat told her, "Yes, but I made the same mistake. Years ago, I was told to always shoot Troc officers at least twice in the head and I failed to remember and act."

"I was the only one present who knew about Biikidori. I should have checked. The error is mine and mine alone. May the gods protect the innocent" Auntie Tara responded.

Chapter Forty-Five –
In Space Aboard *Dark Song*- 12-01-518

Three weeks after the capture of the Count's son, *Dark Song* accelerated out of the Nameless One system. In the control room Niikia Kaiii-var turned to Artystaar, "Count-Viceroy Markiii ought to have killed us for losing his son. Instead he chose to send us after the raiders who took him. We search alone. The rest of the fleet is preparing for war. The Count gave us a free hand to do whatever is needed. We Will!"

The new ship's doctor was a free human and intended to stay that way. As the ship's doctor, he performed complete medical checks on two Troc officers and changed their medipacks each day. The Count sent the doctor with them to ensure their recovery. If Count Markiii wanted these two healed so be it, He was the man for the task. Conversely, before they shipped out, the Count told him to kill Kaiii-var and Artystaar if they tried to break off the pursuit and run. After a few days with the Trocs, the doctor was sure he would not need the second option.

Niikia addressed the crew gathered on the mess deck, "You all know our mission is to find Lord Markiii. I intend to push this ship beyond the limit in this quest. However, when we find him alive, the reward will be one million imperials for the crew to split. More if we capture the raider's commander and officers. Lord Count-Viceroy Markiii has special plans for them. "

"Here is what we know about the raiders. They may have come from a ship called *Outcast Lady*. Whatever the ship's name it escaped the Nameless #8 system. Based on what Lord Sunstar, the Prime Minister of Horizon told us the ship is an old League built escort and the commander is named Kat and the first officer could be named Watkins. Lord Sunstar told us they are killers and tough. Kat and Watkins killed Major Karrack Rayyan, who was known as the 'Hand of Death'. Our first task is to find where they staged the raid. We will see just how tough they are!"

****

After traveling over a month in the High Wave, Kaiii-var placed *Dark Song* in orbit well out beyond Blue Port's moons. The plan had been simple. Artystaar lead a team who repainted the ship to appear a contract warship. They cleaned up the crew by removing the red dye marks and covering kill dots. Clean new light gray utilities completed the illusion.

The *Dark Song* docked at the Blue Port Station. Soon the first watch of the crew was given station leave. Artystaar and Niikia proceeded to the station master's office on the pretext of looking for a new contract. Eight crew members, including Xiggott their new sergeant, drifted into the area near the office. Two guards were stationed at the entrance. Artystaar and Niikia walked through the door and asked to speak to the station master. One of the assistant station masters asked if he could help them. Niikia said, "We really must speak to Ms. Bradshaw."

After ten minutes, it became apparent Amy was not going give them any information about the raiders. Artystaar signal Xiggott and the crew. Thirty seconds later the crew killed the two guards. Charging into the outer office the pirates met gun fire. Three of Amy's staff chose to fight. They drew pistols from their desks as pirates rushed in. Xiggott was killed outright.

In the inner office, Amy drew her compact pistol and fired one round before Niikia and Artystaar slammed her back into the wall. Artystaar turned Amy's right arm back forcing the pistol into Amy's chest. Artystaar yelled, "Now you'll tell us what we want or die. "Amy looked into Artystaar's eyes inches away, yelled in Noble Trocnavar, "Bitch, may your children be born colorless armless slugs". A second later Amy pulled the trigger sending a rocket into her own chest.

It is a warrior's death, thought Artystaar. Station Master Amy Bradshaw died a warrior's death even if she died in her office. The same could not be said for some of her staff. Three of the staff killed two more pirates before they died fighting, but two hid beneath their desks. Half an hour later Niikia and Artystaar knew a great deal about the *Outcast Lady*, Kat, Tracey, Peter and the rest of the crew. The pirates only had to rip out the scum's nails and sliced open

an eye ball before Artystaar threatened to usemotans
in a jar to break him. Once they finished the
interrogation, Artystaar killed both of the cowards
using motans in jars.

.

Three of the staff killed two more pirates before
they died fighting, but two hid beneath their desks.
Half an hour later Niikia and Artystaar knew a great
deal about the *Outcast Lady,* Kat, Tracey, Peter and
rest of the crew. Once they finished the interrogation,
Artystaar killed both of the cowards using the motans
in jars.

Chapter Forty-Six –
In Space Aboard *Outcast Lady*- 01-01-519

Tracey watched Lotus, the little girl with the c-cat kitten, sleeping on the bench in her quarters. The c-cat kitten curled up with her and Purple Cat. Lotus refused to sleep anywhere else. After all the child had been through, Tracey did have the heart to make her sleep in the children's quarters. Lotus named the kitten Blue Cat to match Purple Cat.

It was a long voyage. Three months in the Wave was almost unknown. The children were holding up. Probably because ship life was better than the living hell of bound labor. Supplies of dark matter, water and food rations would be near exhaustion by the time they reached Green's Four. Anna Morgan, daughter of an innkeeper, used all her skills as Sergeant of the Mess to provide for thirty-nine extra mouths. She was already tapping into the emergency rations that all ships carried. She was mixing emergency rations with the standard food supply.

On New Year's Day Tracey took Lotus for a tour of the Control Room. The little girl was awed by the operation and asked question after question. On another day, while in the Navigation Station, Lotus studied Spider for a time and asked, "Is she going die?" It occurred to Tracey what a strain the time wave navigators were under. Riding the high narrow wave drained their minds and bodies. *Gods help us if we lose a navigator,* Tracey thought. A new year had begun but with months of space travel ahead.

Chapter Forty-Seven
– Aboard the *Outcast Lady*& the *Lady Delapasse*- 02-20-519

After three months, Peter brought the *Outcast Lady* out of the wave. Tracy checked their position. They were a light hour out from Green's Four. It was an incredible piece of navigation. Tara and Kat sent a tight beam message to the planet side base. Two hours and ten minutes later General Bridgeford's reply was received.

"Congratulations, Major Freeborn and Commander Jang! Our deepest thanks to you and your outstanding crew. We all mourn the loss of Colonel Chahill. Baryic was a friend and a fine officer. We will miss him.

The summary report of your interrogations of Lord Markiii Count and the information on his data pack is of the greatest value. Please send the full report on the contents the Markiii's data pack and the details of your interrogation. Attached you will find our plan to resupply *Outcast Lady* and offload the children. Green Fleet will be outward bound as soon as possible. Once the more, the thanks all of Green Fleet to each of you."

Tracey read the note then asked Peter who was next to her in the control room, "Green Fleet thanks us; way too late for that. What is this Colonel

Chahill? It's is second time I've heard him called Colonel. "

Peter replied, "I believe we have not yet begun to understand the Baryic mystery."

Cici read over Tracey's shoulder and whispered to Nirabella, "Whatever Baryic Cahill's rank, a thousand women on a hundred planets will mourn him."

Nirabella whispered, "You and I among them."

****

Days later, Kat took *Outcast Lady* around the Green's Star. They were now on a vector to match Green Fleet's outbound course. The General's plan was to have a merchantman *Fast Friend* and *Outcast Lady* meet in space. Tracey carefully matched course and speed with that of the merchant ship *Fast Friend,* a mixed passenger and cargo ship. Both ships raced outward from Green's Star.

Colonel Chung, the Executive Officer of Green Fleet contracted with the merchantman to meet them before they reached Green Fleet. The merchantman was loaded with new missiles, supplies, water, dark matter flasks, spare parts and small arms. Everything that was either used or lost during their odyssey to find Auntie Tara was replaced. *FastFriend* also carried a team of social workers, teachers, and medical people. They would take the children to safety at the Free Space Force ground base. Chung also offered additional personnel but Kat told him no thanks; his crew was outstanding.

Tracey said goodbye to Lotus and her c-cat kitten before she went on duty. She hoped the little girl would find a loving home. When this all was over she would try to check on Lotus and Blue Cat.

Both ships exactly matched speed then cut acceleration Tracey said, "Match complete, Commander. You may deploy the transfer tube." At this speed, the tube was only way because no lifter would work at the ship's speed. Slowing would delay catching Green Fleet.

The commander of *Fast Friend* transmitted, "Deploying tube. Let us hope the front shields hold on both ships. At these speeds a grain of sand would destroy us if it hit the tube." In the open main hatch Cici and several crew members worked in space suits to capture the tube being deployed from the other ship. Once the tube was locked into place, Nirabella and Shadow lead small groups of children through. When the transfer of the children was completed Cici supervised the flow of supplies. As they struggled to transfer the dissembled missiles, Cici was surprised to see Spider in the tube working with the crew. *How times have changed,* Cici observed.

Once the transfer was complete and the tube retracted, the merchant commander began to slow her ship and follow an orbit back to Green Four. Kat told Fidelity, acting engineering officer, "Full power on the plasma drive then go to the dark matter drive as soon as *Fast Friend* is clear. We have a date with Lady *Delapasse* and Ax!"

****

A day later, the officers, and sergeants of *Outcast Lady,* Major Freeborn and their prisoner Lord Markiii, crossed over to the *Lady Delapasse* via transfer tube. General Bridgeford had made a specific request for each of them by name. Major Freeborn joined them. Captain Montgomery, Kat's old friend, met them just outside hanger bay. He told them, "The old man requests this meeting."

Ten minutes later Kat, Peter, Tracey and Spider sat across the table from General Bridgeford, Colonel Harrison Chung, Major Tara Freeborn and Capitan Gunson Montgomery. The General specifically asked that Spider attend.

The General began, "Once more let me offer my apology. I read the report by Major Freeborn of the raid on Nameless One. Also, I read key parts of your logs. Before that, I saw reports of your defense of *White Star,* and your actions on Horizon. Mr. Jang, you command the finest escort of all the contract warships and of escorts in the Free Space Force. *Outcast Lady* is a good ship. But the officers and crew make her the finest. We need you with the Green Fleet. What can I say to convince you to rejoin the FSF? Mr. Jang, I am offering you a Major's Parliamentary Commission."

"NO!" was Kat's immediate reply. Silence filled the office.

After a minute the General continued, "Mr. Guderian, what will change your mind? I offer you a Captain's Commission and FSF will pay off your bank loans."

"Ax you always said I never quit," Peter replied.

No junior officer ever called the General Ax to his face. Bridgeford ignored Peter's remark and moved on to Tracey, "How do we move you Ms. Watkins? Command of your own ship?"

"You can't move me." was her reply.

He turned to Spider and said, "Captain Constantine you were not part of the original group; will you do us the honor of rejoining Green Fleet as Chief Time Wave Navigator?"

Spider replied, "I find greater honor as Third TWN on the *Outcast Lady*."Shock filled the room; the most driven and ambitious officer in Free Space Force just said no to what had previously been her dream.

Auntie Tara stood and said, "For the coming battle I am going to serve on the *Lady Delapasse*. I will not ask you again to join us. All of us know the League of Free Stars needs you. I hope you will reconsider. If not, go with the god's speed and a fair wave."

Twenty minutes later *Outcast Lady* detached from the great battle cruiser. Kat set a course away from Green Fleet.

Chapter Forty-Eight –
Aboard *Dark Song* in Space 02-21-519

Niikia and Artystaar docked first at Horizon then Schwaigerland. At both space stations, they found people willing to sell them information on the *Outcast Lady.* Kat had not stopped at either planet on his way back to the main trade routes. Niikia said, "I think he is rushing to sell Lord Markiii to Green Fleet. If he is going to Green Four without stopping how is he doing it? What other planets can he head for? Where do we head Artystaar?"

"I say we meet the Strike Fleet at the target planet. The distance is shorter than the voyage *Outcast Lady* is making. The humans will have Lord Markiii aboard one of the major ships. Our best chance is to find which ship he is on and take his lordship back." Niikia directed their CTWN Robert Jones to set a high wave to take them to the target site.

Chapter Forty Nine –
Outcast Lady in Space - 02-21-519

A day after they left Green Fleet, Kat lay on the wide bunk in the commander's cabin The *Outcast Lady* neared transition speed. He was drunk, totally and completely drunk.

I haven't been drunk since the day Light found me, what was the planet's name? Free something. Why do this now? Because Ax made me feel like space marsh or is trash? We did the damn contract. All of us were rejected by the Free Splace Farce. I maybe got drunk because - know did wrong thing. Auntie is going with Axie. By gods I love Tracey and can't fell tell her. What did I do to save her? His thoughts were incoherent in his drunken stupor.

Kat fell back into sleep. Ten minutes later there was a ripping sound as the locked cabin door was torn open. Tracey and Nirabella stepped in. Tracey carried a six-foot pry bar and Nirabella carried a full med kit. Tracey looked down at Kat. "Time to get sober, handsome. You've got two hours to be in the control room."

Nira got out a medipack and administered any meds that would help. Kat did not respond. Nirabella applied a medipack and gave him three shots. Nirabella told Tracey, "The medipacks aren't designed to sober someone up. However, I think it will figure out the problem and do everything it can. The med shots should help."

"Thanks, Nirabella," Tracey said. "He is the finest officer I have ever known. All the gods of Far Star know I love him and can't tell him. He is the Commander, I am First Officer; on a League ship, you don't mix those two in a personal relationship. No one on the ship knows I have feelings for him."

"Tracey everyone on the ship knows you have feelings for each other. It could not be more obvious. It is also obvious that you never act on them. Except, well maybe, that time on Blue Port."

Minutes later Kat opened his eyes and asked, "What you say?" Tracey replied, "I said get your ass into the shower and turn it up hot. Don't you dare take off that medipack. Shadow will be here with hot Gubble brew before you get out. Nirabella and I will stay to make sure you get to the Control Room. I dumped out the yellow spice including the hidden bottle. In one hour and fifty minutes you will walk into the Control Room sober."

In two hours and seven minutes Kat walked into the Control Room ahead of Tracey's demanded schedule of two and a quarter hour. "Ms. Stone, you have control. All other officers and sergeants join me in the ward room," Kat confidently ordered.

Anna Morgan had hot coffee and Gubble brew waiting as they filed into the Ward Room.

Kat opened the meeting, "I had a drink, which for me means I got drunk. Many of you know I am an alcoholic. I could not live with what I did. I turned Bridgeford down. We don't care about Ax or Green Fleet, but the faces of the children that we endured so much to save, haunted me. In turn, the faces of all the children of the League of Free Stars haunted me. If the Trocnavar Empire and their pirates win, hundreds of thousands of children could end up dead or living as bound labors. Your efforts saved thirty-nine. What would you have us do about thousands?"

There was no cheering, silence filled the ward room.

Finally, Peter said, "I better go lay in a new course."

They walked out of the ward room to tell the crew.

Chapter Fifty-
Death's Hammer &Outcast Lady in **Space- 03-19-519**

A few light-years away another meeting began. "If this information is correct, you two may not live out your lives as blind laborers in a Uiikaien slime mine." Niikia and Artystaar stood before Count-Viceroy Markiii Commander of the Strike Fleet. Senior Trocnavar officers, pirate commanders including Garman Rayyan Warlord of Pirate Fleets and a Tri Star Army General filled his office. They were aboard the Count's command ship, an Imperial battle cruiser renamed *Death's Hammer* and thinly disguised as a pirate ship. The fleet orbited three light hours out from the target. It was an impressive fleet.

The Count continued, "So you believe this Kat has sold or plans to sell my son to Bridgeford. You also think Bridgeford will obtain our plan of attack. Finally, you think this Kat will join Green Fleet. I have known from the night my son was taken, Bridgeford could gain our attack plans. Let him come and bring his little fleet." Standing behind the Count, Lord Clovis of Rarkiikar Clovis was silent.

Warlord Rayyan spoke "This scum Kat and his bitch Watkins killed my son in barehanded combat. They are light years tougher than you imagine. I relish their deaths. However, we must never forget the Empire's target."

Count-Viceroy Markiii stepped forward "Well said, ladies and gentlemen but we must not lose sight of the goal. We are here to take and hold Pangerbar, not to kill Kat and destroy his ship. With Pangerbar we control shipping along the Green Line. The Empire and our allies can strangle The League of Free Stars. As we conquer Pangerbar we may save my son, if not, so be it. The Emperor ordered the conquest of Pangerbar."

****

Light years away the *Outcast Lady* raced toward its new destination. An hour after the meeting in the Ward Room, the hanger bay was cleared for a meeting of the crew. Kat outlined the plan and spend two hours going over it. Kat, open the meeting for questions. Mark Bittman asked, "Sir with the deepest possible respect, what in all the hells are we doing? You are going to take *Outcast Lady* into battle to save Pangerbar, are you crazy Sir?"

Kat replied "I know it is damn hard to fight for a planet that kept many of you in abject poverty. But we fight for the League not Pangerbar. Because Pangerbar is an important trading center on the Green Line, the Trocs chose to seize it. Pangerbar is a pinch point in the flow of trade. It is also a perfect base to launch an invasion of Green Four. Once Green Four falls the backdoor to the League will be open. Do you want the death for so many?"

Centari Shamir said, "No, we don't want those deaths. I hate Pangerbar as much as anyone. But, I have family on Sander's Planet near this edge of the League's star cluster. Sander's would be one of first planets to fall."

Anna Morgan called out, "I vote we fight! My mother, her companion, family members and friends live on the Pangerbar space station. I say fight."

Kat took over, "The truth is Green Fleet, even with the contract warships, is weak. The Troc Strike Fleet with the pirates and Tri Star ships is twice the size. Our escort could turn the battle. The course I ordered Peter to set will bring us out of the wave in the Pangerbar system. We will exit the wave in Battle Alert. I could have no better crew. I believe each will do their duty. Thank you," Kat concluded.

At the back of the hanger bay someone called out, "Victory Honor Ship." It was Cici.

Chapter Fifty-One
Pangerbar System *Dark Song & Outcast Lady*
03-30-519

Dark Song cruised in high orbit above Pangerbar. Artystaar watched as the invasion fleet dropped toward the doomed planet. Lord Clovis's spies reported the government was unaware of the invasion plans. It was widely known Pangergar's military force was almost nonexistent. The merchants of Pangerbar did not spend money unless it returned a profit. The Count chose not to use an opening bombardment. Ten troop ships from the Tri Star Republic led the assault. 10,000 shock troops using both lifters and combat gliders dropped on Pangerbar City. A second force of five hundred troops attacked the space station.

Protecting the troop ships, the Strike Force warships dropped into orbit eight light seconds out from the planet. The fleet formed a cloud formation. Artystaar scanned the fleet with the ship's sensors. There were two battle cruisers, three heavy cruisers, and three light cruisers including the new imperial cruiser brought out by the Count's son, eight destroyers, two supply ships and finally ten fast escorts including their own ship *Dark Song*. It was an imposing fleet. *Dark Song's* assignment was one of four ships protecting *Death's Hammer.* The only action so far was annihilation of two ancient destroyers as they powered out from the space station.

Artystaar watched the sensors go wild. Ships dropped out of the wave less than a light hour out. Their orbit around Pangerbar would be in the direction of the Strike Fleet. Flares of dark matter engines blazed as the incoming fleet decelerated. After two plus days of deceleration the League fleet would pass through the Trocnavar fleet. The first round of this battle would be quick and deadly. The fleets closing speed added the ship's velocity to the missile's velocity. The kinetic energy of a missile hit would be huge. Artystaar signaled battle preparations. She then requested Niikia join her in the Control Room. The sensor data showed Green Fleet to be half size of Strike Fleet. *By the gods, I love this! May we meet Mr. Kat and company,* Artystaar thought.

****

Outcast Lady dropped out of the wave well behind Green Fleet. With a double jump wave ride Peter had brought them off the wave in the planet's orbital direction and light hours out. Kat addressed the crew, "Peter dropped us out of the wave at just over three percent of light speed. That is still 10K plus clicks per second. We are flipping and decelerating to drop into orbit and catch Bridgeford and company. The Green Fleet is decelerating into orbit well ahead of us. We will orbit around the sun at max deceleration then drop into orbit around Pangerbar behind Bridgeford."

Tracey scanned the sensor information. "Kat does this look like the Spearing the Oiifen maneuver? Is Bridgeford going try it?" Oiifen were a large round fruit so light it floated in the wind. Troc children used Oiifens for targets during spear games. At officer training school, they only spent a few hours covering the Spearing the Oiifen explaining that it was a high-risk attack formation and never to be used. *So much for never,* Tracey thought. With an enemy ship in a Oiifen shaped cloud formation, the attacker formed a single line and speared the cloud. Two heavy well-armed ships were placed one behind the other at the point of the spear. The lead ship was not expected to survive.

Spider, who was handling communication, called out, "Tight beam message coming in from Bridgeford." She flashed the message to all screens:

Commander Jang. It's about time. We are using the Spear with a twist. We don't have two heavy warships, so we will drive *Bighorn Bull,* our armed supply ship in front. Chung volunteered to command her and Montgomery volunteered as XO. A handful of volunteers will crew her. Undoubtedly the *Bull* will be destroyed.

You are following our fleet; I ask *Outcast Lady* to pick up any of the Bull's survivors. Your contact point should be about half way through the Troc cloud. Kat I am asking, not ordering. It's a damn dangerous assignment.

Kat said, "Spider, tell Ax we accept. Then send a message to Montgomery. He should not expect a formal tea when we pick them up."

Chapter Fifty-Two
- Pangerbar System *Outcast Lady & Bighorn Bull* - 04-01-519

A day later the *Lady* completed its deceleration and locked in orbit behind Green Fleet. Kat told Tracey, "Trace, set a course following the fleet into the cloud. For the brave women and men out there, may the gods of Far Star protect us all."

"Fidelity, full power."

"Done," Fidelity responded

"Cici, power up all weapons. Light and Shadow are your missile racks ready?"

Light responded, "Yes sixteen are ready. Peter is clear to drop."

"Ok, Peter are you ready?"

"Do c-cats kill motans?"

"Cici, the rail guns ready?"

"Ready, Commander".

"Spider is com ready?"

"Always."

"Nira, medical deck ready?"

"Ready for casualties."

Kat continued over the ship's com, "Go to Standby Alert. We close on the enemy in an hour. I have accepted a difficult assignment. Green Fleet is attacking using the Spear of Oiifen. We cannot reach the fleet in time to join the spear. Ax is using supply ship *Bull* as a battering ram at the spear tip. The *Bull* will be destroyed or heavy damaged. It's crewed by brave volunteers, some of which we know. Fighting our way into the Troc cloud, *Outcast Lady* will match speed with the remains of the *Bull*. Then we launch both lifters to rescue survivors. Not an easy task. I expect the Troc fleet will have plenty of fire power left. We will rescue everyone we find and kill Troc ships when possible."

"For the Children!" Kat called over the com system.

****

Aboard the *Bull* Gunson Montgomery was too busy creating a storm of missiles and space junk to be terrified. Working in space suits, he and the volunteer crew were pushing missiles out the hanger bay and into space. The *Bull* carried spare missiles for fleet. They pushed out the thirty fourth missile and fired it via a makeshift cable. Accuracy was impossible, none of the controls of a warship drop existed on the *Bull*. However, thirty plus missiles would keep the

Trocs busy and give Ax's spear a chance to penetrate deep within the Troc Fleet. If a missile was destroyed, it transformed into a mass of high speed space junk flying into the back of the enemy formation.

Gunson thought; *let's get number thirty-five out the door. How many missiles and cables do we have? Just keep at it and don't let me feel fear. Within minutes we will take enemy fire and be forced to close the hanger bay. The two forward rail guns will be firing, and then joined by the aft guns as we near the cloud.*

****

Kat called, "Full battle alert!" Tracey tracked the two fleets via sensors. The fleets almost touched less than two hundred kicks separated them. Chung and Montgomery were putting up one hell of a fight. Somehow, they fired missile after missile without any launch system. The *Lady Delapasse,* behind the *Bull,* fired missiles and rail guns. The *Sea Goddess* and *Lady Montoya* light cruisers were next, then the *Republican Lady.* After that there was a contract light cruiser, *Winged Shield.* Ax's four destroyers and four fast escorts along with one contract destroyer and three contract escorts were arranged in the gaps in the line of big ships. This both protected them and protected the heavy line.

The spear of ships plunged into the Troc cloud. A Troc light cruiser shifted orbit to attack the *Bull*. The closing speed was fantastic. One of the swarm of missiles launched by the *Bull* hit the aft section of the cruiser. The Troc ship was enveloped by the explosion. As the two ships passed each other the *Bull's* rail gun shells rained into the Troc ship. Tracey watched as the cruiser veered off course. Then two targeted missiles from the *Lady Delapasse* hit the damaged cruiser and she began to breakup, her weapons silent.

Kat called out, "Nice shooting Ax! ... Peter, Cici, if you get a clean kill shot, fire on targets of opportunity. "An hour and half later they plunged into the cloud. A sea of damaged ships and space junk surrounded them.

Peter exclaimed, "Drop two missiles. Have lock. Drop Now!" In the missile bay the drop crew watched as two missiles dropped clean. The *Lady* closed on a pirate destroyer. Peter spun the missiles ninety degrees launching broadside. Light and Shadow yelled, "Drop clean, engines fired." Two missiles accelerated away locking in on the destroyer. Tracey tracked the two missiles as they closed in. Antimissile fire disintegrated one. The second missile struck one of the destroyer's time wave drive pods. Tracey called out, "Major damage but no kill," then she realized everyone in the control room could see the sensor data. It was over in seconds. They raced further into the cloud.

The sensors showed the *Bull* ahead of them taking heavy damage and falling behind Green fleet. One of the Troc battle cruisers launched a fan of missiles into the *Bull*. Three slammed into the big ship blasting sections of her away. Peter launched two missiles at the battle cruiser. A pirate escort swept in and destroyed both missiles. The battle cruiser and her escorts were gone into the cloud as the *Lady* swept past them.

Tracey locked sensors on the *Bull* and set an intercept course. The *Bull* appeared dead, no weapons fired and no signals. As she did for the glider, Spider began calling out distance. "Ninety-seven clicks out. Debris directly ahead; relative speed of the junk low." Tracey maneuvered the *Lady* around it. Spider called out, "Seventy-six". Kat said, "Switch to visuals." The armored shield over the control room was closed but massive vid screens filled the inside of the cover. "Fifty-six." Small bits of debris hit the front of the *Lady* as Spider called out, "Thirty-seven". Tracey slowed further to match speed with the remains of the *Bull*. As Tracey slowed the ship, Spider called out, "Nineteen" then "Zero".

****

The *Lady* floated half a click off the wreck of the *Bull*. Kat scanned the hull. *She is League built sphere, must be over three hundred meters in diameter. Debris everywhere. The great hanger doors are blown open. Her armored hull is pierce by multiple missile and rail gun hits. The Control Deck*

286

*is gone. The time wave drive surface has a hole
blown in it the size of a big lifter. Can anyone be
alive?*

"Peter, you have the control deck. Fidelity, you
have engineering. Czajka, you have the rail guns.
Erica, you have our TWD. Spider and I will take the
mini-lifter back to engineering and ensure the dark
matter flasks are intact. If the dark matter is stable,
we will search for survivors in the aft section. Tracey,
you Cici and Nirabella will take the big lifter and
check the main section. Light and Shadow shoot
transfer lines across and standby with a transfer tube.
Once we see how determine the number of survivors
and if the ship is stable, we may bring the *Lady* in
close enough to deploy the tube. Tracey also take
Bittman for another set of hands."

As she flew into the *Bull's* main hold Tracy
realized the gravity generators were out. They would
do this operation in zero G.   She dropped the lifter to
deck, although it did not matter there was no up or
down.

"Ok we start our search on this deck. Look for
anyone alive in a space suit, then check for airtight
compartments. Mark the dead with a red X. Mark
anyone alive with a blue X. Mark any airtight
compartments with a blue X."

Within twenty-five meters of the lifter, Cici found
two bodies. Both suits were ripped open by shrapnel.
Light found the next body, helmet gone along with

287

the head.   After finding and marking twenty-three bodies, Nirabella found an unconscious survivor. She had taken a hit in the leg, patched it with plasticine before blacking out. Her suit had a minor air leak and the suit tanks wouldn't compensate for long.

Nirabella told Mark, "Take her back to the lifter and out of her suit. Slap a medipack on leg. Then get back here quickly because we are going find more wounded." Mark picked up the woman and headed toward the lifter.

Five dead bodies later Cici heard a knocking. They found the knocking coming from a ten-meter pressure sphere. There was only one opening, a cargo hatch sealed from inside with plasticine. Tracey hit the sphere with three taps. Four taps came back. Free Space Force code for survivors inside.   Tracey considered, *how in the hells are we going to get them out? No air lock on the sphere. It's a storage tank. The temp airlock will not fit over the hatch. We can get a person inside lock, but it only holds three at max. We have only two spare spacesuits.* Over the com unit Tracey told Mark to help Shadow bring the temp airlock across on the line. "Also, from lifter, bring a power drill and saw, pry bars, spray plasticine and all extra space suits and whatever suits Shadow can bring over," she directed.

Over the com Light responded, "Shadow is loading your requests. He should be there in twenty minutes."

Tracey turned to Cici and Nirabella, "We can't attach the temp air lock over the hatch. We will attach it over a smooth section of the sphere. Once it's airtight and I am inside with space suits, I will drill a hole into the shell of sphere thread a mike inside. Next I will cut a hole in the shell big enough for someone to get out of. Then I'll pass two space suits to the survivors. As soon as they suit up, we cycle the temporary airlock. Mark can move survivors quickly to the lifter. If we find more than five survivors we'll bring back the suits. As soon as I am out Cici, jump in with more suits and cycle the airlock. Nirabella set up medical treatment in the lifter. You will be able to treat them there."

Mark and Shadow arrived with the temp airlock and began installation. Cici built up a ring of plasticine to provide a flat circle on the sphere's curved surface. They then assembled an airlock and placed it on the ring. Cici and Tracey sealed the airlock rim with tube after tube of plasticine.

Once the installation was complete they jammed tools, two suits and Tracey into the airlock. She only had just enough space to drill and cut. Keeping her space suit on and as soon air pressure reached normal, Tracey open the inner seal of the lock and began drilling a hole. She quickly broke through and pushed the mike inside. "Hello, anyone able to speak?"

The response came back, "Seventeen of us, two dead, three badly wounded including Mr.

Montgomery. I am fleet officer Benjamin Newman. We put up a damn fine fight. How can I help get us out of here?"

"I am Watkins, first officer of the *Outcast Lady*. If there is no problem inside, I am going cut a hatch. Get everyone away from the mike hole. Next question: do you have spacesuits?"

Newman replied, "Everyone has a suit, but most of them have damage."

"I am in a temporary airlock; we have good suits. We'll cycle you out three at a time."

Newman was silent for a moment then answered back, "Temporary airlocks are fragile. Don't cut the airlock wall and we'll be Ok."

Deafening noise filled the little airlock as Tracey cut into the sphere wall. Slowly she cut along the pattern drawn on the wall. After minutes the blade began to dull. She finished one side. *How much longer will the blade last? Did Mark think of bring extra blades? I need to cycle the airlock to get them. Will the plasticine seal hold when I close my side of the airlock?* Tracey thought.

****

Spider maneuvered the six-person lifter through the hole in the TWD shell. Kat directed her to the dark matter storage vaults. They passed by four bodies, all with their suits blow apart. No saving them. The lifter came to rest floating above the deck ten meters from the vaults.

One at a time they cycled through the tiny lifter airlock. "Let's go see the condition of the flasks," Spider said. Floating across to the hatch of the sealed room marked **Dark Negative Matter Authorized Personnel ONLY,** they saw a hole the size of the small lifter. The metal bent outward. "Spider, it's an exit hole, must be major damage inside," Kat observed.

"Kat, if a flask is breached the ship would be gone. Try the hatch, "Spider suggested.

"Locked and sealed."

Kat knocked three times. In response came four knocks. Then two knocks, a pause and two more. They looked at each other. The signal was 'don't open the hatch.' Whoever was inside did not have working spacesuits. Their lifter was too small to carry a temp airlock.

Spider said, "Kat, I have an idea of how get them out. Its high risk, but if the gods favor us it might work."

Chapter Fifth-Three –
In Orbit Aboard Bighorn Bull, Outcast Lady
&*Dark Song*- 04-01-519

Niikia ordered an attack on the enemy destroyer identified as *Fire Dancer*. She was a sphere ship. The destroyer dropped six missiles as it raced toward *Death's Hammer,* the Count's commanded ship. Niikia ordered Jones the chief time navigator and pilot, "Mr. Jones, full acceleration. We can't match the scum's speed. But we can extend our firing widow. Artystaar, missiles and rail guns ready?"

"Yes commander. I Have missile lock. Dropping two now!"

"Dropped clean, engines fired," the drop bay crew leader responded.

"Drop two more now!"

"Dropped clean, engines fired."

The Green Fleet destroyer closed in on *Death's Hammer*. The quick-fire rail guns of the battle cruiser put a wall of projectiles taking out five of the missiles fired by the destroyer. The *Fire Dancer's* final missile was hit by rail-gun fire from one the other pirate ships escorting the *Hammer*.

Artystaar tracked her four missiles' trajectory. *Fire Dancer's* rail-guns began to fire too late; they got two of Artystaar's missiles. The other two struck the sphere at mid ships blasting a hole the size of a house in the hull. As the enemy ship raced past, Artystaar ordered the rail-guns to rake the crippled ships. Rail-guns from the *Hammer*, *Dark Song* and another pirate ship tore into the helpless *Fire Dancer*.

Niikia called out, "Good kill Artystaar and crew! She is a dead ship now nothing but scrap in orbit. The Dark Goddess has blessed us." *Now if we can find that bastard Kat and his Outcast Lady and open her like a rotten Papiii fruit, thought* Niikia.

****

On the *Bighorn Bull,* Tracey finally finished the four cuts in the sphere wall. She had dulled three blades cutting the pattern. Hands from the inside pulled away the metal square. A grizzled man of fifty took her hand.

"This is Benjamin Newman, Fleet Officer Ma'm. We jammed Mr. Montgomery into my suit. He is in bad shape so take him first; along with Sergeant Patel she also has serious injuries. We put her in the other good suit."

"Thanks, due the Fleet, here are two new suits! Get the next two into them. I should able to cycle the airlock with three people in suits next time." The next cycle went well. Without the cutting tools, Tracey was able to packed herself and three suits into the airlock and brought out three more injured.

In the lifter Nirabella, with Shadow's help, dealt with a flow of wounded. The first was the girl in the leaking suit. Her leg was broken at the point where she sealed the suit with plasticine. Nirabella used a medipack to form a temporary cast. Shadow got her into a new spacesuit and sent her across via the cable to Light.

The first survivor from the sphere was lucky to be alive. Capitan Montgomery was ripped by a single tiny piece of shrapnel moving at hyper velocity. Someone had gotten him inside the sphere, then got the old suit off and did their best to stop the bleeding. Newman got him into a new suit, which Nirabella now cut him out of. The new suit was already blood soaked. She could see even more damage from the milliseconds exposure to the vacuum of space that his right hip was hacked open. Someone patched the hole within seconds or Montgomery would be dead. Shadow placed him in one of the bunks setup in the lifter. Nirabella used two medipack and pain-stop to stabilize him. She then turned to the third survivor. *By the gods, we are NOT losing anyone today!* she thought.

****

Back in Engineering, Spider brought the min-lifter as close as possible to the hatch. She then turned it so the back was facing the hatch. "Kat, deploy the transfer tube with you inside. Then seal it to the hatch and pressure it up. Open the hatch and pull out whoever is inside. Finally, return to the min-lifter and close the rear hatch on the lifter. Then we'll head back to the *Lady*."

"Sounds good with one exception. I will go back in and check the dark matter flasks. I can ride back on outside of lifter." Kat said.

Half an hour later Kat open the hatch to find of the three of the engineering crew. They had only minor injuries. However, they appeared disoriented. A short grey haired engineer told Kat, "Don't go back in, massive, D427 Gridall Particle leak. The dark matter will go unstable unless the Prime Z-valves 14 and 15 and 16 are closed." Then he said, "and the Motan bats are freed and painted pink." Kat knew the engineering was suffering D427 damage. Sufficient Gridall Particles left one completely unable to function mentally. The effect lasted for days. The brain would reestablish pathways but it took time.

Spider asked, "Is he right about the valves? Everyone knows Motan bats do not exist."

Kat responded, "I am going in and see. If I am not back in fifteen minutes, get back to the *Lady*, recall Tracey's team and get the ship far away. "

In fourteen and half minutes Kat was back. He carried one more survivor. Spider saw the dazed look on Kat's face and she knew that he got too much D427. It would be days before he could command. Spider strapped down Kat and the four survivors and headed the min-lifter back toward the *Lady*.

****

Two hours later, after finding only two more of *Bull's* crew alive, the search concluded. Tracey and Shadow were the last two on board the *Lady*. They came across on the cable after Cici flew the lifter over with the injured and the medical team. Light triggered a small charge blowing the far end of the cable and started the power reel.

As soon as the platform closed and pressurized, Spider stepped through the hatch and waited as Tracey removed her helmet. Spider then gave a sharp salute and said, "Welcome aboard Commander. Ms. Watkins! You are now acting Commander of the *Outcast Lady*." Spider then outlined Kat's condition.

"Spider, as of now you are acting first officer. Assemble everyone, not critically needed, in the hanger bay in thirty minutes. I will be in the control room until then."

Tracey walked quickly up to the control room. Peter greeted her, "Your orders, Commander?"

"First my thanks to each of you for manning the control room during this operation. Now we shall get the *Lady* moving. Peter, lay in a max G course away from the *Bull* and toward Green Fleet. Then bring me up to date on ship's status."

A half hour later, Tracey walked into the hanger deck. Spider formally, called out, "Attention! Commander on the deck!" Tracey stepped onto the platform and turned to the assembly. To her surprise, all the crew stood at attention.

"At ease, find a seat," Tracey ordered. "First, congratulations everyone! We rescued twenty-one souls. Some like Captain Montgomery have life threatening injuries. Also, as some of you know, Commander Jang was exposed to dangerous levels of D427 Gridall Particles. His brain and nerves are damaged. He will make a full recovery in time. In addition to those two, we have a total eighteen other people with injuries. Nirabella needs all the help she can get. Cici is setting up a schedule for the medical support team."

"Next point, Spider is now acting first officer and pilot. She will take over my duties. Give her the excellent support you have given me. All other officer's and sergeant's will cover her duties."

"Finally, we will join Green Fleet and engage the enemy at every opportunity. There is an archaic saying Bob Redding our stable man and a space veteran, taught me. Words are so ancient that it may date back to Home World a thousand years ago or more. - **I intend to take this ship into harm's way.**"

Aboard Dark Song the Com Officer and relayed a message from the Count Markiii:

To all commanders: Green Fleet is decelerating and their next pass at our fleet will be at a much lower velocity. I plan to accelerate our fleet to match their speed. We will destroy the *Lady Delapasse*. All ships escorting us will ensure protection from other enemy ships while we blast Bridgeford to the Tenth Hell.

"Crew, this is Niikia Kaiii-var. We are ordered to protect *Deaths Hammer* in the coming battle. May the dark gods send us Kat Jang and his egg ship. The long elliptical orbit of Green Fleet means hours until their next pass through. Stand down from battle alert. Get some rest. Bonk a crewmate; it may be your last chance."

Off the com Niikia told the Control Center team, "Artystaar set a course matching *Deaths Hammer's*. Full power engineering. Recheck all weapons systems."

****

Hours later at orbit apogee, the *Outcast Lady* caught Green Fleet. Within two hours they transferred the rescued survivors to the heavy cruiser

Republican Lady with one exception. Benjamin Newman the fleet officer, asked to stay with the *Lady* for the coming battle. With Fidelity, up in the Control Center, Engineering could use the help.

As she supervised the transfer, Nirabella encounter Doctor Tommy, her old flame. "By the goddess of beauty, you look good Nirabella. You have developed the élan of a pirate queen. I have missed your body in my bunk," he said.

Nirabella gave him a cold stare and said, " Tommy, the body I miss is sure not yours. Listen up doc rat face, Capitan Montgomery is the most critical. Next, is Commander Jang he has D427 damage. Also, many others are serious. Do not fail to take damn fine care of these people. Pirate queens have been known to kill people for less. A whole lot less!"

****

As soon as they detached from the *Republican Lady,* Tracey brought the crew up to date on the new assignment Bridgeford just sent. "We are assigned to be one of two ships escorting the *Lady Delapasse.* The general's plans to vector his battle cruiser into a low orbit and destroy the Tri-Star troop ships, cutting off support to the Tri-Star troops on the planet. The destroyer *Gold Arrow* will take a position off the *Delapasse's* bow and we will take a position aft. Battle standby for now. 1st watch is on Alert. Get some rest. We are going into the biggest space battle since Morgan's Abode thirty years ago.

All three ships were traveling stern first with dark matter engines at full power. Tracey was staying a thousand clicks out from *Delapasse's* stern. Major Sasha Kedrova, Bridgeford's new XO transmitted verbal information outlining the mass of data coming into *Lady's* navigation computer. Tracey saw the outline of a Troc Battlecruiser on the sensor's screen. As Bridgeford decelerated, Count-Viceroy Markiii accelerated. The two battle cruisers would cross paths just as they reached the troop ships. She watched as five tiny dots appeared on the screen. A total of five escorts and destroyers were defending the *Hammer*.

"Battle Alert! Inform Major Kedrova we will attack the closest destroyer." Tracey called. The crew pulled their space suits from the packs. "Spider, set in a course to intercept our target."

Spider responded, "Course set. Intercept in thirty-four minutes, missile range in ten. We will run a parallel course matching speeds at intercept."

Tracey said, "Peter launch two as soon as you have lock. Missile bay, are you ready?"

"Bay open to space and ready," Light answered.

Ten minutes later Peter called out, "Have lock dropping two, permission to drop one more."

"Yes," Tracey said. She was not yet sure if Peter needed more missiles. Then she saw the traces of a dozen large F1 heavy missiles launched by the *Delapasse* at the Troc Battlecruiser. In an instant, she knew what Peter saw. They were down to their last seven missiles.

Chapter Fifty-Five
– Off Pangerbar – *Outcast Lady & Dark Song* -
04-03-519

Aboard Dark Song, Niikia could not believe it.
An egg-shaped escort was attacking one of the
destroyers protecting Count Markiii. Was it Kat? Did
it matter? The pirate destroyer *Frozen Blood* had
twice the missiles and much heavier guns.

Artystaar tracked the two F2 medium missiles
launched by the little egg. Then the *Delapasse*
launched twelve F1 heavy missiles. They appeared
on the sensor screen headed for the *Hammer*.

"Crew, this is Kaiii-var, target and destroy the
twelve F1 heavy missiles."

Artystaar launched four Trocnavar X2 missiles
each aimed at an F1 missile on a vector for the
Hammer. Two lost the target and disappeared. The
two others hit a missile however, they both hit same
missile. The other ships protecting the battle cruiser
went crazy launching missiles. Some ships were
already firing rail guns. In turn, each of remaining
eight F1 missiles launched at the *Hammer* were
destroyed.

Count Markiii launched sixteen heavy X1
Troc missiles in response. Before Artystaar and
Niikia could Track them, their attention was grabbed
by the sensor display. The destroyer *Frozen Blood*

was so busy firing at the F1 missiles, they made no effort track the third F2 missile launched by the egg. It ran behind the remaining spread of missiles launched by Bridgeford. The weapons officer on the egg had programmed in a last second change. The missile shifted course. It hit the *FrozenBlood's missile* bay. The sensor image became many, and then the *Frozen Blood* was gone. In a flash, Niikia knew the egg was in fact the *Outcast Lady* and the infamous Peter was the missile officer. She would see them all dead and in the tenth hell.

Artystaar and Niikia saw that seven of the incoming Space Force F1 missiles survived. Artystaar launched two more missiles. They watched on sensor screens as five more missiles from the *Delapasse* were destroyed by other pirate ship's missiles and rail guns. Next the rapid-fire rail guns from the *Hammer* cut down one more. A single missile got through and hit one of the *Hammer's* Time Wave Drive pods. Artystaar knew that it would mean little in a battle fought at sub light speed. They watched as the *Delapasse* fired a salvo of F2 missiles to intercept the sixteen X1 missiles from the *Hammer*. Then *Delapasse* slowed matching speed with the troop ships.

****

Aboard the *Outcast Lady* Tracey told Spider, "Vector to incept the missiles from *Hammer*. Peter, launch at will. Cici, fire rail guns as soon as we are in range. Bridgeford is using his F2 missiles and rapid fire rail guns to take out Troc missiles. He is launching his F1 missiles to target the closest of the troop transport."

The crew in the Control Center watched as Peter launched four F2 missiles. Tracey began counting off the distance to the incoming X1 missiles. 100 hundred clicks, then 90,80,70,60 - Cici began firing the two rail guns' turrets that could be brought to bear. A cheer went up as they watched their missiles hit three X1 missiles. The F2 missiles from the *Delapasse* took out six more. But seven of the big X1 were still on course. Even at this distance Cici's rail gun fire got one. Bridgeford, using small rapid fire rail guns took out three more. Next the last three were destroyed by a spread of F2 missiles from *Gold Arrow*. The Battlecruiser *Delapasse* was safe for only a moment.

They watched as a pirate vessel closed on *Delapasse*. She was a Trocnavar built escort. She accelerated as the *Lady* slowed. The Fire Control Computer identified the ship as *Dark Song*. The information in Lord Markiii's data pack and the information tortured out of him was damn useful, how else would the computer know. Tracey thought *you two Troc bitches did survive.* "Spider reset our vector to put between *Delapasse* and *Dark Song.*"

"Resetting!"

Fidelity called out, " Spider, Tracey, these maneuvers are pushing the control jets beyond the max. Don't know if they can hold together."

Peter sent a message to all their screens: "On my signal I will drop two missiles. We are now switching to the last of Troc X2 missiles we got when purchased the *Lady*"

Three minutes later Peter called, "Drop NOW!"

In the Missile Bay Light and Shadow watched air jets push the two missiles out of the bay. Their engines fired driving the missiles outward toward the *Dark Song*. Shadow held up two fingers signaling two missiles in his rack. Light held up three. Just five missiles left.

****

Niikia could not believe their luck; the course setting put them in direct conflict with *Outcast Lady*. Behind the *Song* the pirate cruiser *Death Kiss* - who was in fact the Imperial heavy cruiser *Blue Countess* with a pirate paint job - would blast the *Delapasse* and also destroy Kat and his ship.

Artystaar called out, "Two missiles from *Outcast* tracking us. But the electronic signature is of a Trocnavar X2."

"Confirm Identification," Niikia said.

"Still Tracking us," The Com Officer called out.

Artystaar yelled, "Launching two missiles, power up all rail guns."

****

Over the com link Tracey said, "Peter, change the missile's course. The heavy cruiser behind *Song* is the real target. Spider, vector for the big cruiser. Damn, I have should have seen it! The Troc plan is to keep us busy with the escorts then slip the big cruiser in to destroy *Delapasse* while Bridgeford battles the *Hammer.*"

"Done," said Peter. "I should tell everyone that the first three missiles we launched were F2s, after that we used the converted Troc X2s we got when we bought the *Lady.* I kept the Troc identification codes and can switch the code when needed. I used the codes when we destroyed the *Frozen Blood.* It confused them just long enough."

Cici said, "All rail guns ready, targeting the incoming missiles."

Fidelity said, "Lost one control jet in sector one. Others may fail at any time."

"Fidelity, just hold us together," Tracey lamented.

Cici broke in, "Firing bearing rail guns' turrets number one and two and the rear gun"

Within a minute the com line carried a quick message. "We have a jam on turret number two. This is Gun Captain Shamir."   Like larger war ships escorts had a gun crew in a compartment just below each turret. The leader, a Gun Captain and three other crew members were expected to clear jams and fix any other problems.

"Centari, this is Cici. Are both guns jammed?"

"Yes, it must be the ammo feed. We are cycling the airlock. Cici, are both guns powered down?"

"Both are powered down. Capacitors fully discharged."

Spider said, "Rolling ship to bring turrets one and three to bear."

Centari looked around as her team slipped out of the airlock and into the turret. Behind her two young crewmen emerged with a tool box as big as an ox head and a third with a new drive belt. Centari called Cici on the com, "We are in and starting."

Tracey thought, *by the gods how far has Centari come, from refugee to gun captain. Now fighting to save a planet that treated young ones as disposable labor. How far all of us have come!*

"This is Centari, the ammo feed belt came apart and jammed into the gears. The cover is mangled."

Pulling out a cutting laser, Maxwell, one kids from the Lost group, said, "I'm cutting the cover off. We should be able to free the steel drive belt."

Centari unboxed the massive drive belt. She felt shocks as the two other turrets and single rear gun fired projectiles one after another. If they did not get the rapid fire dual turret up soon they all could be dead. In Turret two they cut the cover off, pried the ruined belt out of the gears and installed the new belt. There was no time remaining for a new cover.

As the Centari's crew worked to finish repairing Turret Two, the single mount rear gun in an open barbette got one of the two missiles. Tracey said, "Cici and Spider nice shooting; one incoming missile is gone." Gun Captain Czajka and crew, my thanks. An open barbette is tough place to be." Tracey knew it was the pilot, weapons officer and the gun crews working together that made it all operate.

"Gun Team dropping through the airlock, fire when ready," Centari signaled. The two repaired rail guns began firing. With a key control jet down, Spider fought to roll the Lady to bring the rapid-fire guns to bear. Decelerating the *Lady* slowed to match the speed of the *Death Kiss* and the *Dark Song.* As the three ships closed in on each other, Tracey knew the escort *Song* would do anything to protect the cruiser. The two escorts began a dance of death. Spider rolled to starboard and Cici, using the rapid-fire guns, sent wall of projectiles into path of the second missile.

****

Niikia, on the com line said, "The scum got both our missiles. Launch two more."

"Acknowledge," Brains replied. With Artystaar fully occupied piloting, he took over missile control.

Within limits of orbital mechanics, Artystaar turned the *Song* into the course nearest to *Outcast*. The two would pass within two clicks of each other. As she watched the two incoming missiles, *Dark Song* shifted course a few degrees and headed for the big cruiser. Niikia ordered, "Brains retarget our last two missiles. Target the two missiles they launched. Artystaar, take us as close as possible. Damn, Kat is targeting the cruiser not us."

"It's not Kat commanding!" their com officer yelled over the com. "I picked up a tight beam intercept. Watkins is commanding."

Niikia yelled, "What the hell! A new grad from the League's Officer Training School is commanding? We will cut the bitch to pieces."

The whole Control Room on the Lady watched as two X2 missiles from the *Dark Song* collided the two sham X2 Peter targeted for the Kiss. "OK everyone, were down to five missiles, let's make them count," Tracey said over ships com. *By the gods could I have said anything more trite?* "Cici, keep up the rail gun fire at the *Song* and any missiles she launches at the *Delapasse*. Peter, launch our missiles only at the *Kiss*. Use your best judgment on timing. Fidelity, keep us ahead of Delapasse. We must arrive first at the *Kiss*. Spider, get us in closer. Missile Drop Bay, are you ready? Light and Shadow? Gun Captains, you all ready?"

All replied, "Yes!"

Tracey watched the sensor screens as Fidelity cut back on plasma drive slowing the rate of deceleration. They dashed toward the Cruiser and *Dark Song*. Tracey saw that they would pass *Dark Song* within ten minutes. Peter launched three of the missiles and they dropped heading toward the *Kiss*. Each missile was masquerading as Troc controlled X2s.

****

Artystaar felt the missiles rather than heard the light rail bolts hitting the outer hull. So far, the armor held. However, soon the larger rail run bolts would hit and break through the hull. She spun the *Song* moving her out of the path of oncoming bolts. She also wanted to give the Assistant Weapons Officer a clear shot at the *Outcast*.

310

Niikia said, "Three missiles launched by *Outcast* all vectored for the *Kiss*. Launch four to intercept."

"Launching four," the weapons officer responded. "That will only leave us six missiles."

Niikia scanned sensor screens then roared, "Damn Commander Friisiek! He's not taking any actions to stop the incoming missiles." She punched the ship to ship com line. "This Niikia Kaiii-var Commander of *Dark Song* we are tacking three missiles on course to hit you."

"This is First Officer Heciir Saiitiagi, why are you bothering us? They are Imperial X2s. Now get off this com line and find some real enemy missiles." The line clicked dead.

Niikia said to the Com Officer, "Send this text to Saiitiagi: **Urgent! They are X2s but are targeted and controlled by Green Fleet.** Niikia tracked the three missiles *Outcast* had launched and also the four *Dark Song* had launched.

****

Tracey watched, as the three missiles they launched and the four missiles from the *Song* closed on each other.

Peter asked, "Free Hand?"

Tracey said, "Yes!"

Peter turned one of the missiles toward the oncoming missiles from *Song*. The missile raced toward the group of four Troc missiles *Song* had launched. Just before it hit, Peter detonated his missile. This sent a spray of fragments into the group of missiles. Three of the four went off course. The last Troc missile hit one of their two remaining missiles. Tracey watched as the Troc missile turned to follow Peters' fakes.

"Cici, keep up with all guns as long as we have the *Song* in range. Fidelity, reduce deceleration. We are going to blast past her and go in for the kill of *Death Kiss*." They all watched as Peter's final missile vector honed in on the target. The *Death Kiss* launched no counter missiles or rail gun fire. The missile blasted *Death Kiss's* port side main turret. The turret exploded. Wreckage and one of rail guns flew into space as the other gun was disabled. But, the heavy armor of the cruiser held and the hull was not breached. She was still a powerful warship.

****

"You dumb colorless idiot Saiitiagi! Now will you believe us about the missiles? Send the following text: **Enemy ship *Outcast Lady* is launching "real" X2 Trocnavar missiles. Commanding Officer Niikia Kaiii-var.**"

"*Outcast* is cutting deceleration and they will flash past us quickly at twice our speed. Launch all six missiles at *Outcast Lady*, two in a first group and a second group of four thirty seconds behind. We are going to overload their defenses. Max rail gun fire until the ship is destroyed."

Artystaar watched as the *Outcast* spiraled on a path taking them past *Song*. Whoever the pilot was, he or she was doing one hell of a job keeping *Outcast* out of the path of the mass of rail gun projectiles. Then the sensor screens showed a bright flash. Their human weapons officer got at least one hit in. She called, "Good hit, but you better get more, you crazy human bastard."

****

The shock of the rail gun hit reverberated through the ship. Tracey thought, *thank the gods we are ready.* "This is Tracey. Damage reports as soon possible. Tell us what you need."

"Erica Nguyen Damage Control reporting. Major hit to the mess deck. I can seal the entrance hole, but the exit hole is a full meter across. Air tight doors closed to hanger and missiles deck below and to crew quarters above. We need at least two three people from engineering to help."

"Fidelity reporting, all communications and controls to aft sections intact."

"Nirabella reporting, in air lock to mess deck. Expect losses and injured."

"Mark Bittman, reporting engineering has no damage."

"Shadow reporting, the two missiles and launch gear undamaged."

"Cici reporting, all rail guns functioning"

"This is Tracey ----"

Peter interrupted. "We have six missiles coming at us and only two left in our racks. Holding them."

"Good. Peter go to the Plan."

Quietly Spider moaned, "Oh gods, not that".

****

While others were fighting the enemy, Nirabella was fighting for the lives of the crew. The one good thing was at Full Battle Alert almost none of the crew was stationed on the Mess Deck. As soon as she and her assistant Rhonda Santacruz were out the airlock she understood she would be blessed to find any of the crew alive. On com Erica Nguyen told her that she believed nine crew members were on the Mess Deck when the hit happened. Anna Morgan and an unnamed crew person were sucked out the exit hole. Both were in spacesuits. The two might survive if

314

picked up quickly after the battle, but the odds were small for a rescue.

Nirabella found two more the crew dead, spacesuits ripped open by shrapnel. Five were alive, one with a broken leg inside an intact spacesuit, four were in damaged spacesuits and slipping fast. Rhonda and she slapped temp patches over the holes. But they all had leaked too much air for suits to remain safe. The air gages showed air supply near an end. If she did not get into the airlock soon they would die.

****

Niikia and Artystaar watched the sensor display. Tracey did not launch the remaining missiles at the six Niikia had just fired. Yet Tracey rushed onward toward the six. Blinding flashes sent all the sensors into over load. At least four missiles appeared to come out of nowhere. There were no ships and no orbiting launch platform. The missiles raced toward the six missiles blasting the six missiles and sending a wall of shrapnel back toward *Dark Song.* Artystaar turned and rolled the ship in a mad attempt turn her away from the oncoming shrapnel.

"This is Commander Niikia; prepare to take major damage in 90 seconds." Metal and plasticine chunks slammed into *Dark Song* ripping holes in her hull, blasting away turrets, and cutting an unarmed missile in half inside the missile bay. Artystaar's roll kept the ship from being totally destroyed.

"This is Commander Niikia. Damage reports now. We are no longer a fighting ship. Prepare to ram *Outcast Lady.*"

****

Tracey watched her sensor displays and said, "Drift missiles always are a bitch. Prepare to hit *Dark Song* with all rail gun fire. Peter, you did great job of calculating where the drift missiles were orbiting."

"Where in all the hells did the drift missiles come from?" Fidelity shouted.

Tracey answered, "Delivered by dead heroes. The two old Pangerbar destroyers we thought were fleeing the space station were in fact dropping these old drift missiles. The Pangerbar Space Force salvaged them after our first battle with the pirates. Both the destroyers were blasted into space dust, but not before they released a dozen missiles running dark and powered down. They were launched into orbit where the Pirate Fleet was expected. Peter picked up a tight beam communication telling us their orbits."

A sudden shift in the gravity field occurred as Spider spun the *Lady* onto a new course. She yelled, "They are going try to ram us!"

Tracey opened the ship's com and calmly said, "Cici, fire all rail guns at will. Give our gun crews your full support. Everyone stay steady. If we get passed *Dark Song,* we will attack *Death Kiss.* If we can disable her, the *Lady Delapasse* can fight the Troc battle cruiser *Death's Hammer* one on one. Ax will win that match."

Chapter Fifty-Six
- Pangerbar Orbit - *Outcast Lady* & *Dark Song*
04-03-519

Artystaar set a vector toward the orbit of *Outcast Lady*. The *Song* was coming apart under them. The missiles ripped open the hull armor. Rail gun fire from the *Lady* cut holes through the ship. The issue was control not power. Many of the control jets were out. Niikia ordered max power. The plasma engines drove them toward the other ship. Their erratic course moved them closer to the *Lady*.

Artystaar cried, "She is coming apart under us!" The *Song* broke into wreckage fragments. The Control Room crew, Niikia and Artystaar watched the sensor displays go dark. The armored Control Room drifted onward with them as unwilling passengers. Niikia cursed until she could no longer speak.

****

Aboard the *Lady* a cheer when up as they raced past the debris field that had once been the *Dark Song*.

Tracey's mind was already racing to the next fight, the pirate heavy cruiser Death *Kiss*. She must be destroyed. Unless she was smashed, Ax's battle cruiser *Lady Delapasse* would fight two heavy warships.

The destroyer *Fire Dancer* and the fast escort *Summer Storm* had already engaged the *Death Kiss.*

Over the com, Tracey outlined the plan, "While she is fighting our two ships, we are going in as close to the *Kiss* as possible. We will launch our last two missiles right up her ass."

And they almost did just that!

Half an hour later the *Lady* closed on the *Death Kiss*. The *Fire Dancer*'s Commander, sent via tight beamed, "We just blew off the right-side turret. Only the open mount is left. We're out of missiles. *Summer Storm* was destroyed. Launch anything you have."

Tracey told Spider, "Close on the damaged turret mount." The Lady raced toward the damaged ship. As they closed Peter launched the last two missiles. The missiles drove into the open turret mount. It was not quite up the ass, but close enough. The heavy cruiser *Kiss* came apart at mid ships. The *Lady Delapasse* would only fight the Troc battle cruiser *Death's Hammer*. It would be a sure victory for Ax and Green Fleet.

Minutes later in moment of calm, Tracey thought, *we have our victory but all should know that the asking price of this star is dreadfully high.*

Chapter Fifty-Seven
Lady Delapasse at Pangerbar Station04-24-519

Two weeks after the battle, the Outcast *Lady* was docked alongside the *Lady Delapasse* at the Pangerbar space station. The Station had been repaired enough to allow ships to dock. At first watch Ax sent over a skeleton crew to man the ship so the whole of *Lady's* crew could be present onboard the battle cruiser. They were welcomed at the transfer tube by Major Sasha Kedrova in full dress uniform. She was now acting XO for Ax.

"The general has setup a bit of a ceremony for you." As they walked toward the hanger bay, Kedrova asked, "What are those dots on your shoulders?"

Kat smiled and said, "Best you never have to find out."

Kat and Tracey led the crew into the hanger bay. 'A bit' of a ceremony was an understatement. All available crew members from the *Lady Delapasse,* in new utilities with boots and buttons polished, were lined up on both sides of the aisle in the center of the hanger bay. Kat was damn sure they would have been in formal dress uniforms if the fleet had not been recovering from the battle. At the far end of the bay awaited General Bridgeford, Auntie Tara and the senior officers of *Lady Delapasse*. The ship's band played "Gods Give Us Freedom" as Kat and the company walked down the aisle. A wave of shock and a buzz of sound ran through the assembly. Each of the *Outcast Lady's* crew had chosen to dress in full pirate regalia. No one aboard the *Lady Delapasse* expected this.

Kat lead them down the aisle dressed in the outfit he wore on the raid on Nameless, with two exceptions. He wore a black leather vest open to the waist which showed both the red kill dot on his right arm and scars on his chest. Scarves and marking on the right side of his head were yellow and black. The crew voted to make these their colors based on their use at the field ball tournament on Blue Port. The great antique sword was on slung on Jang's back.

Tracey walked beside Kat in her cut down utilities. She had replaced the utility top lost on the raid with a sleeveless one showing her red and a black kill dots. A rocket pistol was strapped to her right leg.

Peter and Fidelity were behind them in the brightly colored utilities that they wore on the raid. They also wore the yellow and black scarves and markings. Both were armed; Peter with a hand axe and Fidelity with her compact pistol.

Cici and Nirabella, with yellow and black markings, followed. They were armed and in colorful utilities from the raid. Cici's had replaced her lost top with a new bright yellow one. Strapped to Cici's right leg was a large rocket pistol. Nirabella carried a compact pistol on her belt.

Spider, Centari and Mark were next. The two young crew members wore their rocket pistols and their utilities with holes and wear. Yellow and black marked them. Everyone expected Spider to return to type and wear a dress uniform. Nothing could have been further from the truth. The side of Spider's head was marked with a big splash of yellow and black. Yellow and black scarves wrapped her upper right arm. She wore her brightly colored camouflaged utility top and pants. The pants were cut down to shorts. High black boots completed her outfit. A machete hung across her back. Her dress was far, very far, from Space Force regulations.

The next two in the procession was Light and Shadow. They wore their colored raid utilities with Shadow's black kill dot showing. Light wore the black tank top she had worn during the raid. Both wore rocket pistols strapped to their leg. The other members of the crew followed, each in some form of black and yellow and armed to the teeth.

Tracey heard someone in the ranks yell, "It's them; the outcasts Ax sent to the hells. They saved Green Fleet at Pangerbar. It's Mister Jang and Lieutenant Watkins!"

Then from the other side of the aisle there was the cry of, "Light and Shadow, by the gods welcome back!"

An old fleet officer yelled, "It's Kill Dots! They have Kill Dots. By the gods, I never thought I would see a Kill Dot!"

As the cheering started, Cici heard, "Who the hells is the beauty in black boots?" Cici thought *Spider has come a long way.* The band finished "Gods Give Us Freedom" and stuck up a jauntier piece called "Dance in The Stars Young Heroes". The sound of cheering rose as they walked forward to where General Bridgeford, Major Tara Freeborn, Gunson Montgomery in a medical walking frame and the rest of the senior staff awaited them. Tracey noted Gunson was now a Major.

As Kat and company approached, Ax raised his arms asking for quiet. The sound dropped to a muted roar. Ax stepped forward and in an extraordinary act, saluted them. None of the crew returned his salute.

Bridgeford began, "I should have expected that. You have no reason to return my salute. However, I have every reason to salute you. Your actions saved Green Fleet and the League's hold on the Green Line. You may have just saved the League of Free Stars. The information in the data pack and from the prisoner you brought was invaluable. No one else could have followed the trail through the pirate held fringe to find Major Freeborn. Next, your actions ensured our victory at the battle for Pangerbar; both at the rescue at the *Bighorn Bull* and the final battle. Your action in destroying Trocnavar ships was a key part of our victory."

"You have the deepest thanks from me and all of Green Fleet. I have publicly apologized for the Free Space Force's actions. Once more I offer to restore your commissions and ranks and see the public is informed of your service to the League of Free Stars. Each of you will be able to select your new assignments."

Kat responded "Damn it! No! We did what was necessary to save Auntie Tara and to protect friends and family at home. We expect only three things from the League. First, ensure our wounded received the best Fleet medical care. Second, help the children that we brought back find safe and loving homes. Finally, we expect to be paid in full for both our contracts with you. Beyond that, we want nothing." Shock ran through the hanger deck; none could believe what Kat said.

Ax responded, "We of the Free Space Force and all of League of Free Stars owe the officers and crew of the *Outcast Lady* so incredibly much. You shall have those things. However, after the ceremonies and dinner, I request another private meeting." It turned out to be a very interesting meeting.

****

Tracey watched as the stewards brought in cups of hot Gubble brew along with shots of aged Blue Spiced Liquor. Dinner was over and the officers of *Outcast Lady*, Auntie Tara, Gunson Montgomery and the General were gathered in Bridgeford's private ward room.

Auntie Tara began, "A toast to Colonel Chahill. The bravest damn man I ever met. Most of you may have guessed the man you knew as Sergeant Baryic was much more than that. He was an intelligence officer working undercover to find Trocnavar agents within Green Fleet. When Spider chose to call a Board of Inquire for trumped up reasons, he saw an opportunity to gather information deep within the pirate community."

"Think back, was it not Baryic who suggested you buy a warship and go contracting? And even with Peter's resources how could you get a loan commitment for sixty million Stars? Did you really think it was luck that the Free Space Force just started to install a new navigation and new weapons computers before they decided to sell her? There are many more unique events if you review the last months."

Auntie Tara continued, "Before he died Baryic he told me you where the finest crew he had ever known. If he had to die, it was an honor to lose his life with you. The last words whispered to me were 'Victory, Honor, Ship'."

Bridgeford said, "His name will be carved in special place on the high stone walls at the Space Force Officer School."

All raised their cups, "To Baryic the Brave"

Epilogue –
Planet Assurance - *The Tavern* - 10-13-519

At the very edge of known space, Assurance was the farthest and latest planet to be colonized on the Green Line. The town was located on a ridge of hills overlooking a wide valley of rich farm land. As on most newly colonized worlds, the town of Our Haven was not much. Twenty-nine tiny homes, half dozen barns and workshops, a store, and the tavern comprised the town. All of it built out of colonial glider parts, packing materials and local wood. The town and the lifter port were situated on the ridge. The Valley below flooded each spring bringing precious new soil but making it impossible to build permanent structures. The farmers built camps down on their plots below and lived there during the short summer.

Just after noon local time, Tracey, Kat, Peter, Nirabella, Cici, Light and Shadow sat at a long table on the tavern porch. They were guests of Bob and Deborah the colony leaders. The *Lady* had delivered a critical shipment of new seeds and plants cuttings to the farmers there. After the failure of the first summer's crops, Pangerbar Trading, the merchant bankers of the colony, found a new agronomist. No colonist would pay to settle on a planet without crops. The merchant bankers rushed aid to protect their investment. To get the new seeds and plants before the planting season was over, The *Lady* brought agronomist out at triple rates.

The tavern owner Big B. had set out cold beer, dill pickles and boiled potatoes. Only potatoes and cucumbers thrived from the first crops. Kat asked for tea. Big B. and his wife were making sandwiches of local roast meat of an unknown source. He claimed it tasted just like Vraciek. His wife spooned a deep blue sauce over the open face sandwiches. The sauce smelled wonderful.

It was six months ago that the Green Fleet won the Battle of Pangerbar. It was a great victory for the Free Space Force. They all were gratified to have been a key part of the victory. But sadness also marked the victory. Many crew members had not survived. Anna Morgan and others were lost. Anna was never found. Kat and the other wounded had recovered and most rejoined the crew.

While they awaited the sandwiches, Tracey noted an old man sitting at the far back of the tavern. Big B. said, "He is an old man who ended up here somehow too busted up to work much. Ms. B. keeps him from starving."

Purple Cat lay curled up on Tracey's lap. As Tracey rose from her seat, the c-cat jumped down and sauntered with her. Tracey walked back to the old man. *By the gods, he is very old* she thought. He was slowly eating a single potato and sipping a cup of tea. "Would you like to join us? We have beer and meat sandwiches. We would be pleased if you could join us," Tracey said.

He looked up at her and then rising to his feet said in a clear voice, "Thank you Ms., but I cannot afford the cost of beer or meat. I don't take charity for more than my needs."

Nirabella joined Tracey. She touched the old man and said, "Our First Officer has asked you join us; it is no charity. The honor is ours."

The old man picked up his cane and walked slowly to the long table. Tracey noted, in spite of his physical issues, he carried himself as a spacer. He sat down between Tracey and Light, took a sip beer and dug into his meat sandwich. When he finished, Kat asked, "Please tell us who you are."

"My name is Eric Van Eyke," the old man said. "I came here on a cargo supply ship. The captain needed less crew for the return and thought I was too old. So, he dumped me. In my time, I shipped with most of the adventurers to run beyond the known Green Line. Some were traders, some pirates, others merely curious."

Tracey asked, "Are you saying you have been further out on the Green Line than here?"

"Yes," he firmly replied.

Big B. said, "Eric spins some wild stories. I would be careful about believing any of the old man's stories. Eric may not be all together."

329

The old man pulled his chair back from the table and stated, "My body may be weak but my mind is clear and what I am about to tell you true is to the last word."

For the next two hours, the old man told his story. He spoke of far planets controlled by races other than Trocs or humans; of creatures, so strange they wore spacesuits while in good air; of rich cities with great spaceports and a myriad of goods for trade and of noble lords who ruled planets. Pirate fleets and warlords who killed and were destroyed. Planets existed that were rich in agriculture and planets which were all ocean. Planets flourished where wonderful things were manufactured.

Finally, he told an astonishing tale:

I shipped out years ago with a commander called Morgan on his ship the *Running Star*. She was an ancient imperial destroyer converted to an armed merchant. The commander was a secret trader. He traded far out on the Green Line hundreds of light years beyond where the Free Space Force had control or even any knowledge. The risks were exceedingly high, but the shares were ten times normal.

We reached the planet Aalvake. It was so distant they almost never saw a human or a Troc. The planet itself was mostly desert with less than a third covered by seas. The local people looked very much like us and Trocs, but soft down fur covered their heads and backs. The great city of Aalvake is the center of trade. It is on a green island in one of few seas.

There was a small space station to control traffic. But, all trading was done on the surface. We brought our goods down by lifter. Many of the ships landed directly on spaceport field. A few landed in the harbor. That is right, on the water!

I found one of the few humans on Aalvake running a tavern near the harbor. His name was Braunfels. One night it was just Braunfels, me the ladies, and too much local wine.

He began, 'Son you think you are far out of the Green Line; you have only just started. The line goes out through ten thousand stars. A trader traveled here years ago and told us far, very far out other humans live. They know nothing of us. But the kingdoms and empires ruled by these people fill a section of the Galaxy. Their language is nothing like Standard Common Com, or any of the Troc languages. Their ships always land on water. And even more astonishing is that they have ships which sail through space without time wave drive.'"

****

Twenty-four hours later in the Command Center, Kat said, "If you please, Tracey take the *Lady* out of orbit."

Tracey said, "Final Checks".

"Second Officer Spider reporting, all ships systems are stable and fully functional."

"Medical Officer Nirabella reporting, crew is berthed and ready for acceleration."

"Weapons Officer Cici reporting, all weapons at Battle Standby."

"Engineering Officer Fidelity reporting, the Plasma Drive powered up and ready. Dark Matter Engines ready at standby."

"Chief Time Wave Navigator Peter reporting Time Wave Drive ready at standby, Mr. Van Eyke's course is laid in." Peter smiled and winked at Eric.

Over the com system they heard as Light and Shadow yelled, "Victory, Honor, Ship!"

Tracey piloted the *Outcast Lady* outward toward unknown space.

The End

About the Author

John Baeyertz is an Engineer who came to writing via a long and strange path. He grew up in Southern California surrounded by a bright and curious family. When John was seven his father papered the wall of his bedroom with National Geo maps. Next his favorite aunt bought John a membership in a Sci-Fi book club. The gifts lead to a lifelong love of travel and Sci-Fi.

After attending a plethora of colleges studying art, photography, and whatever else came along. He then stumbled into working in advertising, a chemical plant, and as a journeyman electrician.

John then made a transition, which few if any humans ever make. He changed from liberal arts to engineering. This lead to a BSEE and a career at computer companies and an electronic game manufacturer. Which in turn brought chances to travel and meet people throughout the world. He even got to live in Minnesota, talk about exotic. You can read a lot of Sci-Fi books in a Minnesota winter. The idea of writing books was always there but never fulfilled.

After returning to California and retirement, came more travel. John then lost Ruth his beloved wife of many years. He focused on a project beyond grief and began writing. Today John lives in Southern California. He recently married Janice, who fully supports all John's various obsessions. They live life writing, traveling, drawing, photographing, reading, and appreciating life.